Emmie and Roger
A Thermonuclear Romance

by

Richard S. Greeley

To

Tony and Pat

my very best critics

Dick

DORRANCE PUBLISHING CO., INC.
PITTSBURGH, PENNSYLVANIA 15222

Dorrance Publishing Co., Inc.
701 Smithfield Street
Pittsburgh, PA 15222
Visit our website at *www.dorrancebookstore.com*

ISBN: 978-1-4349-6980-4
eISBN: 978-1-4809-0049-3

The dedication of this book is in two parts

The first is to Earl Forrest "Frosty" Lockwood, my boss and carpool mate at the Mitre Corporation from 1961 to 1967. He obtained our contract with the U.S. Air Force Electronic Systems Command to develop the Nuclear Detection and Reporting System (NUDETS), System 477L, to provide detection and instantaneous report of the detonation of any nuclear weapons within the continental United States to the National Command Authorities (NCA). When President Kennedy decided to test many of the U.S. nuclear weapons just off the coast of Christmas Island in the Pacific Ocean, Frosty and I determined to test the capabilities of a prototype of the NUDETS to detect actual nuclear weapons bursts. I volunteered to take the prototype system to Palmyra Island, four hundred miles northwest of Christmas, since the Air Force requirement for the system was to detect the bursts at that distance. Frosty was indispensable in making all the arrangements to get our team to Palmyra in time for the tests.

This book also is dedicated to President John F. Kennedy; his brother, Attorney General Robert F. Kennedy; and Secretary of Defense Robert S. McNamara (and others who spoke up forcefully). They decided to seek a peaceful resolution of the Cuban Missile Crisis in October 1962. The prevailing sentiment of almost everyone whom the president spoke to during the crisis—including members of his cabinet, the Joint Chiefs of Staff, senior members of the Congress, and even former President Dwight D. Eisenhower—urged that he promptly order air strikes against the Cuban missile and air bases and supporting anti-aircraft sites. Kennedy did not listen to his generals, as more recent presidents have done or said they would do, or to the senior persons noted above. Instead, he asked his brother Robert, Secretary McNamara, and other members of the ExComm (a select group of top officials advising him during the crisis) to determine a set of measures to delay the need for the air strikes and give Nikita Khruschev, chairman of the Soviet Union, time to consider the ultimate effects of the possibility of all-out nuclear war.

At 9:00 A.M. on Sunday, October 28, 1962, Khrushchev's reply agreeing to end the crisis was broadcast to the world. The U.S. air strikes scheduled to begin on the twenty-ninth were hurriedly called off. The president's caution and adroit diplomacy may well have saved the world from World War Three—most likely a thermonuclear war.

Contents

Cover Photo: U.S. nuclear weapons test Bluestone, 1.27 megatons, airdrop from a B-52 bomber, detonated 10,000 feet above the ocean, off the southern tip of Christmas Island.

Preface

This is a romantic novel. The basic events, the U.S. thermonuclear weapons tests off Christmas Island from April to July 1962 and the Cuban Missile Crisis of October 1962, form the backdrop for the romance between Emmie Trowbridge and Roger Malcolm. She is a very bright Englishwoman who agrees to teach elementary school on Christmas Island. He is a very bright American scientist sent to monitor the tests by Secretary of Defense Robert S. McNamara. They are swept up in the two signal events of 1962.

Emmie, her family, her mentor Professor Chebandrov, and the romance between Roger and Emmie are completely fictional. The character of Roger Malcolm is based on that of the author, and much of the episodes typify his actual experiences. It should be understood that his activities as described are fictional. However, he did witness a one-megaton nuclear weapon, called Shot Alma, from Christmas Island, thirty-five miles away from the actual burst. He also was present in the NUDETS trailer on Palmyra and witnessed a number of visible flashes of light from the nuclear bursts four hundred miles away.

The nonfictional characters depicted in this novel are Earl Forrest "Frosty" Lockwood, based on the author's boss at the Mitre Corporation at that time (with his permission); Dick Johnson, the Mitre representative at Hickam Air Force Base in Honolulu (now deceased), as well as his superiors Robert R. Everett and Charles A. Zraket ("Caz"), the Mitre president and executive vice president, respectively. Also mentioned in the novel are the senior U.S. officials President Kennedy, Attorney General Robert Kennedy, Secretary of Defense Robert S. McNamara, and members of ExComm, the committee set up by President Kennedy to handle the Cuban Missile Crisis. Also mentioned are Anatoly Dobrynin, the Soviet ambassador to the U.S.; the Office of the Director, Defense Research and Engineering (ODDR&E), Harold Brown ("Bowen" in the text); senior analyst at ODDR&E Willie V. Moore; and the commander of Task Force Eight, the nuclear testing organization, Lt. Gen. Alfred D. Starbird, U.S. Army. Also mentioned in passing are President Kennedy's private secretary, Evelyn Lincoln, and his personal aide, Kenneth O'Donnell.

The situations and the conversations involving these officials are fictional, although based on the author's experiences and, in some cases, on transcripts from tape recordings in the White House of the actual events and other published nonfictional sources. Others mentioned in the novel are based on real persons but given fictional names to protect their actual identity.

Acknowledgements

I am deeply indebted to a knowledgeable British woman who, at her request, must remain anonymous. She provided to me her personal account of the mandatory evacuation of schoolchildren out of London starting just as, or shortly before, World War II was declared by Great Britain against Germany on September 1, 1939. This was done to attempt to ensure the safety of the children from the presumed bombing of London and other areas by the German Luftwaffe. Many, if not most, of the children returned home only in the spring of 1945. My British acquaintance also provided to me her personal knowledge of the British school system. (I was privileged to have visited Girton College of Cambridge University in 1971.) She also provided material on Stacey Cunliffe ("Stacey Conover" in the novel), who had been leader of the Girl Guides in England before World War II.

I acknowledge the use of Google Wikipedia on the Internet for additional information on the British school system, Girton College and the professors of mathematics there, the Roedean School, Christmas Island (Kiritimati), and the Cuban Missile Crisis.

The nonfiction book *The Kennedy Tapes: Inside the White House during the Cuban Missile Crisis* was used to accurately describe the conversations that went on between President Kennedy, his brother Robert, the attorney general, and the several members of the ExComm during the Cuban Missile Crisis. Other nonfiction books on the crisis that I considered were *Thirteen Days in October: A Memoir of the Cuban Missile Crisis* by Robert F. Kennedy, *Eyeball to Eyeball*, and *October Fury*, among many others available. The layout of the West Wing of the White House, including the Oval Office, the Cabinet Room, the Situation Room, and the Roosevelt Room, was obtained from Google Wikipedia. The information about the U.S. nuclear tests was taken from my experiences on Palmyra and Christmas islands during the tests, as described in my nonfiction book, *NUDETS: Cocking the Trigger on Nuclear War.*

Prologue

Way across the world in August 1961, Chairman Khrushchev was busy taking the measure of President Kennedy. The chairman and President Eisenhower had made a tacit agreement not to test nuclear weapons in the atmosphere. Ike was working hard to make it permanent when their summit conference failed, due to the Soviets shooting down a U.S. U-2 spy plane. President Eisenhower was caught in a lie about it being a weather plane when the pilot showed up live and on Soviet TV. Khrushchev feigned great anger and stalked out of the summit meeting. He soon determined to take direct action. So suddenly, not even a year after President Kennedy's inauguration, the U.S. sniffer aircraft aloft over the Arctic and other sensors detected a Soviet nuclear test—then another, then another. There were about twenty in all, ending like any good fireworks show: with a monster, fifty-megaton thunder-bumper!

As soon as the U.S. Air Force sniffer plane detected the radioactive cloud from the first Soviet weapon test over Novaya Zemlya in August 1961, General Curtis LeMay, chief of staff of the Air Force, was notified by coded message directly to his office at the Pentagon. LeMay was more than a bit startled. He hadn't expected this. He picked up his secure phone and punched the number for Major General Jermaine Rhodenhauser, director of the Air Force Technical Applications Center (AFTAC), the organization that monitors all nuclear weapons' release of radioactivity worldwide.

"Jerry, have you double-checked this?"

"Yes, this is for sure. Doyle went over the data with a fine-tooth comb, and he's positive about this. It's been his whole life, as you know." Doyle Northrup was the Air Force scientist who initiated the sniffer plane flights over the Arctic to detect Soviet nuclear tests. "Initial measurements put it at over a megaton."

"Thanks. Stand by for some urgent orders." General LeMay pressed a button that sounded in Secretary of Defense McNamara's office, then he got up and strode the few feet past the startled colonels in each adjoining office and went directly into the SecDef's office, shutting the door firmly behind him.

"Curt, what's up? What's wrong?"

"Mr. Secretary, those bastards have done it. They just set off a big nuke over Novaya Zemlya. They just broke the test ban—thank God for that! I'll get our plans together and be ready in the morning to get our test site out at Eniwetok refurbished."

"I was just on my way over to the White House. This will really break him up! Come along."

The SecDef's limousine quickly brought them to 1600 Pennsylvania Avenue, and the two men were immediately ushered inside. As they settled into the Oval Office, the president's aides having been dismissed, McNamara told President Kennedy the news.

"Those bastards!" the president exclaimed. "Those dirty, conniving bastards! Well, we'll have to test our own weapons. Curt, how soon can you guys be ready?"

"Well, I'll have to send a crew out today to Eniwetok to look around. Probably a couple of months. Goddamn it, those Commies really blindsided us!"

But President Kennedy suddenly realized he had a different problem. Eniwetok was out!

"Curt, the Marshall Islanders will have none of it! No way! They stood right here in the Oval Office and told me most emphatically, 'You radiated our islands, gave us cancer, killed those Japanese fishermen, and ruined our livelihood. Take your nuclear weapons and leave us alone!' Get that globe over here. What about Guam? Too inhabited? Wake Island? Too small. Johnston, likewise; Australia, too far away; Hawaii, I'd never get reelected. Wait! What's this? The Line Islands. There's Christmas Island. Didn't the British just test their weapons there?"

McNamara answered. "They shot off several over Christmas Island in the Pacific near the equator, but stopped in 1958. They're still arguing about the natives getting cancer."

"Get the prime minister on the horn. We're gonna have to twist his arms."

Prime Minister Harold Macmillan was not at all pleased. He had had bruising fights about the British nuclear weapons and their testing just three years previously. Finally he gave in, but it took President Kennedy until October 1961 to get his full agreement to use Christmas Island for the U.S. nuclear tests. He had already gotten Major-General, now Lieutenant-General, Alfred "Dodd" Starbird organizing the full task force for the testing. Finally the president could say, "Go to it, Dodd, go to it." Actually, the president held up the final go-ahead until March of 1962, but by then Dodd had already made every preparation needed to start the tests within the next month.

Little did the president know that Premier Khrushchev had another surprise in the making, one which would bring the world to the brink of nuclear war before the year was out.

MAP OF THE PACIFIC OCEAN
SOUTH OF HAWAII

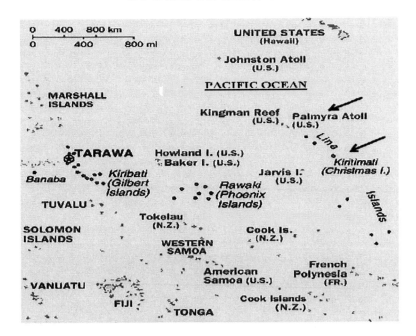

CHRISTMAS ISLAND

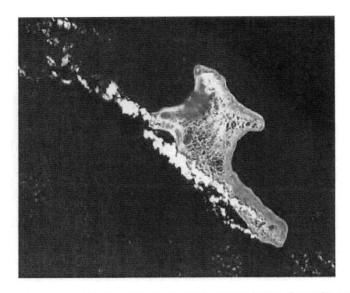

Aerial photograph of Christmas Island taken by a NASA Space Shuttle.
Note the white cloud cover and the lagoon structure through the centre of the island

PALMYRA ISLAND

Northern Arm   Trailer Site   Note Runway

Ship Channel   Southern Arm (Google Earth Photo-Author's Arrows)

Chapter 1

Emmie's Arrival

Emmie was roughly handed down from the C-124. Landing on the ground, her knees buckled slightly, and she had to take a step forward to regain her balance as the rest of the passengers swept past her, all U.S. airmen except one navy captain. She ached in every extremity after sitting in that damned bucket seat during her six-hour flight from Hawaii. She took a deep breath and immediately regretted it; the air was filled with dust. She coughed, caught her breath and, not wanting to spit, swallowed the dirty saliva. *Yuck*, she thought. She looked up in amazement as the whole front of the plane was raised hydraulically, cockpit and all, and the forward off-loading ramp came rolling out and down. Just then, a huge truck loaded with broken coral swept past, much too close for comfort. She recoiled in horror at the scene in front of her: men in uniform and construction vehicles of every sort in constant motion, dust everywhere, and the cacophony of noise as a plane took off, roaring past her. The stifling heat and humidity of the tropical island brought an immediate rush of perspiration to her face and underclothes. *I've landed in hell* was her second thought. In a panic, she turned and tried wildly to get back on the plane. At about the third step, she heard a voice.

"Miss Trowbridge! Miss Trowbridge!" a man shouted as he came toward her from around the front of the plane, dodging the ramp. "I'm so glad you've arrived. I wasn't sure which plane you would be on. I'm William Duxbury, the school principal. Welcome to Christmas Island."

"Oh, Mr. Duxbury! Thank God you're here. What's going on? This is complete chaos!"

"I hate to tell you this, but we are being blessed with another round of nuclear weapons tests, courtesy of the United States of America."

****

Mr. Duxbury led Emmie to his car, a tiny, vintage British Austin, and told her as he drove, "I'll take you to London—no, not your London, but the main town of Christmas Island. It's just a couple of miles north of Banana, the village we just left where the airport and much of the chaos is centered. London has the port facility, so over by the waterfront there is also considerable chaos, as you have said. I've arranged for you to stay in the home of the governor of The Republic of Kiribati. That is the name of the group of islands including Tarawa, where the government sits. The governor is there now. His wife died a few years ago, so there is a caretaker family in the home here on Christmas with the governor's son, Te Raoi, or "Peace" in Gilbertese, or "Terry" as we call him in school. Unfortunately he acts nothing like "Peace," being a typical rambunctious kid, but he is smart and very friendly. The natives speak Gilbertese but most understand, and many speak, English, which we primarily use in school. We have the elementary school adjacent to the high school. I hope you can teach both math and science in the elementary school and help me with those subjects and perhaps others in the high school. It may be quite a load, and you must tell me if it's too much, but you come extraordinarily recommended. I understand you have a 'first' degree in math from Cambridge."

"Well, actually, it's from Girton, the women's college of Cambridge University, but"—she chuckled, despite feeling clammy all over—"I like to think that we women are just as smart as men."

Mr. Duxbury chuckled too, and thinking of his wife added, "How true, how true." As they passed the high school in the car, he turned to Emmie and asked, 'Now, can you tell me why, with your background, you agreed to fly out here to teach elementary-level kids? Please don't think I'm trying to pry into your private life, but it just struck me as, first, wonderful for us here, but second, quite a shift in outlook for you."

"Oh, as I told Mrs. Wentworth at the foreign office who also wondered about that, I had been teaching math and science at a prestigious elementary school, Roedean, but I suddenly received some very unwelcome publicity in the tabloids in London. I felt I had to resign from the school to protect its reputation, and one thing led to another, and here I am. I do so want to help the kids and will do everything you ask me to. But I must admit, no one so much as breathed a word about what was going to happen here with these tests. I was appalled, totally appalled, when I stepped off the plane." She looked around at the small city of London. "Here, things are a bit more peaceful, but still nothing like what I expected. I'm sure this is a lovely island, perhaps close to a paradise to some people, but how do the children learn? The bombs going off must be a complete distraction."

"Oh, Miss Trowbridge, please believe me, I only learned about the tests myself, as I said, earlier this week. If I had known sooner, I surely would have notified Mrs. Wentworth, and through her, you. We are totally devastated but have been told there is nothing that can be done. The final decision was made just recently by agreement between the U.S. president, Mr. Kennedy, and our prime minister, Harold Macmillan. I can't understand how Macmillan could have agreed with Kennedy. Obviously, the president applied enormous pressure. As you may know, the British tested their nuclear weapons here in 1957 to '58. We've suffered from increased cases of cancer already. How anyone could subject us to further risks is almost unbelievable. But here we are. We must just suffer in silence for the present."

"But how do you protect the natives here when the bombs go off, particularly the children?"

"Oh, that was tough. Everyone had to stay at home and put their face into a pillow when the sirens announced an imminent blast. It was awful! I don't know what precautions the Americans will take. I fear the worst. Oh, here we are at your home. After you are settled, I'll take you over to the schools. I hope you are prepared to start teaching immediately."

Emmie greeted her hosts and Terry, and after being served a simple but hot meal of fish and rice, she said, "Good night. I'm so very tired" and dropped onto her bed and promptly fell sound asleep.

Chapter Two

Roger's Arrival

That same day, Roger Malcolm had jumped down from a similar U.S. Air Force C-124 cargo plane carrying his nuclear detection equipment to Palmyra Island. He had high hopes that his system could detect and measure the size and location of the weapon bursts accurately enough to satisfy the stringent requirements placed on the system design by the secretary of defense, Robert McNamara. Palmyra was four hundred miles northwest of Christmas Island, giving the equipment a very realistic test to detect and measure the many U.S. thermonuclear tests to be detonated. Just a few minutes later, Roger thought that his entire project was doomed to failure.

* * * *

Roger had seen the news about the Soviet nuclear tests in the morning *New York Times* at the end of August '61 and rushed to tell his boss, Earl Forest "Frosty" Lockwood.

"Frosty, Frosty, look! The Soviets have broken the nuclear test ban! Now Kennedy will have to do the same. We here at Mitre will have a chance to test our nuclear detection system—NUDETS—for real! Quick, call Willie Moore at the defense department! We've got to get started!"

It took a while to reach Willie since the whole Pentagon was in a complete dither. Willie promised to send a top secret message as soon as he found out anything.

Roger added, "Let's find Colonel Jones. He's going to have to modify his plans." The good colonel, the Air Force system program officer for NUDETS, was completely behind the curve.

"I have a directive from the Air staff to install a prototype nuclear detection system around Washington, D.C. in a year and a half at a cost of no more than $1.8 million. Until I get a different directive, I will proceed to do just that, and only that!" He would hold to that position for the next three years.

Willie, on the other hand, one of Secretary of Defense (SecDef) McNamara's whiz kids in the Office of the Director, Defense Research and Engineering (ODDR&E), knew his way around the Pentagon, but it took him from September 1961 to April 1962 to get Roger and his Mitre Corporation team out to the actual U.S. nuclear test range in the Pacific Ocean. Roger, for his part, got the General Electric Company promptly to design and build a "brass-board" prototype set of instruments—electromagnetic, optical, and seismic—that would determine whether these sensors would achieve the SecDef's requirements. Roger picked Palmyra Island, a thousand miles south of Hawaii and four hundred miles northwest of Christmas Island in the Pacific Ocean, as his location to give the equipment a very realistic test.

****

As Roger jumped off the stairs, an airman had unfolded from the C-124, and he stepped aside for the other men on the plane to disembark also. He straightened up and felt stiff in every extremity of his body after the five-hour flight from Hickam Air Force Base. *Oh, those bucket seats are cramped,* he thought as he looked out at the familiar scene before him. He had flown to Palmyra Island just four days previously, a quick round-trip with the owner of the island, Leslie Fullard-Leo, to get the lay of the land, so to speak, and to get the owner's permission to use his island for Roger's tests. Palmyra was part of Honolulu County, the southernmost part of the U.S., privately owned, and until the tests were announced, completely uninhabited. On this trip he thought he had everything he needed to fulfill his mission.

Roger had been enormously relieved to find Holmes and Narver there in full force and well established. H&N was the civilian firm contracted to provide complete logistical support to the personnel on all of the islands involved in the nuclear tests—food, water, tents, electricity, transport, and even movies each night for the men's diversion. He learned that there were also shuttle flights between and among the islands and Honolulu. On the return trip, Fullard-Leo told Roger he could do all the experiments he wanted—he had just taken the opportunity to get a free ride down to check on his island property. So the view from where Roger stood was familiar: the cluster of the tents set back from the runway, the dirt path leading along the narrow island past the one house still standing after many years of abandonment, and the many palm trees ringing the lagoon. He mused for just a minute about seeing a movie with Dorothy Lamour in a skimpy bathing suit slowly immersing herself in such a picture-perfect lagoon. *Come off it, Rog,* he thought. *I know there are no natives on this remote island, and certainly no women.*

Roger stomped his foot to ward off any cramp and took a few steps toward the front of the plane, carefully avoiding the prop-jet propellers and the huge forward part of the fuselage being raised hydraulically to make way for the forward unloading ramp. Roger called out, "Mr. Myers! Mr. Myers, over here!" Roger immediately felt the heat and humidity of the equatorial sun and ocean breezes. He struggled out of the jacket he had worn in the chilly plane. He and his teammates had on khaki shorts, a khaki shirt, sturdy boots, and a pith helmet. The shirt almost immediately became damp with his sweat. The flight had departed Hickam Air Force Base at 6:00 A.M., so the sun was in full force almost directly overhead just an hour before noon near the equator, a few days after the spring equinox.

Paul Myers looked up. He was the man in charge of the Holmes and Narver team on Palmyra.

"Oh, there you are, Mr. Malcolm. Hello again."

"Hello again to you, too. I trust you're ready to help off-load our trailer. I see that the crew chief has lowered the front ramp, so I suppose he is attaching the fifth wheel to the front of the trailer. Where is your truck to pull the trailer off?"

"We never did get any trucks sent down here, despite my many urgent requests. We're evidently at the tail end of the logistical wet noodle. All we have is that old, decrepit fire truck left over from the thirties back by the camp. It runs, but it has no brakes. I thought you knew that and would bring your own truck."

"What? No truck?" Roger said in great surprise to Myers. He added to himself, *Jeezus H…hullabaloo! Now that's put the kibosh on the project!* He looked around in desperation, trying to think how to get his trailer off the plane. He saw nothing that might work. Out loud he went on, "Sorry, I really didn't know. Well, how are we going to pull the trailer off the plane? It certainly can't go back to Hickam."

After some discussion, Lee Turner, Roger's right-hand man on his team, came to the rescue.

"Look, there's a jeep over there," Lee said. " Hopefully it has reasonably good brakes. Back the truck up the ramp with the jeep following in reverse, bumper-to-bumper. Get the fifth wheel connected to the truck, and then slowly let the jeep go down the ramp forward with the driver standing on the brakes, and inch by inch get all three vehicles down onto the ground."

"Lee, you're fabulous! Don't you think that will work, Mr. Myers?"

"I don't know what else to suggest. Let's try it."

Soon the truck and the jeep were backed up the ramp.

Roger climbed back into the C-124 and saw the Air Force crew chief underneath the front of the trailer. He and another crewman had jockeyed the fifth wheel into place. The fifth wheel allowed the two front wheels to support the trailer, which had only its two rear wheels. The fifth wheel was a horizontal metal plate attached to a regular trailer hitch to connect to a truck to pull it. The horizontal plate could be slid underneath the front of the trailer, which was supported by two stout arms that reached to the floor of the plane. The horizontal plate had a notch and a locking bar to connect to the trailer's underside between the vertical arms.

"That should do it," the chief said as he straightened up and moved beside Roger with the crewman. He took a step forward and shouted to the driver of the truck, "Okay, put 'er in low gear and start down the ramp!" He took another step and shouted to the man in the jeep, "Let up on that brake just a tad! Take it slowly." At that moment, the jeep moved, the truck moved, and the fifth wheel moved, but the trailer hesitated—and then its forward end crashed with a tremendous *bang* and a *crunch* onto the deck of the aircraft.

The crew chief jumped back and swore a string of swear words Roger had not heard since he left the navy eight years before. Then the chief quickly shouted, "Stop the jeep! Stop the truck! Stop! Stop! Stop!"

They both stopped.

"Ye gods!" shouted Roger. "What happened? Are you hurt? Is anybody hurt?"

"My filter! My filters!" Lee Turner exclaimed. Roger didn't know what that meant, and he didn't find out until later.

"I'm okay!" shouted the crew chief, as did the crewman. "That goddamn fifth wheel pulled out from the trailer! The goddamn lock on the pin didn't hold! Keerist a'mighty!"

Shortly, the plane's pilot and copilot, the jeep and truck drivers, Paul Myers, Roger's teammates, and a few stragglers climbed up into the plane and looked at the mess. Roger felt sick. *That's done it! Jeezus!* He saw the two support legs on his trailer had plunged right through the deck of the plane. That was the *crunch* he had heard. *Holy crimoly,* he thought. *That's the ground showing right through the holes in the deck. Now what are we going to do? How can they fly a plane with holes in the fuselage?* He shivered in the tropical heat of Palmyra Island swirling up from the open ramp of the C-124, and he suddenly realized that his whole project, directed personally by Secretary of Defense McNamara and authorized by the commander, Task Force 8, Lieutenant General Starbird, was most likely finished before it had even started.

Everybody swore and offered suggestions.

"Get another plane to fly in a crane that can raise the front of the trailer," said one.

"Nah, we're blocking the runway and can't take off," said the pilot.

"Get two jacks and raise the front of the trailer so the fifth wheel can go back under," said another.

This sounded more reasonable. Paul Myers sent two guys off to find a jack or two. There weren't any in the jeep or the fire truck.

Suddenly, the crew chief, who had disappeared behind the trailer to avoid being blamed for the accident, reappeared. He held the controls to the electric hoist that was installed in the rear of the plane. He was edging along between the trailer and the bucket seats very calmly, trying to coax the hoist along toward the front of the plane. It ran on two rails at the top of the cargo space where the trailer sat. Roger thought, *It won't clear the top of the trailer, and besides, it's too puny to lift this heavy trailer.* But the crew chief persisted, and it just cleared the whole top of the trailer. He lowered the hook, fastened it securely to the bottom of the trailer, and pressed the lift button. Every breath was held as the trailer slowly was raised. The hook held, the hoist cable held, the hoist kept hoisting, the rails fastened to the plane held, and the top of the plane held. The crew chief casually put the hoist on "stop," stepped to the edge of the ramp, and got the two drivers to get back in their vehicles. He motioned and shouted to them and slowly, slowly, had them move in reverse a foot or two back up the ramp as he guided the fifth wheel under the trailer again. With calm bravado, he ducked under the suspended trailer, shouted to the drivers to move another inch by inch, and finally was able to fasten the pin that would keep the fifth wheel from slipping out again. Every breath was held once more as the two vehicles inched forward, down the ramp, and—wow!— the trailer was on the ground.

Roger jumped into the fire truck and told the driver, "I'll show you where I want it. I marked the place down the dirt path about a thousand yards when I was here before." He heard the C-124 take off to return to Hickam as he had the trailer maneuvered into place. When his team walked the short distance to join him, he joked, "I'll bet those pilots will cook up quite a story about returning with two holes in their fuselage. Something like running into some fierce natives who shot at them as they escaped with their lives."

After the contretemps of getting the trailer off the C-124, they immediately set up in order to detect the first nuclear weapon explosion. Roger still didn't know the schedule of nuclear tests. His crew consisted of Hal Leach, the General Electric Company team chief; Joe Henry, the electronics whiz who had designed and built the NUDETS prototype system; and Lee Turner, the Mitre senior technician. Ultimately, Roger's team would record the sensor signals from twenty of twenty-six nuclear weapons tests detonated just off the southern tip off Christmas Island and one high-altitude burst set off over Johnston Island a thousand miles to the northwest.

Chapter Three

Emmie's World War II with Professor Chebandrov

I t was the spring of 1945. Emmie told herself, *Now, don't cry. Don't even think about crying. You're grown-up now; you mustn't cry.* But then she burst into tears, and so did everybody else. She soon choked them back, sniffled, took out her hanky, blew her nose, dried her eyes and cheeks, and managed to say, "Oh, dear! Now I've spoiled everything."

"Oh, no," said Margaret Hawthorpe, her wartime mother. "Oh, bother! You're just you, my beloved Emmie. You've promised to write—and to come visit every summer. So there! Be off with you. London-town is where you belong now. Go and enjoy your own home, and give our best to your parents."

Christopher Hawthorpe, her wartime father, stood on the train platform looking rather miserable. He piped up, "Yes, Emmie, come visit us often. We are sure going to miss you behind the counter at our store. Please write," he added, shedding a few tears into his handkerchief as he blew his nose.

"Yes, write. Write often. Tell us all about your life in London," added Mrs. Hawthorpe, giving Emmie a strong hug.

The train's whistle tooted and the conductor shouted, "All aboard!" Emmie grabbed her suitcase stuffed with all of her belongings, swung up into her compartment, and all too soon, she was under way.

Mary-Ellen Islington Trowbridge, "Emmie" as she was affectionately called, shivered in the train carrying her to London. It was late April in 1945, and the war against Germany was just about over. Her parents had agreed that she could come home now. The last of the V-1 buzz bombs and V-2 missiles had landed in March; incredibly, none had hit their home directly, although one of the last V-1s had hit nearby, knocking the side porch and chimney askew and blowing out all of the windows on that side. No one was hurt, but her father had only had time to put cloth over the window frames. Window glass was as scarce as putty, or mortar for the piles of old bricks lying around. She shivered more from the prospect of coming to a home she scarcely knew and to her parents, who suddenly seemed remote, than she did from the lack of heat in the train. It was a long journey with several changes of trains from Keswick to London Bridge Station, well over four hours.

* * * *

She had been evacuated from her cozy home in the London suburb of South Oxney as a ten-year-old child in early September 1939, when the British authorities feared a German Luftwaffe attack at the outset of World War II. Many schoolchildren were sent, school by school, into the strange countryside where families, many in quite rural farm settings, had to make room for them. Not a year later, France fell and the false lull in the war against Germany ended in a bang as the Luftwaffe suddenly appeared over London, raining bombs down on the populace. The RAF flew up to meet the bombers, guided by the new radar system, and made life short for many Nazi aircraft crew, but the response of the government was likewise prompt: "Get the remaining children out of London!" There ensued chaos at the railroad stations as the mass of children and their parents assembled for the relocation. Attempts were made to get the kids to queue up, hold onto their meager sandwich for lunch, show their letter of destination and receiving family, be given a train number, and six-by-six get into a compartment on the correct train. Then it was chaos at the other end, as one train pulled in at various cities and emptied its human cargo, and another pulled in right behind it. Volunteer women from the Red Cross and the Girl Guides were there with their lists, and they shouted over the din to get children and foster parents together. Tempers flared, kids got shoved, and most of those under ten cried. It took too long for everybody, but finally the pairing-off succeeded.

Luckily, Emmie's school in London, on the other hand, was the prestigious Francis Holland School at Clarence Gate near Baker Street in London. The girls in this school were sent in 1939 to Roedean in Brighton, an even more prestigious school for girls that had been founded in 1888 to prepare its students for entrance into Girton or Newnham colleges at Cambridge. Since Brighton was on the seashore when the blitz by the Luftwaffe had started in earnest over London in 1940, Roedean was commandeered by the Royal Navy for their mining and torpedo school, and the Roedean girls were sent all together to the small village of Keswick in the Lake District for the duration of the war. The trip was well planned but very long, over six hours. They went by train from Brighton to Southampton, to avoid London, changing to go north through Birmingham to Manchester, where they caught a slower train. That one took them through Preston to Penrith, where they were loaded onto a creaky, very old single-car rural train, finally arriving completely exhausted at Keswick. It seemed that the entire Keswick community was there to greet them, and everyone responded promptly to make the new girls welcome. Emmie was taken in by the Hawthorpes, Christopher and Margaret, who had a small, typical yarn and knitting shop right in Keswick. Some of the other girls were similarly located in town, but others were taken in by farm families not far away. Mrs. Hawthorpe fussed over Emmie and took her right over to their shop, fed her a sandwich and some soup, and then took her up the stairs to their living quarters and showed her to her room. It was awfully small, but as soon as Mrs. Hawthorpe left her alone, Emmie dropped onto her bed and was sound asleep.

The next morning was Sunday, so after breakfast the three of them went around the corner to the Anglican Church. After dinner Mr. Hawthorpe asked Emmie to join him in the kitchen. He said, "The woman organizing your trip told me yesterday that your headmistress plans to start school right away. The Roedean classes are to be held in the Keswick railroad station waiting room and in the local hotel's conservatory. So tomorrow morning I'll take you over there, and I believe that you will start your school year right where you left off. You'll be in the A form, I believe."

Emmie hoped that the rigorous academic standards and classroom behavior instilled at Roedean would not suffer by the change in location. In fact, she knew that she was bright and had maintained honors in all of her courses. Soon she was studying hard to keep up with the Roedean school's demanding curriculum, but she still managed to keep busy outside of school by helping in the Hawthorpes' shop and by playing games, swimming in the lake in the summer and skating on it in the winter, and hiking in the hill country around the lakes with the other girls.

* * * *

The war years went by slowly, but Emmie had what would turn out to be great good fortune. By one of those amazing coincidences that she never could quite comprehend, Professor Alexander Chebandrov had become the math teacher in the Upper School at Roedean in 1940. After a couple of years, Professor Chebandrov despaired of finding any student in Roedean truly interested in math, but having no choice, he stuck it out there. To his great surprise, in 1943 he found out that he had a prize on his hands: Emmie. Despite her being in her last year in the middle school, he just happened to see her grades on the Oxford and Cambridge School Certificate (O&CSC) and spotted her top score in math. Wondering if she really was interested in that subject, he arranged for her to meet with him in the upper school and began tutoring her in algebra, and then calculus and right up to Riemann Surfaces. "Call me 'Prof,' I'll call you 'Miss Trowbridge,' and we'll get along just fine," he said. And they did.

During the next several years, while he tutored Emmie in math, she came to hear his story. "I was a young Russian mathematician at the Lomonosov Moscow State University in the early 1920s and certainly had a flair for math," he told her. "I managed to get several notable papers published in international math journals, so I was offered a prestigious position at the University of Berlin in 1926. I accepted it, thinking I would stay in Germany for just a few years. But when I learned of Stalin's totalitarian rule, I forsook my Russian roots and took out German citizenship in 1931. Suddenly, as a Jew, I realized I had jumped from the frying pan into the fire. Desperate to get out of Germany, I appealed to my British acquaintances and with great relief was offered a junior professorship at the University of Edinburgh. Again, the frying pan sizzled, and I was judged an enemy alien when England declared war on Germany in 1939. As I listened to the British bureaucrat assigned to handle my 'alien problem' tell me that I would be sent to Canada for the duration of the war as soon as transport became available, I protested vigorously. I was told I would no doubt have to work in a factory or on a farm. 'I'm too old for that,' I said loudly. 'I'm fifty-nine and have never done things like that. All I know how to do is teach mathematics to young students and write scholarly articles on advanced topics such as topology—two- and three-dimensional surfaces, to be exact.' The bureaucrat said, 'You don't have to shout, sir. Let me ask around the office to see what other officers are doing in situations like yours. What kind of surfaces, did you say?' I replied, 'Riemann and…well, you know…like saddles.' After a short time he returned and said, 'Well, perhaps we could use a man like you in our farm country. You could possibly teach a few youngsters some arithmetic as well as caring for the horses saddles.'"

Chuckling to himself as Emmie smiled, the professor continued telling Emmie how he got to the Roedean School in Keswick. "The bureaucrat made some telephone calls, hemmed and hawed, filled out some forms, and finally gave me a one-way train ticket from Edinburgh to Penrith and a paper with the name of the headmistress of the Roedean School on it with a telephone number and directions from the train station at Penrith to the train to Keswick. The bureaucrat said, 'Actually, I think you may like it at that school. It's not the university, but it does provide a college curriculum, and I'm sure they need teachers.' Shortly, after more bureaucratic delays, I got off the train from Edinburgh at Penrith. Caught that awful train to Keswick, and looking at the map I had been given, walked the couple of steps up to the station waiting room and found Headmistress Lawrence. She welcomed me right away and seemed overjoyed to meet me since her school staff was sorely depleted. She promptly got me settled as a boarder with the Woodsons, that farm family near the school. I was just as promptly appointed head of the math department for the upper forms at the beginning of 1940. As you know, in my off hours, I do care for some horses and their saddles on the farm, and ride one to school almost every day."

* * * *

The train to London in 1945, which Emmie had changed to in Birmingham, slowed and broke Emmie out of her reverie. The thought of Prof had warmed her, and now she could face her parents with the calm and daughterly fondness they expected. She had been back to London twice before, when her parents thought it was safe, but then hurriedly sent back to Keswick when the buzz bombs, and later the V-2s, began to rain down. So she had seen the devastation in London before and was not completely shocked as the train pulled in to London Bridge Station.

"Oh, my darling Emmie," said her mother as she got off the train. "It's been much too long. I've missed you so completely." Her mother couldn't help breaking out in tears.

"Welcome home, Emmie. I hope to God it's for good." Her father too had to get out his handkerchief.

"Oh, Mummy and Daddy, yes, yes, now I can believe I'm home. Is the terrible war truly over?"

"Yes," said her father. "It should be over for sure in a few weeks. Now we just need to get you home and settled. I will still be commuting to Bletchley Park but am hoping to get a position here in London soon."

"And I have finished my war job with the RAF and will be staying home for a while," said her mother.

Emmie was shocked as they approached their home on the tram, since the house hadn't had maintenance for five years and the sheeting over the windows made it look even more dilapidated. A V-1 buzz bomb had hit close to the house next door, and the ruins were likewise shocking because she had known the neighbors well. Luckily they had survived the V-1 blast since they were not at home at that moment and had then moved in with relatives outside London.

After getting Emmie unpacked, Mrs. Trowbridge prepared a lunch as best she could, what with the rationing and shortage of meat, fresh vegetables and fruit that Emmie had enjoyed in the farm country around the Lake District. Emmie's father then spoke what was on each of their minds. "So, what will you do this summer until school starts again in the fall? You know you could enroll right now for the last of the spring session. You would surely qualify for the fifth form, from what your professor and Headmaster Barron have written me."

"Oh," replied Emmie, "I was hoping to study at home until fall. Prof has given me the fifth form curriculum and said that I surely could go right into the sixth form. I will just need to get the right books from our local school."

"But dear," said her mother, "that would put you two years ahead of your age group. Do you think that's wise?"

"I know the professor thinks most highly of you, but school is a social as well as an academic place," added her father. "To go from even the fine Roedean School in Keswick to the rough and tumble of an urban school may be awfully tough on you."

"Oh, but I know I can do well. The Hatch End School is close by, and they have a good reputation; the prof checked, and he said so. He expects me to take an A in math—in fact, in every subject I take."

"Why not continue at Roedean?" asked her father.

"The navy still hasn't cleared out from Brighton, and may never do so. Roedean is still looking for a place to move back to."

"Well, go to it, Emmie," said her father. "I am so delighted that you are home here with us and that you are so confident in your abilities. We love you so and will support you in anything you do."

Chapter Four

Roger's World War II and the Korean War

O n December 7, 1941, Roger Malcolm was in his family home's basement working on a balsa-wood model of the new battleship, USS *Washington*. He and his buddy Richard "Dick" Mullen had been fascinated by a news story about the latest and largest battleship, just commissioned at the Philadelphia navy yard in May 1941. The two friends were thirteen years old and in the ninth grade at the local junior high school in Framingham, Massachusetts. Roger suddenly perked up. The radio in the living room upstairs was blaring forth. He put down the wooden model with its hull partially shaped and ran up the stairs. "Turn that thing down!" he shouted at his younger brother. "What are you doing?"

"It's Pearl Harbor. The Japs bombed Pearl Harbor. What's Pearl Harbor?"

"It's not *what's* Pearl Harbor, it's *where's* Pearl Harbor," Roger shouted, just as his brother turned the volume down.

"All right," his brother said softly. "*Where's* Pearl Harbor?"

"It's in Hawaii, in the Pacific Ocean," Roger replied just as softly. "It's our naval base out there. I doubt that the Japanese would attack it. It's too heavily defended."

"Well, I'm just telling you what the radio announcer said."

The next day Dick and Roger pedaled back from the morning session at school and sat by his family radio as President Roosevelt gave his "A Date Which Will Live in Infamy" speech to Congress, and they knew they were at war with Japan. Three days later, the U.S. also was at war with Germany and Italy—the Axis powers.

They lingered for a bit, stunned at the news. Roger thought out loud, "I doubt that we, you and I, will have to get in to it. America's wars last only four years. We'll be just graduating from high school by then."

"Four years! There's nothing in the history books that says our wars last only four years! We just lost our Pacific fleet, and surely we'll have to fight Hitler and Mussolini as well as Japan! God! Look," added Dick, "my two brothers are in the Air Corps. They'll be in this right from the start. We could be joining them all too soon, probably as soon as we turn sixteen. Four years, my eye!"

"Gee," replied a chastened Roger, "I didn't know…I didn't think…gee, you're right, Dick. This could involve everybody. So what shall we do? Just sit and wait to get drafted? Do you want to be a grunt slogging through the mud and living in a foxhole?"

"Yeah, but remember what our assistant scoutmaster Ricky Whitney said: 'Join the navy and see the world—through a porthole!' The navy has lost a bunch of ships already. Do you want to drown? I say let's get appointed to the naval academy, get a free education, and become an officer way after this war is over."

"Oh," replied Roger sarcastically, "that's easy. Just appear in Annapolis and join the midshipmen."

"Well, let's think about it."

* * * *

The war actually lasted just a little under four years. Neither Roger nor Dick were drafted or had to serve in the military. They were good Boy Scouts, collecting newspapers, bacon fat, toothpaste tubes, tin cans and other metals; learning close order drill; riding the bus or their bicycles to save gas; observing the blackouts; and doing whatever ever else they were told to do.

Earlier in the spring of 1945, they had applied to college, having taken the Scholastic Aptitude Tests and scored well. Roger had achieved highest scholastic honors as well as honors for leadership and service at high school. He also had played varsity football, hockey, and baseball and had been captain of the ice hockey team. He figured he was a shoo-in to get into either Harvard or the Massachusetts Institute of Technology. When the acceptances came out, Dick asked Roger, "How'd ya do?"

"You know that I applied to Harvard and to MIT. I got admitted to both," Roger replied a bit sheepishly. He knew that Dick's grades had not been as good as his. "I've decided to follow my father's and brother's footsteps to Harvard. What about you?"

"Oh, I did much better. I'm going to Dartmouth. No pansy John Harvard for me."

"Pansy? Pansy? Just wait until I get out my hockey stick, and we'll see who's a pansy!"

They graduated from high school just after the war ended in Europe and took summer jobs. After V-J Day in 1945, both went to college.

Two years passed. Roger plunged into the life at Harvard, signing up to major in chemistry. He knew it was tough on his father to pay the bills, so he took summer jobs to help pay them. With a wary eye on the debates in Congress about the military draft (which was actually abandoned in 1947, but reinstated in 1948), Roger, at the end of his sophomore year in June 1947, noticed an advertisement in the Harvard Crimson daily newspaper for the "Admiral Holloway Plan," the renewal of the Naval Reserve Officers Training Program (NROTC, or "Rotcee" to some). He responded immediately. The notice read:

> Admiral Holloway, the Chief of Naval Operations, is convinced that the NROTC Program is required to fill all of the officer slots in the post-war navy. Any high school graduating senior who passes a rigorous academic and physical exam and be admitted to one of the colleges accepting such students could be selected. The student will receive his full tuition and fifty dollars per month for books, fees, and living expenses. Following graduation, he will be liable for naval service for eighteen months, or at the pleasure of the president, three years.

"Now that's a dream come true," Roger thought. His father had paid for one year, 1943–1944, at Harvard for his older brother, who then got into the navy V-12 program. He had just returned from his service in the navy and re-entered Harvard on the GI Bill. Roger's thought was, "Now I need the NROTC for myself, with brother Walter coming along."

His father was, of course, delighted. "Do you think you can make it, Roger?" Dad was scrimping by with his small appliance store. He needed all the financial help he could get.

"Oh, sure, Dad, no problem." Roger had raced over to the navy office in the yard as soon as he saw the notice and breathlessly asked for the application forms. They required a multiple-choice exam covering a wide range of topics presumably included in a good academic high school, and a stringent physical. Although the navy notice read "any high school graduating senior," no one questioned that he was entering his junior year at Harvard. He took the exam and aced it, and he was accepted pending the results of a physical exam. He passed that without a hitch. Roger and his dad were exultant.

"Now I can finish Harvard and have two more years to get an advanced degree somewhere," Roger said. "Then it's only an eighteen-month stint in the navy—perhaps at the Naval Research Lab. We're not likely to get into a war by then, so what's to lose?"

Two years later, after the commencement exercises at Harvard in 1949, Roger was admitted to the graduate program at Northwestern University in Evanston, Illinois, which also had an NROTC program. He received a research assistantship and had a chance to conduct an experimental project that would lead to his master's degree in physical chemistry.

The very next year, in June 1950, North Korea upset all his plans. Their army had launched an unprovoked attack upon South Korea. President Truman had obtained the agreement of the United Nations (UN) to declare war on North Korea and had sent troops immediately to reinforce the badly outmanned and outgunned South Koreans. After retreating to a tiny foothold on the South Korean peninsula, General MacArthur, in a stunning move, sent a strong invasion force directly from the U.S. to land far behind enemy lines. The North Koreans retreated under fire, pursued by the American-led UN forces almost to the Yalu River, the border of Korea with China. An army force of about a million Chinese suddenly swept across the river and forced the UN army back. The front line went back and forth, settling finally at just about the original border between South and North Korea at the thirty-eighth parallel.

In early 1951, worried about where the navy might send him when he got his ensign's bars, Roger had his adviser in chemistry write the Bureau of Naval Personnel (BuPers) to recommend that "Mr. Malcolm should be given a position with naval research to take advantage of his advanced knowledge of chemistry." Despite having received his master's degree in physical chemistry with his set of ensign's bars in June, Roger was surprised and chagrined when the commanding officer of the NROTC unit at Northwestern handed him his official orders from BuPers. It read:

> Upon successfully graduating from Northwestern University and receiving your commission as ensign in the United States Naval Reserve, you shall report to the commanding officer USS *Vector*, at the U.S. naval base, Norfolk, Virginia. You are hereby granted twenty days' delay in reporting. You shall serve at the pleasure of the president of the United States for three years or until otherwise relieved of duty as an officer in the United States Naval Reserve.

Roger reported to the USS *Vector* on July 20, 1951. Roger was going to sea and to war.

****

Ensign Malcolm stirred restlessly in his bunk in early August 1952 aboard the USS *Vector*, one of the last Fletcher-class destroyers built during World War II. She had five single, five-inch, 38-caliber gun mounts for her primary armament. Roger had just come off watch at 4 A.M. in July 1952 after one of those surprising and potentially deadly episodes in the waters close to shore behind enemy lines in North Korea. The *Vector* had been surprised by an enemy 90-millimeter gun on shore as she steamed casually north, a bit too close to shore—actually, to rendezvous with the U.S. Marine special forces for night actions behind enemy lines. The *Vector* had evaded the 90-millimeter shells and poured a torrent of five-inch shells back at the offending gun, silencing it. Roger thought, "What a crazy set of circumstances led to my being aboard this ship—just missing the draft for World War Two, joining the NROTC at Harvard to escape the post-war draft, the North Korean invasion, Truman's decision to intervene, and the start of the Korean police action, my failure to get assigned to naval research, and now trading gunfire with the enemy. In a way, I'm surely lucky to be still alive! What's next?"

His ruminations finally allowed him to sleep, but that was suddenly and rudely interrupted. "Mr. Malcolm, Mr. Malcolm, wake up! You're the boat duty officer. You have to get on deck immediately!" The seaman had turned on the lights in the stateroom, blinding Roger temporarily.

"What? What are you talking about?" Roger sat up and looked at the seaman shaking him.

"You know. The ensign just coming off watch becomes the boat officer. There's an emergency! Get your clothes on, grab your helmet, '45 and life preserver, and get topside!"

Still buttoning his jacket, Roger staggered onto the main deck. It was completely dark, of course. They were in a war zone accompanying the Marines. The chief gunner's mate poked him in the ribs. "Here, Mr. Malcolm, take this automatic rifle and a spare magazine. You may need it. That .45 on your belt won't do you much good in a firefight."

"How do you work it? I've never shot one."

"Oh, it's simple. Just click it here to put the first shell in the chamber, flip off the safety, aim it, and pull the trigger. You've got twenty-four shots in each magazine."

Just then, the chief bo's'n mate grabbed Roger, shoved him toward the motor whaleboat, and said, "Get in." Roger awkwardly complied. Four sailors and the boat engineer followed. The deck force swung the boat out on its davits free of the ship and lowered it roughly into the sea. The motor roared into life, and they were off into the darkness, a brisk sea causing them to plunge up and down as they motored at top speed.

"Where are we going?" Roger shouted to the coxswain. As the only officer aboard, Roger suddenly realized that he was in command of the boat and responsible for whatever happened.

"I'm following a compass course we just got over the radio toward shore," replied Cox'n First Class Bingham. "The marines are already there and will guide us in. They've been in a firefight and taken some casualties. We have to get them to our ship's corpsman and later have them airlifted to a carrier or to a hospital in Japan."

Roger still couldn't see a thing but turned toward Bingham and told him, "I should know, but I've never fired this thing," showing him the automatic.

"Here," said the cox'n. "I'll click the first shell into the chamber, and here's the safety. Turn it off and try it out to sea away from the ship." Roger found the safety, flipped it, and sure enough, managed to fire a couple of rounds. He had to rub his shoulder where the force of the recoil of each shot surprised him. "Now you've got it," said Bingham. "Just pray we don't have to shoot our way in or out."

Soon they all saw a tiny light flash a coded signal. "That's it," said the cox'n. He aimed right toward it and directed the engineer to slow as they plowed through the surf. The engineer cut the engine as the bow slid ashore, and all four seamen jumped overboard and sloshed out to grab the forward painter and haul the boat as far as they could up the beach with the motor still in the surf ready to pull back out. The cox'n and Roger jumped into the surf and helped secure the boat on shore with the anchor while the boat engineer remained on board ready to start the engine once they were back in the water. A marine lieutenant appeared out of the darkness, saw Roger's ensign bars, and said in a whisper, "Thank God you got here. We have two men down with serious injuries and will get them onto your boat immediately. We'll need your men to help. All I've got left are five of us, including me. We've also got two captives that we grabbed off the road and have trussed up. The enemy is all around us, so we've established a four-man perimeter to hold them off until you get away, and we can do likewise. Be ready to respond to my orders to fire at anyone I indicate."

Roger realized that the cox'n had already motioned to his four seamen to move forward to where the injured men lay on two stretchers. One by one they lifted them and carried them as tenderly as they could and lowered them into their motor whaleboat, placing life preservers under and around them. Just then, automatic rifle fire erupted from the left side of their perimeter, but it was aimed at the shore some distance away. The marine lieutenant whispered to Roger, "We placed some booby traps over there in the hope that they would think we were behind some rocks in that direction. Our man on the left may have lobbed a grenade as far over to the left as he could throw it to draw them further off. I guess they took the bait. Quick now, before they discover we're over here."

Roger tapped his cox'n on the shoulder and motioned toward their boat. "Get the anchor out of the sand and have the men start shoving us off. I'll be the last man aboard." As his men moved quickly, Roger stood looking back toward the darkness. Four figures appeared sprinting for their own boat on the beach besides Roger's. Two stopped, turned, and fired their automatics behind them, spraying the entire perimeter. Then they sprinted, and the other two repeated the firing. When they got to their boat they repeated their shooting as they heaved their captives onto the boat without much care how they landed, shoved the boat off the beach, and jumped aboard. Last in was the lieutenant, who stood in the bow and fired his entire magazine into the dark, just missing Roger, who luckily had bent low next to his boat. One of the marines started their boat's diesel engine, and the engine caught and roared to life. They backed away, swinging around and heading out to sea.

Roger suddenly realized that his boat was already in the water and moving away, so he shouted, "Here I come!" He clicked a shell into his rifle, managed to flip off the safety, turned, and fired the whole thing the way he had seen the marine do it. He was answered by a burst of fire from the darkness. His engineer, standing in the rear of the boat, let out a cry and fell into the well of the boat onto one of the wounded men lying there. Roger clambered aboard the bow, found his spare magazine, managed in his desperation to get the empty off and the full one onto his rifle, turned toward the beach, and fired again, sweeping from one side of the boat to the other but stopping after expending about a dozen shots.

Meanwhile, the cox'n had scrambled aft past his four crewmen, trying not to step on the wounded men, and bent over the engineer. "He's been shot, and it's pretty bad."

"Let him be! Get the engine running and get us out of here," Roger shouted as another burst of gunfire from the shore erupted. Roger saw several figures come running out of the dark toward his boat and let loose the last of his bullets toward them. The cox'n had trouble starting the diesel engine. He pushed the throttle all the way forward and tried again. This time the diesel caught and roared to life. As the cox'n threw it into reverse gear, the boat lurched backward, almost throwing Roger forward over the bow, bent double. At that moment, as he caught hold of the gunwale, a searing hot pain went through the entire right side of his chest. *Jeezus!* he thought. *Goddamn! I've been hit.* But he steadied himself by holding onto the gunwale and slumping down onto the forward seat on their motor whaleboat, and didn't cry out.

The cox'n got the boat clear of the beach, swung it around, and headed out to sea after the marines' boat. He called to the seaman next to him, "Here, Mike! Take the rudder and try to catch up to the marines." Then he called to the second mate, a pharmacist second class who was attending to one of the wounded marines, "Quick! Come look at George, our engineer. See what you can do for him. I've got to radio our ship and get a compass bearing to head for." As they got abreast of the marines, he called out as loud as he could over the noise of both diesels, "Are you guys okay? We've picked up another casualty—our engineer!"

"Yeah, we're okay, but our mission is sure blown. At least we snatched a couple a guys for intel to work over. How bad is your man?"

"Don't know yet. I'll give you a compass heading to get back to our ship and on to your island in a minute." As he groped for their boat's radio, he shouted, "Mr. Malcolm! How're you?"

Roger shifted his position on the seat, sat up, turned to face aft, and managed to shout back, "I caught something in that last exchange of shots, but I seem to be okay. Just need a few Band-Aids. I'll come back aft to help out."

The coxswain answered, "Just stay there for now. Everything's under control. I just need to know how bad George is." Then he said to himself, *Ah, here's our radio. Now I can get our bearing to the ship.* Roger heard the cox'n call their ship and then his reply over the radio: "Yes, I got that bearing, sir. We're under way at top speed in company with the marines. We have three, maybe four wounded and two captives. Quite a haul!"

Roger felt blood running down his side. He stripped off his jacket and shirt and in the dark tried to staunch whatever flow of blood there was with the shirt. He had been sweating heavily, but now he was chilled by the night air whistling by him as the boat rushed along the ocean. He threw his jacket over his shoulders and hunched down to get out of the wind. *Some boat commander I am,* he thought to himself. *I'm just a wounded duck. Thank God for a competent cox'n.* The dawn was just breaking, and Roger anxiously scanned the horizon, hoping his ship was not far away. He now realized he was hurt pretty badly.

When they reached the *Vector,* Roger waited in the motor whaleboat while they hoisted George Briggs, their boat engineer, and the two marine casualties aboard the ship and took them into the wardroom, which had been hastily changed into a medical emergency room. Roger followed the rest of the men after the boat was hauled out of the water by the davits, clambering down onto the quarterdeck, where he promptly collapsed. Mike Dunnan, the pharmacist mate second class who had been on the boat, kneeled over Roger and quickly saw the problem. "He's lost a whole lot of blood. Quick, get him into the wardroom too and get him on plasma."

A few hours later, Roger awoke in his bunk. As he tried to turn over and get up, his whole body rebelled. His roommate, Lieutenant Clemmer, the chief engineering officer, was standing there and responded immediately. "Whoa there, Malcolm, you've had a rough night. Just lie back and take it easy."

"What happened? I remember climbing down from the motor whaleboat, but that's all. "

"Yeah, you were in a bad way—blood all over you and the boat. Luckily, a few bags of plasma and then a blood transfusion brought you right around. The chief pharmacist mate sewed up that huge wound in your side, but pronounced you whole otherwise. Now that you're awake, we'll get some hot soup into you, and as soon as you can handle some real navy chow, you'll be up and ready for more escapades."

"Golly, dingbat, and dooly-whistle," said Roger, lying back down and remembering that he never swore. "My first solo mission and I blow it. I've got to see Bingham, the cox'n, and praise him to the skies. He really saved the day for all of us. You know, if he hadn't revved up the boat engine so that when he put it into reverse gear it surged so suddenly I fell forward, I probably would have taken that bullet right in my chest. How lucky can I get? But how's George Briggs, our engineer, and the others, the marines we brought back?"

"They're all okay, at least as far as we know. George took a bullet right in his upper chest, but it missed his heart and he made it by chopper to the hospital ward on the aircraft carrier *Philippine Sea,* along with the two marines. They all will probably have to be flown to the navy hospital at Yokuska in Japan to be sure of their recovery. They are not out of the woods yet, that's for sure. But you—you're too ornery to get off this ship so easily. That's how lucky you are. But I must say, that's a hard way to get a Purple Heart!"

Later it turned out that the mission to get intelligence about the enemy behind enemy lines was so top secret that no one could report his, or Briggs', injuries to be awarded the Purple Heart award.

Roger recovered quite nicely, as his boss had told him. The USS *Vector* was relieved of her duty with the marines and close-in fire support to the UN forces at the bomb line where the two opposing armies faced each other. They were now assigned to plane guard duty with the two aircraft carriers operating in the Sea of Japan off the coast of North Korea. After a month of that arduous steaming back and forth, they went south to patrol the Formosa Strait. From there they set off to complete a trip around the world, stopping at ports from Subic Bay in the Philippines to Hong Kong, Singapore, Ceylon, Arabia, and Aden, and transiting the Suez Canal, Naples, Cannes, Gibraltar, and home to Norfolk. He wrote to Dick Mullen, now flying Corsair aircraft off one of the carriers behind them still bombing North Korea:

> Dick,
> Hope you are well and enjoying your chosen duty. I just completed an around-the-world cruise courtesy of the U.S. Navy, doing what Ricky Whitney told us to do—enjoy the view from a porthole! Actually, though, I am spending most of my time below decks since I'm in the engineering division. Hades couldn't be much hotter, but the shore liberty has been fantastic! Check in with me when you get back.
> Cheers,
> Roger.

Roger still had eighteen months left on his three-year hitch. Lieutenant Clemmer, the chief engineer, a reservist who had just completed his tour of duty, sprinkled a glass of holy water on Roger, and speaking very solemnly intoned, "Ensign Malcolm, I now dub thee 'chief engineer of the USS *Vector*.' Thank God for a capable replacement. Now I can get off this bucket and be with my family again." The paperwork, including his promotion to lieutenant junior grade, followed promptly, and Roger was soon in charge.

Roger wrote his parents, "I now know every nut, bolt, pump, pipe, and gizmo on this ship. I know all the one hundred forty men in the engineering department. But that doesn't tell me how to manage everything and everybody. I just hope it all works together." Later he wrote again, "On our very first trip out of the harbor at Norfolk, the ship began to fall apart—bricks fell out of one boiler, we got water in the oil and stopped dead for a time, one of the main turbine steam lines leaked—what turmoil! But the men were outstanding. They seemed to know just what to do, did it, and did not complain, and we got back in to port safely." The reports Roger made to the commodore had quite an impact, and the ship was ordered to be mothballed and put out of active service into the reserve fleet at Portsmouth, Virginia. Roger oversaw the entire operation.

Chapter Five

Emmie's 'First' at Girton

England had won the war, but in the summer of 1945 it was still in deep distress. London and other cities and port areas had been heavily bombed, and reconstruction was barely under way. The cream of English manhood had been decimated for the second time in less than three decades. The returning veterans had to fit back into an economy that was barely functioning. Rationing all essential goods was still necessary. The transportation system, electricity grid and other utilities, roads and bridges, and so many government buildings, residences, and factories that had escaped destruction from the air were very much in disrepair. The electorate, tired perhaps of his overbearing personality, threw Winston Churchill out as prime minister and elected Clement Atlee. An entirely new government had to handle these domestic challenges, as well as the problems abroad with France, the Soviet Union, China, the restive British Commonwealth, and the defeated Axis powers: Germany, Italy, and Japan. The English public had to muddle through.

In the fall Emmie took the local bus to Hatch End High School and registered for the sixth form. Several weeks later her mother found her after school in her room crying.

"Oh, Mummy, you were right. The girls at school are awful. I try to sit with them at lunch, but they just turn toward each other or move away. If I ask them a question, they either give me a sassy response or again turn away. 'MKIA,' they snicker—Miss Know It All."

"What about your teachers? Aren't they respectful to you?"

"Well, most of them. But the math teacher, Mr. Humphrey, is surely mad at me because I'm smarter than he is. He said, 'Just because you know some big math professor up north, don't think that impresses me.' He gives me tons of homework; I know it's much more than he gives everyone else in the class, and it's all just trivial problems. I can do them easily, but there are too many of them. I'm not learning anything, and I hate to waste my time. I thought he would help me get ready for my Oxford and Cambridge Higher School Certificate exams, but he has made no mention of them."

"Do you still think you can get into college? It's so competitive, and you want to study math. Isn't that still basically a boys' field?"

"Oh, Mummy! The prof—Professor Chebandrov—says I can make it if anyone can. He has been so very supportive, and I really do love math. It's…well, it's regular, it's totally rational, you can figure things out. The prof showed me how purely mathematical equations suddenly show up describing real physical data, like Newton's Laws, like alternating current and its imaginary components, like quantum mechanics and Schrödinger's equation with its Hamiltonian and Lagrangian solutions."

"I'm sure I don't know what you're talking about, but you sound so sincere. Your father seems to understand, but he too wonders about your competition. You speak of the Oxford and Cambridge certificates. You know they won't let you into either one. They're still just for men."

"But I can get into Girton. That's almost Cambridge, and there's talk of letting women into both Oxford and Cambridge."

"Oh, Emmie, you're incorrigible! Okay, go for it! You'll have to ignore all those mere mortal students at Hatch, suffer through teachers like Mr. Humphrey, and study, study, study. But we can still go to the parks around London for a picnic on Sundays, can't we?"

****

Shortly thereafter, the prof sent a letter to Mr. and Mrs. Trowbridge saying that he was coming to a math symposium in London and would like to drop by to see how their daughter was getting on. Mrs. Trowbridge wrote back, telling him to be sure to come and stay with them and that the whole family would enjoy seeing him. The prof arrived, walking the whole way from the hotel where the symposium was being held. He had begged off staying with the Trowbridges, saying, "I need to interact with the other mathematicians. I've saved up my ha'pennies and can afford it, but I do want to drop by."

After a Sunday midday meal, he talked to Emmie and her parents. "Emmie, you must realize that just getting top marks in your exams won't get you into Girton, or most other prestigious colleges and universities. You must have advocates to urge your case. I am returning to the University in Edinburgh, and there are still some colleagues from before the war who are graduates of Cambridge, some now quite elderly, but some not so. With your permission, I will speak to them and show them some of your work. Mr. Trowbridge, I understand you too were at Cambridge and may have similar colleagues. I suggest that we work together on this. Unfortunately, with the war and all, I do not know any dons or fellows who are presently at either Oxford or Cambridge. Do you?"

"Well, perhaps a few. We absolutely must make a strong case for Emmie. She has told me about your work on saddles, both on horses and Riemannian." They both chuckled, and Emmie joined in. Her father continued more soberly. "I hope you can get back into your field and start contributing to it again. But my work during, and even before, the war prevents me from saying anything much about math. I truly regret that aspect of my work. You would not believe what we have done these past few years. And it is not just in the work on radar and the atom bomb with the Americans. Someday, the story I must keep hidden will be told. We have saved countless lives and made astounding progress in understanding the relationship between entirely theoretical math and the real world. However, I suspect that very few, if any, of my former colleagues—the ones still at the universities and more particularly the ones out in government, industry, or commerce—would even remember me. I have published no academic papers and have simply a blank page in the academic record. I wish that were not so, but let's be realistic. Oh, perhaps I can find one or two former colleagues who might be willing to help out. So, here's a pen and some paper. Let's start helping Emmie by making a list and deciding what we tell each one."

✳ ✳ ✳ ✳

Emmie did get into Girton, and she secretly always knew that it was because she got all A's in her high school courses and aced the O&C Certificate exams. The prof and her father did contact the men they had listed and each was able to talk to one of them about Emmie. Emmie's father's contact said right away, "But she's a girl. What does she know about math? The men will eat her up!"

The contact at the University of Edinburgh agreed to sign a letter drafted by Professor Chebandrov to accompany Emmie's application to Girton. But when he found out the applicant was a young woman—in fact, a high school girl—and it was to Girton and not Cambridge, he backed way off. "They'd think I've gone all dotty at Cambridge, and probably at Edinburgh too." Finally he allowed a very noncommittal letter to be drafted, which he signed as "a friend of the family," and provided that to accompany Emmie's application.

In 1948, Girton became a college within Cambridge University, but the Girton campus was several miles from the university itself, and the undergraduates did not mingle all that much. Emmie found herself studying extremely hard for long hours and had essentially no social life. The great woman mathematician Mary Cartwright was the leading professor at Girton when Emmie first enrolled there in the fall of 1946, so Emmie looked to Professor Cartwright to mentor her through the difficult course work in theoretical math, which she wanted to major in. The courses were designed to prepare students for the Tripos exams. If a student excelled in these through the first three years, she would receive a bachelor of arts degree and qualify for a fourth year toward the master's degree.

Emmie went home on holiday and excitedly told her father, "Professor Cartwright is so famous, and she is so nice. She helps me whenever I have a problem or a question, and not just in math. I hope she will agree to assist me in my fourth-year research."

"Now, Emmie," said her father a bit patronizingly, "you haven't even finished your Part One and Two Tripos. Don't you have to ace those to get to the fourth year?"

"Oh, sure, Daddy, but so far I have had no trouble with the math. Professor Cartwright has been very supportive already."

"Well," added her father, "Professor Cartwright is an international star. She, along with professors Littlewood and Hardy, have made a huge difference in some of the work we do at Bletchley Park, and the Americans have praised both her and the men to the skies about their impact on radar and computers at the Massachusetts Institute of Technology and Harvard in Cambridge, Massachusetts."

"They all are stars in my mind," said Emmie. "They are the nicest, most pleasant and polite professors you can imagine. Littlewood and Hardy, too, have encouraged me already."

Indeed, there was almost none of the discrimination against women in math, particularly at Cambridge and Oxford, that still existed in the academic (and business) world elsewhere. But Miss Cartwright was made the headmistress of Girton in 1949, just as Emmie was ready to undertake serious research, so she was handed over to John Littlewood, an equally eminent mathematician at Cambridge with whom Cartwright had worked for many years. They had been persuaded to look into the differential equations involved in radio and radar transmissions and reception—subjects that became inordinately important when the war broke out. As the war ended, the two brilliant mathematicians turned their attention to more theoretical subjects, such as the dynamical fine structure solutions to certain differential equations, which later were called the butterfly effect. This is the concept that, in layman's terms, meant the mere flapping of a butterfly anywhere in the world could affect the weather worldwide. This became the basis for chaos theory, which is still a major part of modern mathematics.

Having aced the third year Tripos and received her B.A. degree, Emmie, for her very critical fourth year, 1949–50, she undertook a problem in advanced math that Professor Cartwright had suggested to her: the proof that certain fine structure solutions can be grouped statistically to form a boundary around the end results. But at the beginning of 1950, Professor Littlewood informed her that he would be retiring at the end of that academic year. Professor Hardy, with whom Littlewood had worked very closely over the recent years, had died in 1947. So Littlewood suggested Philip Hall as the professor with whom Emmie should continue after her fourth year.

"I'll see you through until then, Emmie, but you will need someone to advise you on your final Tripos," Professor Littlewood said. "That, as you know, is truly critical to your future career."

"Oh, thank you, thank you, Professor. I'm having trouble with this statistical approach since it means learning an entirely new field. I will need all the help I can get. If you and Professor Hall will both look over my work, I would appreciate that."

Professor Hall had achieved some notoriety at Cambridge and Girton with his marriage theorem, the result of his fully theoretical study of mathematical sets, which he tried to popularize by giving it a noteworthy name. He would say: "Imagine two groups, one of men and one of women of equal number. Each woman would happily marry any one in some subset of the men; and any man would be happy to marry a woman who wants to marry him. The mathematical result of applying his theorem is the finding that it is possible to pair up in marriage all of the men and all of the women so that every person is happy." This was a great icebreaker at any gathering of Cambridge men and Girton (or other institution) women.

However, regarding Emmie's fourth year, Professor Hall was not all that enthusiastic about either Emmie's problem or her approach. Emmie talked to her father about her situation. "He's just not like Cartwright and Littlewood," she complained. "I have a terrible fear that I may be stuck either with an insoluble problem or an inscrutable professor."

"Why don't you write to Professor Chebandrov? He has had a lot more worldly experience than Professor Hall. If Professor Littlewood has become preoccupied with his retirement, maybe the prof could give you some sound advice."

The prof, back at the University of Edinburgh since 1946, was eager to help Emmie. He took the train down to London, using the usual symposium as his reason, and Emmie came down from Cambridge to meet him at home.

"I read your letter, Emmie, with great interest, and even looked up some of the papers your professors Cartwright and Littlewood have written, but your research is so far beyond me now that I just don't know whether I can help you," the prof said. "This butterfly effect appears to be so chaotic that to put any boundaries on it seems improbable. You know, that one mathematician changed his input number by much less than one percent, and the whole function blew up."

"Yes, I've studied that, but if I generalize into additional dimensions, the functions appear to remain confined to the original set."

"That's amazing, Emmie. You may just be on to something. Look, here's what I have often done. Do not try to solve the whole problem all at once. Don't try any and all dimensions. Focus on those that seem to—what are you saying—cluster? You haven't much time left in your fourth year. Many solutions to problems seem to be just around the corner, and then take years to be resolved, if ever. Bite off what you can chew, take the 'first' in the Tripos that

I'm sure you will have earned, and accept the fact that *any* limit on chaos that you can show would be an astounding feat."

In the spring of 1950, Emmie graduated from Girton College with her 'first' in the final Tripos, her master's degree in theoretical math, and a grudging acceptance of her thesis by Professor Hall and the committee formed to examine her and her findings. Her proof was long, detailed, and difficult, but clearly it had succeeded. Her 'first' made news, not just because she was a woman, although that may have helped, but because Professor Littlewood mentioned the butterfly effect and chaos theory, and the reporters perked up. They harped on the butterflies and Emmie's challenge to the chaos theory. As a result, it was good press, but the mathematical world was not yet overly impressed with her results.

During these years of very hard work, Emmie had bicycled frequently over to Cambridge to take courses given only there and to discuss her work with her professors. She also was invited, as an upperclasswoman, to the afternoon or evening gatherings at the junior fellows' common room for sherry and even to a formal dinner at the university. But Emmie did not respond to any invitations to visit the men in their rooms, being quite aware of what might transpire. She was so totally concerned with her math that she denied herself almost all one-to-one contact with men. However, one fellow in economics, James Delavan, took her out to lunch on occasion. She enjoyed his company, but their relationship never went beyond those lunches.

Emmie's 'first' in math made headlines, though small and with short articles in *The Times* and other British papers. They heralded her accomplishment and spoke of following on the "exceptional mathematical abilities of Mary Cartwright, John Littlewood, and Godfrey Hardy."

"Emmie, darling, you're famous," said her mother when Emmie at last packed up her belongings and returned to their now fully restored home in South Oxney. "Oh, it's so good to have you back here at last."

"Yes," chimed in her father, "you truly make us proud. What an achievement, to take a 'first' at Cambridge and make *The Times!*"

"Oh, Mummy and Daddy, I just did what I liked doing. So I get mentioned in *The Times*. I suspect that and a couple a bob will get me a ride on the tube. Now I'm just going to relax and sleep, sleep, sleep. I'm truly fagged. I really need a change. Maybe after a rest I'll do something different."

"Well," said her father, "what about a vacation trip? What about the Costa del Sol, the Riviera? You name it. We'll go, just the three of us."

Just then, the phone rang. It was Stacey Conover. Emmie was not sure at that moment who Stacey Conover was, but she covered up by saying, "Who is this? I didn't get your name."

"Stacey Conover" she said slowly, "you know, captain of your Girl Guides troop way back before the war."

"Oh, sure, Stacey, our captain. It must be ten years ago. How have you been?"

"I've been busy, that's for sure. And you?"

"It's been study, study, study for me the whole time."

"Of course. That's why I'm calling. I saw the item about your 'first' in *The Times,* and it just struck me that you might be the one person who would like to help us out." Stacey stopped for a moment to try to be sure how to proceed with what she wanted to ask Emmie.

"What's that?" asked Emmie. "What do you want me to do? Right now I'm pretty well exhausted."

"I'm head of the Guide International Service. We're volunteers helping with the rehabilitation of Europe. I've been head of the service since it was formed in 1945. Things were pretty chaotic at the beginning, let me tell you."

"What exactly have you been doing?" asked Emmie. "You aren't restoring all those bombed-out buildings, are you?"

"No, no. We were trying to cope with basic services, making sure that no one got left out by the United Nations and the Allied Armies relief services. Right now we're focusing on getting everyone connected with their family, if anyone in their family has survived. If not, we're trying to help them decide where they want to go to pick up on their life. We also help with seeing that everyone able to work has a job, trying to fit their expertise to what needs to be done."

"Wow, that's a tall order!"

"You bet, so we have a continuing need for more volunteers. You talk about being exhausted. Well, so am I."

"Well, what would you want me to do? I can't quite see how a theoretical mathematician would be of use."

"Any former Girl Guide has the ability to help out. But in reading about your research, however theoretical it may have been, I sensed that it might have some relevance to our work. I've been talking to the War Office about their newfangled computers. What you might find interesting, as well as chal- lenging, is to apply your ability to sort through a set of complex variables in a rational, thoughtful, and caring way using those machines. They have agreed to make time available on them."

"Oh, Stacey, I don't know. This is really too much to get my mind around."

"What say I come around to your house in a day or two to show you some of our achievements and talk about what still needs to be done? Don't give me an answer yet."

"Well, I would like to see you again, but it's been ten years. I can hardly remember what being a Girl Guide was like. I'm not sure that has any relevance today. But all right. Come around. How about coming for lunch tomorrow?"

Emmie's mother and father were appalled when she told them about her conversation with Stacey. "It's been five years since the war ended. Things are getting restored pretty well now," said her father. "What can the Girl Guides do that the formal relief organizations can't do? I just don't see this as something you need to get involved with, Emmie."

Her mother added, "My job since the war is trying to help the orphan refugees here in England. You have a brilliant mind, Emmie. We need you here to put it to work on our problems in England, not other countries'. This Stacey woman is preposterous!"

Stacey came the next day and stayed all afternoon going over her work with Emmie. Emmie's parents were cordial but fretted the entire time. Finally Stacey left, and Emmie said to her parents, "Let's take that vacation to the Costa del Sol. I told Stacey that I would give her my decision when we got back."

****

Three weeks later after their trip, Emmie phoned Stacey and said, "I'll do it!" She agreed to join the Guide International Service with Stacey as her boss and mentor. It was a heady time for her. She left home and found a tiny apartment near her work (but never spent much time there with her overseas activities). Emmie spent the next three years finding families, jobs, and housing for every displaced person she could find. The War Office computers, along with staff members who punched the cards with the data Emmie provided, made a huge difference in the process. The trips overseas to deal with the actual refugees were exhausting, gut-wrenching work. Many times Emmie was just about to quit when one of her charges got a break and found a place to go. One young woman had walked with her mother and sister all the way from Breslau to Frankfurt-on-Main to escape the Russians. Emmie found her father and brothers there. Emmie found a grandmother in Potsdam for another young man, a presumed orphan, in desperate condition in Munich. As the years went by, she would receive letters from many of these refugees from the war, praising her for having saved their lives.

Then both Stacey and Emmie decided to move on, the former to a very responsible job as director of statistics at the home office in the British government statistical office. Emmie tried first to get back to her mathematics profession but quickly found that no one had a place for her. Each of the professors she talked to said, "Miss Trowbridge, you've been away from theoretical math for several years now. The field moves on. It will take you quite a while to catch up. I'm afraid I can't take you on under those circumstances." Also, the cost to enroll at Cambridge University was stiff, and living expenses would be high. She couldn't live at home and try to commute from London. She would have to get a job and study part time. She called Stacey.

"Oh, Stacey, I am not sure where to turn. I am going to have to take a real job." Emmie told Stacey all about her failure to find a place to take up her studies of math toward the Ph.D.

"Funny that you should call right now. I need an associate desperately, and I truly was just about to call you to come back to work with me, Emmie."

"Thank God," answered Emmie. "You're in a statistical office, aren't you? What could I do for you?"

"This is real, Emmie. I really need you right away, again. You know, this office is still in the Dark Ages. I've been here only a couple a days. They don't know a Poisson from a Gaussian distribution, and they wouldn't know the Bayes Theorem if they fell over him. It will take a lot of work to bring this place up into the modern world of statistics, and you're the only one I know who can do that. It won't be fundamental or theoretical Ph.D.-type investigation, but it will sure serve Her Majesty's government well. Actually, our office is in The City—the financial district of London—so you can live at home and commute. The hours are nine to five, so you could continue your theoretical work at home in the evenings."

"What's the catch, Stacey? There must be some catch. It sounds too good to be true."

"Well, the pay is modest, you know, civil service rates. But it comes with a pension if you live long enough."

"Okay, I am interested. I'll be over to see you. Is tomorrow convenient?"

"No, come today. We've got a lot of paperwork to get you on board, and time's a-wastin'."

Emmie signed on that very day. She could say within the month, "This isn't too bad." She moved to a much nicer apartment, she began to save money, she began to meet interesting people, and even began to get invitations from men to various functions—for lunch or dinner, museum shows, art gallery openings, the theatre.

Time flew by. Within a couple of years she felt she could say, "You know, Stacey, we might just have created almost a modern statistical service for the British government. That's not too shabby!"

"It's all due to you, Emmie. No one else could have done it."

"Aw, you've been in charge and given me all the support I have asked for, and then some. It's truly been a team effort."

Then James Delevan called her up. "Hi, do you remember me? I've been working in The City now for some time, and as soon as I heard you were too, I thought we ought to try lunch again."

Emmie did, of course, remember James as one of those fellows in the junior common room at Cambridge who had often asked her out. Somehow she knew he was married. It had been a society affair, and the newspapers had been full of it. *But lunch again?* she thought. *Could that be a problem?*

"Oh, James," replied Emmie after catching her breath. "So nice to hear from you. It would be fun to catch up. Is tomorrow too soon?"

"Tomorrow it is. I'll swing by your office and pick you up."

And so the affair started. Before long Emmie rationalized it by telling herself, *A lot of men sleep about. I wonder how "it" feels?*

But James took his time. He kept their meetings to just lunches for several weeks. Then he called her and asked, "What about dinner tonight at Brown's Hotel?"

Emmie figured that this was it. Brown's Hotel was *the* posh hotel in London. "I'd love to," she said, trying to keep the excitement out of her voice.

She told no one, but took off work early, found just the right dress, had her hair done, and was ready at 7:00 P.M. when James breezed to a stop in his Jaguar in front of her apartment.

The dinner was impeccable, with a cocktail to start, white wine with the fish, and then red wine with the beef. Emmie said, "Oh, let's skip the dessert to keep our figures," and James escorted her right to the elevator and up to their room. She had told herself, *Now, don't just throw yourself at him. Let him set the pace.*

He had champagne on ice but said right away, "Emmie, why don't you go into the bedroom and put on the nightgown I have hanging there?" It was a sheer silk, and she noticed that the sheets were silk also.

She went to the bathroom then back to the bedroom, where she slipped off her clothes, put on the nightgown, and slipped between the sheets. She lay back, tingling with excitement. James came in with his robe and nothing else on, bent down, kissed her on the lips, and disappeared into the bathroom.

Suddenly Emmie heard the door to the front room open. Then, with a bang, the bedroom door opened.

"Get out of that bed, and get out of this room!" shouted a woman. "You're Emmie, aren't you?" James opened the bathroom door and stood there transfixed. "I know all about you and James. This has been going on a long time, but finally I've caught you two."

James started to say, "Margo, you've got this all wrong…"

"Oh, no, I haven't!" the woman shouted. It was obvious to Emmie that she was James's wife. "Come on, you slut. Get your clothes on and get out!"

* * * *

The next morning, Emmie went right in to see Stacey. Crying and blubbering, she blurted out the whole story. Finally she stopped and said, "Oh, Stacey, what am I going to do? I can't stay here in this office or even in The City. I'm a ruined woman!"

"Oh, Emmie, stop it! None of that is true. James is a rotter, and you're better off getting away from him. Pick yourself up and after a couple a weeks, start dating other men. Just let me run a background check on them before you go all the way. Better yet, when you find the right guy, wait for him to ask for your hand or at least be very sure he's Mister Right before jumping into bed."

Emmie couldn't get the affair out of her mind. Two months later, she went to Stacey. "I have to tell you that I've been asking around about other jobs. Actually, I think the work here has become a bit, shall we say, humdrum?"

"Oh, Emmie, we've got so much more to do here in this office. Don't leave now."

"I know, Stacey, I know. But you have a lot of bright, experienced girls here in this office. You could promote any one of them and do everyone a favor, yourself included. I'm an old war horse around here now. I need a real change."

"What do you mean by that? You're not giving up on statistics…on math…on everything you've learned, are you?"

"Well, in a way. I called Roedean and spoke to the headmistress, Miss Shaw. She had heard of me and wanted to know what I was doing. After a bit, I asked her straight out whether she had any openings for a math teacher. She practically jumped out at me."

"Oh, Emmie, what do you know about teaching math?"

"Well, maybe nothing, but she asked me to come down tomorrow and talk about it. Roedean is back on the cliffs of Brighton again. The navy gave them some nice rooms when they downsized after the war, and the whole place has been updated."

* * * *

When the next semester started, Emmie was the new math teacher at Roedean for the middle and upper forms, as well as the science teacher for the lower school. She had taken a small apartment in Brighton and could walk to work. Both her parents, and Stacey, were horrified. Emmie was ecstatic.

But it couldn't last. Two years later, she awoke to find on her doorstep a copy of the *Post*, the London tabloid, as she picked up her daily bottle of milk. She opened it warily because she had never subscribed to such a rag. What was it doing here early in the morning? Suddenly she saw it. Right on the front page was a color photo of Margo and James Delevan. They were getting a divorce, and it was big news in The City. How much would she take him for? The corner of an inside page had been turned down. There was a large color photo of Emmie in James's arms, and he was holding her very close in a provocative pose. Other photos on that and other pages purported to show all of James's women. The text accompanying the photos made no distinction between those James had laid and any who may not had been, or not quite had been, such as Emmie.

Emmie could hardly get back in the house and up the stairs to her apartment in Brighton. She sat there a long time, first in tears, then in anger, and finally in a mood to tear Margo and James apart. Suddenly she knew what to do first. She marched right over to Roedean, knocked on the headmistress's door, and walked in. "Miss Shaw, I don't know if you saw this," she said, breathing steadily and holding up the newspaper to show it to her, "but in any case, someone will send it to you, so I am trying to minimize any damage to Roedean that it might cause. I hereby give you my resignation, effective immediately." Holding up her hand again, she went on, "No, don't try to dissuade me. The damage has been done with this photo. You can call the board of trustees and just tell them that I have moved on to other pursuits. When the tabloids call, say the same thing. Someone has it in for me, to be sure, and I think I know who and why. But I also know that I can't fight them. I've had a wonderful time here at Roedean. Everyone, and especially you, has been completely supportive, friendly, and wonderful. I've learned a lot about teaching that will always stand me in good stead. I don't know yet what I will try to do next, but I will have many opportunities despite this awful crime against me. You can reach me at my apartment in Brighton for now, but please don't even try to find me, and don't let anyone else, no one at all, know where I am." Now she had to steady herself against Miss Shaw's desk, but she took a mighty breath, turned, and walked out.

On the way to her apartment, she stopped at the newsstand and bought a copy of *The Times*. Sitting on her bed, she thumbed through it and found a small article about the divorce. "Whew," she sighed, "at least I'm not mentioned in *The Times*." She thumbed through the paper all the way to the advertisements. Idly letting her attention wander down the page, at the bottom she saw, "Teachers wanted for overseas assignments. Experience in math and science at the elementary and high school level desired."

Do I dare? she thought. *Do I really dare?*

The next day, she was in perhaps the smallest cubicle in the British foreign office. The little sign on the desk of the person across from Emmie said, "Mrs. Wentworth—Assignments." Emmie went through her prepared speech about why she was there, saying briefly, "I saw your advertisement in *The Times* and thought that I might be qualified. You see, I would like to try teaching at an overseas location."

She handed over her résumé, and Mrs. Wentworth saw "first in math at Girton, experience in Europe, statistical work in The City, and teaching math at Roedean. Something didn't add up here, but she hardly wanted to dismiss Emmie. She reviewed each item on the résumé with great care. "Of course, I'll have to verify everything, but now, Miss Trowbridge, what say you tell me the real reason you are here."

Emmie tried to stammer out the story she had prepared, but suddenly broke down and told Mrs. Wentworth everything. "Well," Mrs. Wentworth spoke very carefully, "we don't like to solve our teachers' personal problems, but let me try this. We have placed a number of teachers in overseas situations recently since the schools are staffing up for the coming year. Our positions in Australia, Canada, New Zealand, and South Africa have been filled. But we just received an urgent request for a person to teach elementary and high school math and science at Christmas Island, a sort of British protectorate. Here is a map to show you where it is. The native population numbers about fifteen hundred, with 350 schoolchildren, K through sixth form. They speak Gilbertese, from the Gilbert Islands, but most speak and understand English. The island got its name from the Gilbertese pronunciation of "Kiritimati," where the "ti" is pronounced "s." The islanders produce and export *copra,* or dried coconut pulp, as well as aquarium fish and seaweed. Locally caught fish are the primary food, although much food is imported. The entire island has been designated a bird sanctuary, so there is some ecotourism along with anglers. The waves have thousands of miles to build up, so there are often a number of avid surfers. There is an airfield, Cassidy International, with a paved runway of 6,900 feet which is served from Honolulu weekly by Air Pacific

Airlines, as well as charter flights by American Te Mauri Travel, also from Honolulu. We ask for a two-year commitment, although there is nothing to prevent you from simply climbing on an airplane, when one comes by, and flying off home. The salary is set for all of the assignments at five hundred pounds sterling per month."

Looking hard at Emmie, Mrs. Wentworth added somberly, "Miss Trowbridge, I respectfully suggest that you take this information, go home, and think long and hard about committing yourself to such a remote island."

Emmie allowed herself a few moments to think about her response then replied, "If I don't take the job, who would? Wouldn't the children be left without a qualified teacher? You paint a rather bleak picture of an otherwise idyllic island. Are there no other English men or women there?"

"Oh, yes. The superintendent of schools and the high school principal is Mr. Duxbury, a longtime resident. There are six other teachers, all natives, but they've been to high school in Hawaii."

Emmie swallowed hard, thought for one minute more, and said, "I'll take the job."

Chapter Six

Roger Joins the Cold War

Roger was ready to leave the navy. He wrote his parents, "I feel that I got quite an education during my three-year hitch. I sure learned about engineering and how to manage a crew of men. I'm ready to put all that into a career." He prepared a résumé emphasizing both his chemical knowledge and his recent engineering and management experience. He sent it to nearly a hundred firms, big and little, but received very few replies. One of the letters piqued his interest. It was from the Oak Ridge National Laboratory (ORNL) in Oak Ridge, Tennessee, and read: "We have an opening in the Reactor Experimental Engineering Division which might interest you." Roger jumped at the chance. He got a day's leave from the commander of the reserve fleet, flew over to Knoxville, Tennessee, and got the job. Again, he was the low man on the totem pole and was facing an entirely new field. His chemical knowledge was vital, but the job entailed building a brand-new type of nuclear-electric generator requiring him to learn nuclear physics along with all of the innovative engineering that was new even to the existing staff at ORNL.

Unfazed, Roger not only jumped right in but he also noted that he could take courses given in Oak Ridge toward the Ph.D. in chemistry. Five years later, in May 1959, he successfully defended his thesis and received his Ph.D. degree in physical chemistry with a minor in nuclear engineering.

* * * *

A few months later, with his Ph.D. in hand and the reactor project dead, Roger sent his résumé around to half a dozen firms he thought might be interesting to work for. He promptly received a letter from The Mitre Corporation in Bedford, Massachusetts, inviting him for an interview. His nuclear experience, as well as his Ph.D. in chemistry, just happened to be exactly what they were looking for. On April 4, 1960, he started work at this new, not-for-profit, Federally Funded R&D Center (FFRDC) located in a brand-new building in Bedford, Massachusetts. Mitre's sole client at that time was the U.S. Air Force Command and Control Development Division, known as C^2D^2 (later changed to the Electronics Systems Division, or ESD), located on the Hanscom Air Force Base in nearby Lexington, Massachusetts.

Roger was assigned to the advanced systems department, and after a two-month hiatus while waiting for his top secret clearance to come through, he was asked to investigate the effects of nuclear weapons bursts above the atmosphere on Air Force radar systems. Roger told his immediate boss, Earl Forest Lockwood, whom everyone called Frosty, "The Mitre higher-ups must think I know all about nuclear weapons since a lot of work on them goes on at Oak Ridge. Actually, I know nothing at all about them or anything about Air Force radars. I don't know where to start."

"Pish tush, mah boy," Frosty said in his put-on Kentucky accent. "Nobody heah abouts evah knows anythin' about what they ah asked ta study. Ya jus' have ta kip wan step ahead a th' Aah Fawce, who know even less, if anythin'." Even so, Frosty soon had Roger sent to the nuclear weapons course given by the Sandia Corporation in Albuquerque, New Mexico. There he came face-to-face with mockups of the "Fat Man" and the "Little Boy" nuclear weapons that had devastated Hiroshima and Nagasaki in Japan to end WWII. Soon he was expert enough to give written advice to the Air Force about various nuclear matters.

But still, Roger complained to Frosty, "After all the tooting around to various government labs we've done for a year, I don't know what we have accomplished. The main problem isn't extrapolating from the old data from kiloton fission bomb tests, it's that we know very little about the megaton fusion bombs we and the Soviets have."

"Pish tush, mah boy," Frosty replied with a grin. "What we do know shows weah still ahead a the Aah Fawce."

But in March 1961, Frosty got a game-changing phone call from an Air Force civilian at the Hanscom Base he had shared an office with in 1959: Richard "Curly" (only partially bald) Moore. "Whatcha doin'?" Curly asked.

"The usual," replied Frosty.

"That means nuttin', right?"

"Yeah."

"Well, get your sorry ass over here because I've got a real one."

Frosty returned to tell Roger, "It's a brand-new program named NUDETS. That's for 'nuclear detection system.' It's even got a number: 477 L. That 'L' is for 'electronics' in case you hadn't figured that out all by yourself. Here, dig into all this crap and learn what we have to know a'fore the Aah Fawce finds out." Within a month, Roger and their small Mitre team, with the help of a similar team at the General Electric Company research lab in Syracuse, New York, had designed the basic components of the NUDET system.

****

A few weeks later, in the late spring of 1961, Roger Malcolm was in his office at the Mitre Corporation a bit after five o'clock on a Wednesday evening. He was running late for supper, as usual, when the phone rang. "Malcolm here," he answered.

"This is John Golden," the caller said. "I'm working for General Partridge, and we'd like you to come down to the Pentagon to brief our little committee on NUDETS this Friday. We'll start at nine A.M. and you can have as long as you want."

"Okay," Roger replied, not having the faintest idea who General Partridge was, what the "little committee" was, or who John Golden was. "Exactly what do you want to know?"

"Oh, just tell us about the system, its capabilities, and its costs. Then we'll ask questions to fill in the details."

Later that evening Roger got hold of his boss at home, and Frosty commented on Everett, the Mitre vice president, and Charles "Caz" Zraket, the technical director. "Wow!" Frosty said. "Everett and Caz have been trying desperately to get in to see the Partridge committee. They'll turn green with envy, but don't tell 'em until we come back—they'll want to horn in."

Roger and Frosty got to work early the next morning and tried to figure out what to say in the briefing. They decided to stick pretty much to what they and their Mitre group had shown the NUDETS program chief, Lt. Col. Elmer Jones, and his civilian deputy Richard "Curly" Moore, at the previous meeting in the Pentagon with the high level members of the Air Staff the week before. *I'll let the committee members' questions guide us after that,* thought Roger.

The following morning, after an early flight from Boston to D.C., Roger and Frosty arrived at Major Alten's office in the bowels of the Pentagon at 8:00 A.M. to find Colonel Jones and Curly Moore there already, quite nervous. There was no time to change their briefing, and to Roger's relief no one suggested any changes. They trooped up to a third-floor conference room where John Golden greeted them warmly and led them into the meeting room and introduced them all around. There was the white-haired, four-star general Earle E. Partridge, recently retired, flanked by two-star Army Major-General Alfred Dodd Starbird, a civilian named Willie Lee Moore from the Office of the Director, Defense Research and Engineering (ODDR&E), and three or four others. General Partridge had been a widely respected Army Chief of Staff and was known for his common sense and sound advice as well as his firm military leadership qualities. Starbird, also a tall, lean army general, had recently been the director of military applications in the Atomic Energy Agency under commissioner John A. McCone and had worked closely with

George B. Kistiakowsky, President Eisenhower's science adviser on the proposed nuclear test ban treaty. Willie Moore was a long-term member of ODDR&E, a brilliant, quick thinker, well versed in military research and engineering and able to discuss the details of proposed weapon systems with the military service and industrial contractor engineers and scientists. He was a Louisianan with a delightful sense of humor, relaxed and affable, but always ready to insist on knowing the facts and cutting through the rhetoric. Later, Roger and Frosty thoroughly enjoyed working with him, and if it had not been for him and his ability to pull the appropriate strings, they probably would never have gotten the system under way at all or at least not been able to test the system under real, live conditions.

General Partridge nodded to John Golden, who gave a brief summary of the objectives of the committee: "The committee is to determine how to shift the U.S. strategic weapons policy from Mutual Assured Destruction to Flexible Response. The committee was set up very recently, directly by Secretary of Defense McNamara at the request of President Kennedy, and has their full confidence. Whatever the committee decides would be implemented as rapidly as possible with the highest national priority. The committee wants to know whether NUDETS, if it meets the Specific Operational Requirements the Air Force has established already, would provide reliable information immediately to the National Command Authorities so as to allow them to make the decisions required by Flexible Response. These responses could be whether to hold off on a return strike, or to respond with a partial or a full nuclear weapon counterattack. The latter might be counterforce against the enemy's remaining weapons, or countervalue against his cities and industrial facilities. This policy would depend upon the president receiving detailed information immediately after a nuclear burst had occurred within the continental U.S. No false alarms would be allowed, and the system has to survive any follow-on nuclear bursts after the first one."

Roger realized that he was now a direct participant in the Cold War against the Soviet Union. *How soon will it get hot?* he wondered.

After some introductory remarks by Colonel Jones and Frosty, Roger got up to make the primary presentation on the technical capabilities of NUDETS as he had calculated them. He said, "Our long-range NUDET system can meet the technical objectives in the Specific Operational Requirements, as far as, if not more than, four hundred miles away. Roughly thirty primary stations could cover the entire continental U.S." Unfortunately, it would turn out that Roger had no real data on which to base that assertion. Furthermore, he had no idea that lightning bolts would present an intractable problem of false alarms.

The Partridge committee accepted their report, perhaps with some reservations, but appointed Willie Moore, a member of Secretary McNamara's whiz kids, to help get NUDETS under way. Within days, Lieutenant Colonel Jones had received direct orders from the Air Staff to install within eighteen months a prototype system around Washington, D.C. He had $1.8 million to spend.

The System Program Office expanded swiftly in size. Yet, despite the highest priority, progress toward getting the contractor, the General Electric Company, to complete the design and start installing the system slowed bureaucratically to a crawl.

Frosty, Roger, and their now expanded NUDETS team became more and more frustrated. Yet their frustration was soon about to end with a bang— many super-bangs!

Khrushchev's thumper-bumpers got Roger really excited about getting their nuclear detection system tested against the real thing. With clever skul-duggery, he found out where and when the U.S. thermonuclear tests would take place. Thanks to his boss Frosty Lockwood, Willie Moore, a compliant Mitre president and executive vice president, an uncomprehending Colonel Jones, and a willing General Electric Company, within a few months Roger had obtained everything he figured he needed ready to be taken by air to the test site he had chosen: Palmyra Island. At almost the last minute, Mitre received a top secret telegram:

> From: Commander Joint Task Force 8.0
> To: NUDETS Team, The Mitre Corporation, Bedford, Mass.
> You are hereby authorized to join Task Force 8.0, Task Unit 8.1.3 on Palmyra Island. You will provide all of your own supplies and equipment, including electricity, food, and tents. Report to Commander Task Unit 8.1.3 Hickam Air Force Base on or before March 1, 1962.
>> Major-General, Alfred D. Starbird, USA

There were a number of hang-ups along the way, but on April 23, 1962, Roger was aboard an Air Force C-124 cargo plane taking off from Hanscom Air Force Base on his way to Palmyra Island with his team, trailer, a 200-kilowatt diesel generator, one tent, and three fishing poles with which to catch fish to eat. He wasn't at all sure they could survive on just the fish they might catch, or where the fuel for the generator would come from. He was just hoping for the best.

Chapter Seven

Emmie Meets Roger:
The Thermonuclear Weapons Tests Begin

E mmie closed up her apartment in Brighton, had a short vacation with her parents—who were properly appalled about her decision—decided what to pack, got her tickets and a meager travel advance from Mrs. Wentworth, and boarded the huge Boeing 707 for the long BOAC flight from London's Heathrow Airport to Idlewild in New York, transferring to an American 707 flight across the U.S. to Los Angeles. Mrs. Wentworth had wangled an overnight stay at a hotel near the airport for Emmie at LA since her overall flight was so long. She was too tired to do any sightseeing there, so the next morning she boarded another 707 and was soon on her way to Honolulu, Hawaii. She enjoyed the flights. She thought, *I could get used to living like this. It's not like those terrible flights to Europe on creaky DC-3s or C-47s when I worked for Stacey. This plane has plenty of leg room, a pillow, and a blanket, and the food is wonderful and the stewardesses attentive.* She had brought along plenty of silly reading matter, and the layover at Los Angeles had allowed her to walk a bit and then stretch out in bed at the hotel for a welcome sleep. *I wonder what Hawaii is like? she mused. Let me look at my ticket—yes, I have almost a four-hour layover there. I could take a cab in to Honolulu, even to Waikiki.* It was April 1962.

As the 707 noticeably decreased in altitude and speed, one of the stewardesses announced the usual patter for arrival at Honolulu: "Please put your seats in the full upright position, close your tray tables, check that your seat belt is securely fastened, and prepare for landing at the Honolulu International Airport. The pilot will circle as we approach so that you will all have a chance to look over and down to see Diamond Head and Waikiki Beach. Please remain seated until the aircraft has come to a complete stop at the terminal building. Aloha." Emmie was quite delighted at the sights.

Suddenly, as soon as the plane landed and Emmie disembarked, there was a noticeable shift in the air. She had just been greeted with a lei and "Aloha, welcome to Hawaii," when a loudspeaker squawked, "Miss Trowbridge, Miss Trowbridge. Please report to the shuttle to Hickam Air Force Base." She looked quizzically around just as an Air Force lieutenant approached her on the run. "Miss Trowbridge?"

"Yes, I'm Miss Trowbridge."

"Please come with me. Quickly now. You're on your way to Christmas Island, right?"

"Well, yes."

"Your flight has been changed. As soon as we get over to the military base, navy captain Patten will explain everything." The lieutenant whisked her aboard the shuttle, stowed her luggage—which he had retrieved from the 707—and accompanied her as it lumbered around the passenger airport to the military airport and drew up next to a U.S. Air Force cargo plane. The lieutenant helped her off the shuttle, retrieved her luggage, and left her facing the captain standing beside the steps up into the cargo plane. She noted the four stripes on his sleeve, indicating he was a full navy captain, and his name tag, Capt. John T. Patten, USN pinned to his chest along with his many other medals.

"Miss Trowbridge, I'm Captain Patten, and I must apologize for this rude change in plans. Your flight to Christmas Island—in fact, all flights there—have been cancelled until further notice. I will accompany you to Christmas on this, the only flight for now. I only received word that you were booked on that flight a few minutes ago. The manager of Air Pacific Airlines called me in some distress that you had been booked by the British Foreign Service on the cancelled flight. He wondered how you were supposed to get to Christmas Island since there would be no more flights. I checked with my schedules and found this flight ready to go. In fact, my boss down at Christmas had ordered me to fly down from my office here to help him with his project down there, and I had planned to take the next flight myself. Shall we get on board? Your luggage, I see, has already been stowed."

Before Emmie could say a word to object, several hands hoisted her up and led her to a bucket seat facing toward the middle of the plane, which was taken up by several huge containers. Rough men in blue jeans who looked like stevedores were loading the rest of the cargo up a rear ramp in great haste. Captain Patten was the last person to jump aboard. Two men in uniform saluted snappily and escorted him up into the pilot's compartment. He would ride in comfort. Quickly the doors were shut, everyone was told to buckle up, and the plane taxied to the end of the runway and took off. Every other seat was taken by military personnel.

Emmie turned to the person next to her and asked timidly, "Is this the flight to Christmas Island?"

"It sure is, ma'am. It sure is."

"But you're not with the British foreign service, are you?"

"Ah bin with the service in many foreign lands, but not with the Brits—yet, that is."

"What are all these soldiers and this equipment going to Christmas Island for?"

"Thet ah cannot say, ma'am. Ah sure cannot say."

Emmie dug into her purse and took out one of the silly novels she had brought along. She couldn't concentrate. She put it down on her lap. Exhausted, she put her head back, and despite the noise from the engines and the air rushing past the fuselage, she mercifully fell asleep.

Six hours later, someone shouted, "There it is!" Bolting wide awake, Emmie craned her neck toward a window behind the man next to her and could just make out the long, green island as the plane circled for what seemed a very long time. Finally it settled into its glide path, bumped to a rough landing, turned sharply, and taxied off to the side. All of the doors and ramps opened up, and Emmie was unceremoniously handed down to the ground. It was sheer chaos all around. The navy stevedores rushed to unload the plane. Jeeps and trucks roared perilously close to the passengers, now looking for their belongings in a pile of luggage. The vehicles stirred up huge amounts of coral dust.

"Miss Trowbridge. Miss Trowbridge. Over here." There was Mr. Duxbury.

"Oh, Mr. Duxbury. Thank God you're here! What's going on? This is complete chaos!"

"I hate to tell you this, but we are being blessed with another round of nuclear weapons tests, courtesy the United States Air Force."

* * * *

Roger helped his team unlimber all of the equipment from the trailer as soon as the trailer had been set securely within the cleared space Roger had designated. His first task was to get the diesel-electric generator set solidly on the ground and to get it connected to the electric system in the trailer. That went smoothly, so he filled the fuel tank from a canister he got from Paul Myers and tried to start it. It chugged but didn't start. Then he tried again and it did, but it stopped after a minute or two. He banged on everything that had a place to bang. Finally, when he hit the fuel oil filter chamber, it did start, and it ran seemingly just fine. "Throw the switch, Lee!" he shouted, and the lights went on inside. He turned his attention to the air conditioner, which he and Lee wrestled atop the box it came in and connected the cool-air outlet to the trailer inlet. The temperature in the trailer quickly came down to a very cool eighty degrees or so. The six-foot-square crossed loop antenna came next. Roger and Joe hoisted it up to Lee and Hal on the top of the trailer, and they fastened it with prearranged bolts. Lee got out his transit and got it aimed south toward Christmas Island. The photo cells were likewise mounted on top, facing south. Lee took three geophones to pick up the seismic shock motion of the ground from the massive thermonuclear explosions, forced them securely into the ground in a triangular array, and connected them to wires from the tape recorders in a rack inside the trailer. Roger left Hal and Joe to unpack the electronics Joe had designed and get all of that set up, while Lee looked after everything else.

Roger went around the island to coordinate with the other teams, who were already quite established. He quickly ran into a stone wall. Only the British team would let him into their trailer and talk to him. The half-dozen other teams, all from the U.S., asked him brusquely, "Who are you?" When he told them, they barred the door and added, "Get your need-to-know forwarded down here, and then we'll talk!"

The British had a setup somewhat akin to what Roger had and told him to get ready. "The first test is scheduled only two days away, on the twenty-fifth." So Roger figured he had better coordinate with General Starbird down at Christmas Island right away. With his team finishing up their setup, he wangled the last C-130 shuttle flight from Palmyra to Christmas Island for the day, thinking that he could get back to his team on Palmyra without a hitch. Landing at the Christmas Island airstrip, Roger too was appalled at the dust, noise, and general chaos. Several bulldozers were busy at the end of the runway lengthening and expanding it. The makeshift control tower was up and running, and beside it was a construction crew working on a more permanent one. Back toward the town of Banana adjacent to the airport were a set of Quonset huts. Roger walked over there and saw a sign on one that read BOQ, meaning "bachelor officer's quarters." A sign reading "Cafeteria" was on the next, and another said "Headquarters Task Force 8." It was General Starbird's command post and had all kinds of antennas mounted atop it. A noisy diesel-electric generating plant completed the bare-bones complex. Back of that was a tent complex for everyone else. Roger found that he could bunk at the BOQ for a dollar a night, so he had a bite to eat at the cafeteria and settled in for the night.

The next day he asked at the base office, "I'd like to see more of Christmas Island than just this air base. Do you think I could rent a jeep and explore this place?"

"Oh, sure. You're in luck. We just got a shipment and have a few extras. They'll be gone by noon. Just take any one and sign this register, but be sure to be back in an hour or so. There should be a map of the island and the keys on the seat. Just don't go too far south. The road gets pretty bad, and guys have gotten stuck in the sand down there. By the way, they drive on the wrong side of the road—that is, the British left-hand side—so beware of oncoming traffic—and of most of the Americans who can't or won't remember."

Roger drove north past the village of Banana to the main village and commercial port facility in London. The port was a maze of existing piers, piers under construction, three cargo ships off-loading piles of large containers, three more ships just off shore waiting to off-load, and a swirl of men, bulldozers, trucks, and jeeps trying to sort it all out. He didn't want to get caught up in all that mess and figured that Starbird had enough to do without his piddling problems back on Palmyra, so he turned the jeep around and headed south. Once past the airport, the road swung around the lagoon along the eastern shore, driving carefully on the left-hand side, until he could cross over to the western shore and drive south along the beach road. Roger pondered, *What a lovely long, white coral beach, essentially undisturbed. It's picture–perfect: the bright blue sky, the shimmering blue ocean, the waves lapping calmly along the shore. Of course, if this were along the California coast, it would all be beach bungalows and motels by now.* The road began to break up, so he turned his jeep back around and headed north again. He came to where the road crossed over toward the eastern shore and noticed a large concrete culvert, about four feet in diameter running east and west, appearing to drain a swampy area. Roger stopped and walked over to it. There was actually nothing unusual about it. Later Roger found out that Christmas Island suffered strong storms that dumped huge amounts of water on the place in flash floods. The culvert was simply there to drain the water off toward the sea. He got back in his jeep and returned north to civilization. It was still well before noon, so he continued past the jeep parking lot, again past the village of Banana toward London, the main city of the island. Ahead of him was a three-story wooden building with a sign: "Christmas Island Preparatory School." Clustered around the school to the rear were half a dozen trailers, which he immediately took to be the elementary school, similar to crowded schools in the States.

His way along the street was blocked by a young woman holding hands with three children of various ages on one side and holding a parasol on the other side, walking slowly toward the school. Roger pulled off the road and got out. "Need any help with your kids?" he asked airily.

"No, thank you. I'm sorry to hold you up. The children are doing just fine," came the curt reply in a strong British accent.

"Well, would you mind if I walked along? I'm trying to find someone who knows what's going on."

"Ugh!" she exclaimed in some disgust. "You came to the wrong person. I just got here yesterday and know nothing, absolutely nothing. It's a total nightmare!"

"I'm sorry," replied Roger.

"You're an American, aren't you? You're with *them*." She shook her fist at the sky, dropping the hand of one of the children but quickly scooping it up again.

"Yes, but what can I do about it? Is there anything I can do to help?"

"Call up your president and have him call this whole thing off. *That's* what you can do!"

"Only God can do that," said Roger, "and He obviously is nowhere around. Look, I have some contacts and may be able to find some things out. Let me ask some questions back at the base and come around to the school in an hour or so."

"Well, you're the first person on this whole island except for the school principal, Mr. Duxbury, who has taken an interest in my plight. So, okay, the children and I are on our way back to have lunch, and then there will be a short recess. Meet me there in an hour. By the way, my name is Miss Trowbridge, Emmie Trowbridge."

"How do you do, Miss Trowbridge? My name is Roger Malcolm, employed by the Mitre Corporation under contract with the U.S. Air Force. Yes, I am one of *them*. I'll be back in an hour." As he climbed back in to the jeep, Roger turned to look at Emmie directly. Suddenly he was smitten! *What is it about love at first sight?* Roger immediately thought to himself. *That is some feisty girl, and pretty too. I'm going to ask her to marry me!*

As he drove away, he felt himself getting aroused. His thoughts wandered, as did his driving. A truck driver coming the other way blew its horn, and Roger had to swerve sharply back to the left to get out of his way. *What is it about her? Is it just that I'm a randy old virgin bachelor wanting to get my share of sex before it's too late? Or is it some emanation from her that has washed over me, stirring up my baser thoughts—or higher emotions like having a lifetime companion to love, honor, and obey? Jeezus, I surely will have to come back and see her again—and again.*

Luckily he couldn't read her mind. She was furious with herself. *Why did I encourage him to come back? I hate this place. I hate everyone on it except the kids and Mr. Duxbury. And I particularly hate that pushy guy Roger what's-his-name.*

At the BOQ, Roger handed in the keys to the jeep and went over to the command post looking for anyone he might know or be able to collar. As luck would have it, striding out of the post was Navy Captain Patten, whom Roger had met at Hickam. As luck would have it, Captain Patten recognized Roger and greeted him warmly.

"How's Dr. Malcolm, and what are you doing down here on Christmas?"

"Oh, hi there, Captain Patten. I thought you would still be at Hickam, expediting teams the way you did for me. We're all set up on Palmyra, thanks to you. But no one there seems to know anything or is willing to share with me what's going on. I thought I could catch the shuttle and make a quick trip here to find out. Could you give me a few answers? When will the tests start and how many will there be?"

"Why sure, Doctor. Presumably everyone's on a strict need-to-know basis, but here on Christmas we can share 'most everything. We hope to start tomorrow, actually. We have scheduled the tests for every other day. The totals are twenty-four here over Christmas, plus one for-real Polaris submarine-launched missile test in the ocean, and another destroyer-fired ASROC nuclear depth charge missile test also in the ocean. Then there will be ten or more high-altitude missile shots off Johnston Island. We hope to wind this up here by the end of July. The ones here will be B-52 Air Force drops coming from Barber's Point in Hawaii, air bursts at about ten thousand feet. The B-52 will arrive at dawn, enter a racetrack pattern, and if all sensors are ready, drop the weapon, turn, and hightail it for home. Up at Palmyra, you should get a daily sheet with all that information on it. You're lucky you caught me since General Starbird, 'The Man,' just gave me another all-consuming job. That's why I'm here and not still at Hickam. I am to be the task force coordinator for the island. My job, among others, is to see that everyone knows what each test is for and all safety systems are go. Here is a handout I just had printed up. My primary instrument is 'Mahatma,' the loudspeaker that can be heard all over the island through multiple ballpark-type speakers."

Captain Patten handed Roger a sheaf of his Mahatma memorandum. "Here, Doc—if "The Man" can call you that, so can I—on the reverse side, all of the information is printed in Gilbertese, the native language. You can help to distribute them to the natives."

Part of the memo read:

THE MAHATMA COUNTDOWN
<u>Everyone</u> on Christmas Island **MUST** listen to the loudspeaker named MAHATMA when an airborne test is scheduled.
<u>Everyone</u> **MUST** <u>be facing north away from the blast with dark glasses on and eyes closed at the end of the countdown when MAHATMA says "DETONATION."</u>

Captain Patten explained, "The countdown will start when the B-52 carrying the bomb takes off from Hawaii. Mahatma will give a heads-up notice every fifteen minutes: 'This is Mahatma. So-and-so minutes to bomb release.' When the B-52 arrives within twenty minutes of Christmas Island, the bombardier will notify the command center and Mahatma by radio, and Mahatma will switch to every five minutes. When the B-52 enters its racetrack orbit at thirty thousand feet, Mahatma will wait to hear on his direct phone line from Starbird's command post that all monitoring stations, ground-based, airborne, and seagoing, are 'go.' Until then, the B-52 will remain in its racetrack orbit. Upon 'go,' when the B-52 comes around and starts its actual bomb run, at that moment Mahatma will say, 'Everyone on this island must face north away from the burst and cover his eyes—everyone—and the countdown will come every minute. When the bombardier calls over the radio 'bomb released,' Mahatma will repeat 'bomb released' and count down twenty-six seconds by the second. That is the time it takes the bomb to fall from thirty thousand feet to ten thousand feet. At 'one second' Mahatma will exclaim, 'detonation!' At that moment, everyone should be hunkered down with eyes closed facing away from the blast." He added, "I hate to think about anyone with open eyes being blinded by that incredibly bright initial flash!"

"Wow!" Roger exclaimed. "That seems clear."

Roger held the memos and persisted, "I noticed some native kids with their teacher over in that village called London just now. What's being done with them? How do they avoid being blinded by the flash?"

"Oh, that's Miss Trowbridge. She was on the same flight that I caught from Hickam. She was none too pleased to be highjacked, as it were, onto a C-124 instead of an Air Pacific jet. I was told she was a British foreign officer, so I expedited her trip down here, thinking she must be a diplomatic type, but she turned out to be a schoolteacher! I don't know what she made of this situation when she arrived. I'll bet she was appalled. But to answer your question, during the British tests in '57 to '58, they were not evacuated but turned over to their parents to keep their eyes buried in their pillows until the shot had gone off. There are more kids now, so I came up with a navy-style answer. One of those freighters at the dock has been outfitted with a cafeteria, movie theatre, and bunk beds for every child and their parents if desired. The evening before each test, we'll corral the kids and give 'em supper and a show until lights-out. Right after the bomb blast first thing in the morning, and after breakfast, they can all come out and go to the school for their lessons or go home to play. It's all described on the Gilbertese side of the memo."

"Wow, again! I couldn't add anything to those plans. Well, here," Roger said, handing Patten back most of his memos, "I'll keep a bunch of these memos for the teacher to hand around, but I've got to get back to Palmyra. I may be down again later to ensure that our system is working okay. Many, many thanks, Captain Patten."

Roger went back to his jeep, found the keys where he had left them, and drove off to give Miss Trowbridge the news. As he approached the school, Emmie and the kids were just coming out for post-lunch recess. "Miss Trowbridge, here. I have something for you," he said, handing her the sheaf of memos.

Emmie took them and turned to Roger with the same scowl on her face as when he had left her. "Well, thanks, Mr....er, er...Malcolm. That's right, Roger Malcolm, isn't it? Let's see what the Air Force bureaucrats have ginned up for us now." She read the memo in English and perused the Gilbertese side quite carefully, not understanding much of it. "Wow! The great Lord Mahatma is giving us quite a treat: supper, movies, and so to bed. Three months of *hell* as I see it."

The stress on the word "hell" jarred Roger, but he softened up right away. She sure was pretty. "Call me Roger, please."

"Oh, sure, Roger. I'm Emmie." Now she suddenly looked at him with less emotion. Here was a guy who actually did what he said he would do. He was even being helpful. She couldn't help thinking also that he was quite manly, clean-shaven, and attractive in his work shirt, khaki shorts, and pith helmet. She almost laughed out loud at the sight of that hat, but she squelched it and didn't even giggle. She suddenly wanted to see more of him. "Please excuse my reaction to your memo, but I truly did not bargain for this. One minute I'm on a comfortable commercial jet plane from Los Angeles to Honolulu expecting another of equal comfort to Christmas Island, when I'm literally thrust onto a most uncomfortable American Air Force cargo plane. We land, not at the peaceful remote island I had been led to believe awaited me, but into this din, this—chaos! And I'm expected to teach these kids math and science? Nuclear physics and bomb-making, perhaps, but not their number facts and basic machines! Yet I can't just run out on them."

"Well, Emmie." Roger paused an instant to collect his thoughts and to think, *What a nice name! What a nice appearance What moxie!* "I'm sure you wouldn't run out on them, of course, but I can suggest one bit of help. I'll drive you down to meet Captain Patten."

"Captain Patten! Captain god-all-ready jump aboard Patten? He's the one who hoisted me onto that cargo plane. 'Made all the arrangements,' he said. Why did he even bother? When my flight was cancelled, didn't he think even once I might have made other plans—like flying right back to jolly ole England?"

Roger was taken aback at her renewed outburst. "I see your point. But now that you're here, perhaps you might talk to him about this 'Mahatma' thing. I think he's trying to do his best for the kids, and for you, with that ship. Talk to him. Work out how you are actually going to get the kids onto the ship, perhaps with the other teachers and some of the kids' parents, and how the supper, movies, and bed-down will work. He may have some sailors who can help too. He is a full navy captain, which is no small rank, and he evidently has the ear and confidence of General Starbird, who is running this whole task force. Those two have a lot of clout, as we say, and they have an unlimited budget. I've met Starbird. He will do anything to keep this operation on schedule, but he is human and won't do anything to harm the kids and the rest of the natives."

"Oh, Roger, sure, I know you're right. And thanks so much. Yes, let me meet this Captain Patten who's not an ogre, but he sure messed me up. Perhaps he'll realize he owes me one. And I'll remember about General Starbird—the top guy, eh? Maybe I can meet him too and get him to talk to Mr. Duxbury, the school principal, and the natives." Emmie got one of the native teachers to watch the schoolchildren and hopped into Roger's jeep, folding up her parasol. "The wife of the family I'm to be living with gave me this. She said that the sun is brutal to any pale skin that gets exposed."

"Yeah," replied Roger, trying hard to remember to keep to the left. "The sun's right overhead so close to the equinox, and at this moment, just about noon, it's right overhead with no cloud cover. It sure can be brutal. Luckily I had a couple days in Honolulu to get a bit of a tan in preparation." Roger drove on, found Captain Patten, waited while Emmie chatted with him, and took her back to her schoolyard.

As they drove, she told him about their conversation. "He apologized again for the trip down here. He said he had been led to believe I was being sent by the British foreign office, which is true in a way, so he couldn't just let me languish in Honolulu. So I swallowed hard and asked him how we are to handle the kids to keep them from getting blinded by accident. He went through the 'Mahatma' thing and then said he would call for me and Mr. Duxbury as soon as the ship was ready to take the kids overnight so we could check it out. Oh, here we are at the school." She jumped out, turned, and added, "Many, many thanks, Roger. You've been marvelous. See you again on your next trip from Palmyra, and good luck with your project."

He desperately wanted to kiss her goodbye, but stifled the impulse and merely said, "Well, I sure hope you and Patten can work out the details of this jumble. Yes, I'm off to catch that airplane back to Palmyra—that's four hundred miles to the north—where my team is just setting up to record the signals from the nuclear bursts. I'm sure chaos also reigns there. Bye, see you later."

Luckily, Roger got to the airport just in time to catch the afternoon plane going back to Palmyra. As the shuttle flight took off on its way there, he pondered his feelings about Emmie. Why was he so taken with her?

It took a while for the C-130 to grind its way northwest, so his mind brought up Emmie's image as they had talked just a few minutes ago. She obviously had her light brown hair done before leaving England. It was in an attractive short bob parted on one side, but probably her arduous activities since then showed in a number of straggling wisps that curled over her brow. Some even stood up in the back of her head. He recalled that she had the typical British full, smooth, reddish cheeks, but two smudges of dirt had appeared, one on her left cheek and one over her right eyebrow. In his mind's eye, he remembered her face was otherwise smooth and nicely symmetrical. She hadn't bothered with earrings or a bracelet, but an expensive watch adorned her left wrist. He suddenly thought, *I didn't even look to see if she had an engagement or wedding ring on her finger, but of course she's not married...yet.* His image of her refocused in his mind: Her teeth were lovely, even, and white. Her upper lip was narrow with a hint of a notch. Her lower lip was full. In the chaos of her arrival, she wore no lipstick or other makeup. She wore a patterned, short-sleeved dress that fit snugly over a full but not ample bosom, and which showed off her nicely curved rear and well-turned legs, ending in sturdy brown shoes. Her skin was still quite untanned, and Roger was pleased to see that she was so alert to the need to keep from getting sunburned by carrying that parasol. She held her body erect—no slouching for her—and walked with a purposeful stride.

Roger mused some more. *No, her looks and bearing are lovely, but that isn't what draws me to her. It's her feisty attitude that caught me unaware, set me back for just a moment, then allowed me to think I could help her. When I offered my help, she accepted without looking sheepish. The children showed that they already were comfortable with her, and she with them. When I returned with Captain Patten's memo, she at first exploded, rightly so, but when she explained her terrible journey to me I realized the crazy dilemma she is in. I immediately felt her courage and resolve.* Roger brought himself up short, thinking, *Come on. You really are just a randy thirty-four-year-old virgin. On the other hand, she is the prettiest woman around. I truly believe I could live with her the rest of my life.*

He thought some more about love and how he could suddenly think he was in love with Emmie. *I've dated quite a few girls, and more recently grown women,* he remembered. *More than a few of them,* he had to admit. *I enjoyed parties, dances, movies, hiking, and various outdoor activities with them, even sparking with them in my or her car or even apartment, but let's face it, never trying to get into her pants or even her bra.* He thought on, *Oh, yes, what about Janice? I sure was smitten with her after graduating from Harvard. But again, let's face it, after I went so far as to attend a church service of her religion, I was turned off.* Roger felt that, as he often reminded himself, *I really tried to understand Janice, but it surely didn't feel the way I do about Emmie. Is it my biological clock? Is it the threat of a nuclear bomb blowing us up or irradiating us? No! She is different. I want to hold her, feel her, touch her, yes, sleep with her, but also live with her. I know deep down that she is self-sufficient and undoubtedly smarter than I am, or at least more rational and more connected to reality than I am. I don't want to let her out of my sight. I want to be with her always. If that is love, I have it! Now and forever!*

As Roger had surmised, chaos reigned on Palmyra too. Planes were landing steadily on what turned into a gravel patch of broken coral halfway down the island. They taxied back to a coral sand apron, unloaded, and took off for another trip as soon as possible to provide a break for the next arrival. A U.S. Air Force sergeant manned what passed for a control tower beside the runway. Roger walked the half mile to his team's trailer, hopped up the wooden steps, pulled open the door, and stepped inside the trailer, letting out a huge sigh as the cool air hit him. "How's it going?" he asked cheerily.

"Look out!" said Lee Turner, squeezing by Roger in the very narrow aisle, holding a coaxial cable over their heads that he connected to a junction box on the opposite wall. "My 10.5 k filters were crushed when that air force crew chief screwed up, and now we find that none of the pre-installed coax cables go to the right places."

Just then the power went out, the lights and air conditioning went off, and Joe Henry and Hal Leach swore a blue streak simultaneously. "Can't you get that diesel-generator to work for more than a minute or two, Rog?"

"I'll try again." He took off his shirt so it wouldn't get all sweaty and jumped out of the trailer. He went right to the diesel and checked the fuel supply, the air intakes, and everything he could think of, so again he suspected the diesel oil filters. Banging on them produced no success. Having sweat through his undershirt, he took it off. Opening up the cover, he found what looked like two Popsicle sticks, obviously too small, wedged into the filter. The whole filter was cockeyed and blocked the flow of fuel to the cylinders. He ran back to Paul Myers and asked about spare filters. "Not for your model," was the answer. So Roger sent off a message via the shuttle flight to Dick Johnson, the Mitre representative for the project at Hickam Air Force Base in Honolulu: "Need spare filters for diesel. Get them airlifted immediately." He returned to the diesel not knowing that the filters would not arrive until two months later. Needing an immediate fix, he just straightened out the crushed filter, replaced it, propped it up with the Popsicle sticks, and reassembled the unit, and the diesel started right up when he pushed the start button. Later he got an entire professional diesel electric system installed by Holmes and Narver for their use. He walked back to his tent, got another undershirt, walked back to the trailer, hopped back up and in, and when he had cooled off a bit, put on both his fresh undershirt and his khaki shirt. Within a few minutes, his back began to hurt, so he took off both shirts and asked Lee to look at his back.

"Boy," said Lee, "you have some sunburn. That looks really bad. You better go over to the dispensary and get something put on it." Roger did so, but his back still felt as if it were on fire. That night was torture for Roger. That sunburn would give him fits for months.

Captain Patten's schedule indicated that the first bomb would go off the next morning, April 25. Unfortunately, the exact time of the burst would depend on conditions down at Christmas Island. On Palmyra, they would just have to be ready at any time after 6:00 A.M. or so. Working around the clock, Joe, Hal, and Lee got all of the electronics set up, and Joe said, "There, that should work just fine." It was about 3:00 A.M.

The alarm clock in their tent went off at 5:30. As they got up, Roger said, "We're going to hate that alarm before this project is over." The dawn was just breaking, with scattered clouds and the usual heat and humidity increasing rapidly. Just before 6:30, Roger stationed himself so that he could turn on the high-fidelity tape recorders and look out the trailer window to see the flash from the detonation four hundred miles away. They all waited anxiously, when Joe shouted "Got it!" He had seen a signal on the oscilloscope, but the NUDETS electronics failed to trigger. Roger had shouted "There's the flash!" but while the paper tape recorder showed a nice optical signal, the seismic geophones gave no signal. Hal Leach was the one who spotted the trouble.

"Rog, the nuclear burst-emitted radio wave electromagnetic pulse went *positive,* not *negative,* for its initial signal!"

Roger was dumfounded. "Hal, *every* EMP signal I looked at from recordings of previous U.S. test series went negative. It must be that they were all bombs set off from towers on the ground. These tests off Christmas Island will all be air bursts. Now that I think about it, we have to think of a vertical radio antenna and which way most of the electrons are flowing. The initial pulse will be the opposite to the flow of the majority of the electrons, up for ground bursts, down for air bursts."

Hal Leach was furious and said, "I'm disgusted. I feel like a complete fool. We've just wasted the whole trip out here."

Roger felt like two cents himself. He realized to himself, *I should have checked with someone who knew about nuclear bombs, probably at Livermore or at Los Alamos, before I wrote the specifications for the EMP electronics. But what with all of the secrecy, and need-to-know, how was I to accomplish that? Who would have told me? And in fact, did anyone really know?*

Joe Henry saved the day. "Why don't we just change the NUDETS trigger electronics to accept pulses going initially either positive or negative? That should be easy enough." Sure enough, within the hour he had accomplished that.

Roger said, "I don't know what that fix will do with regard to discriminating nuclear burst radio signals from lightning bolts, but if we can at least get the trigger to work and record the EMPs from several of the nuclear tests, I'll consider our trip to be successful."

Hal Leach had to admit the same. "Okay, Roger, I guess you're right. Let's just hope this fix works."

Two days later the second test was detonated, and the repaired NUDETS electronics triggered successfully. Joe shouted to Roger, Hal, and Lee, "Look! Look! Look at the oscilloscope." There, a wave form of about 10 kilohertz was displayed. On the other oscilloscope that was fitted with a Polaroid camera, the photo that Hal stripped off showed the perfect wave-form in permanent form. Roger led a huge cheer by all four, and a wave of relief swept over him. Then he looked at the output of the crossed loop antenna, which was supposed to tell the direction to the burst. He laid the indicated direction out on the hydrographic office map of the area between Palmyra and Christmas Islands. It was pretty close, but he couldn't swear whether it was within a tenth of a degree or even one degree. Of course, he didn't know exactly where on, over, or near Christmas Island the burst actually detonated. Actually, he couldn't even tell whether it had been near one end of the island or the other. *Oh, well,* he thought to himself, *first things first.*

From then on, whenever the nuclear burst occurred before sunrise, both the photocells and his eyes detected the burst. Taking the paper chart that recorded the output of the photocells, Roger could measure quite accurately the difference in time between the first flash and the peak of the fireball's glow. Then he plotted this time difference on a graph of time differences versus the yields of nuclear weapons taken from the RAND Calculator based on Glasstone and Edlund's book, *The Effects of Atomic Weapons.* The yields of the nuclear bursts that he read from the graph corresponded rather poorly with the yields given to him by Captain Patten. Eventually, back at Mitre in Bedford, when Roger had obtained the official yields from the task force records, the yields he had calculated from the optical flashes were in better agreement.

More of a problem was the fact that no observable ground-shaking seismic signal was evident on the paper chart record of the seismic earth-shaking signals from the geophones. Despite a number of attempted fixes, they never did observe a clear seismic signal from any of the nuclear bursts.

Roger sent Frosty, via the shuttle to Hickam, a guarded, unclassified letter telling him, "We had success on the second but not the first item. We had to trigger both up and down." Roger had no way to send classified messages back to the U.S. via radiophone. Because of the intransigence of the system program officer, Frosty wasn't able to get anything done about that problem until Roger got back to Mitre in Massachusetts. The colonel continued to care not at all about the tests.

Chapter Eight

Palmyra to Christmas: Roger and Emmie

The thermonuclear bomb tests continued every other day quite regularly. Roger's team detected them quite regularly as well. The third one was a huge one-megaton weapon (millions of tons of TNT explosive equivalent)— a "city buster" for sure—from which they got a crisp EMP and a superb optical signal. Roger saw the glare from the fireball quite clearly through the trailer's window four hundred miles away!

Roger thought he ought to check with other teams measuring the EMP, optical, and seismic effects from the blasts. Also, he saw on Patten's schedule that the first (and only) live, full-scale test of the Polaris submarine-launched thermonuclear missile system was to occur on May sixth. So on May fifth, he hopped on the shuttle and, leaving Hal Leach in charge, went back to Christmas Island.

Arriving on Christmas, Roger found Captain Patten relaxing at what passed for the officer's club about 10:00 A.M. "Can you get me connected with other teams here on Christmas?" Roger asked. "The ones on Palmyra are strictly need-to-know and don't recognize the Mitre Corp. Also, I would love to see the Polaris test. Can you get me into the command center tomorrow?"

"Doc, I doubt it unless you can get your sponsor to send down a 'need-to-know' message for Mitre here. How about that guy who called me at Hickam and got somebody in the SecDef's office to get you on a plane to Palmyra?"

"Okay, have you got a telephone to the States or Hickam?"

"Yes, but it's not secure. You'll have to paraphrase something."

Roger got to Frosty at work in Massachusetts a little before 4:00 P.M. and told him, "Need to know. Get me a blanket need-to-know about the nuclear tests and send it posthaste to Dick Johnson with a note to put it on the next shuttle to me on Palmyra. Today!"

Frosty mumbled something like, "Don't you know it's close to the end of the working day at the Pentagon? But I'll see what I can do."

After a brief chat with the captain, who told him to forget about seeing anything about the Polaris test the next day but to come around the following day to see if his need-to-know had come in, Roger excused himself saying, "That's okay, I'll check with you then," and rushed off on his primary mission—to see Emmie.

Luckily she was on playground duty and greeted him warmly. She had wondered about him since that first day they met. He was the only person about her age who had spoken to her since she had arrived and, although he was one of *them,* she was curious. He seemed somehow different from all the military and support people rushing about. He was handsome, obviously athletic, trim and strong, and, she felt, interested in her. While he was on Palmyra, she wangled a jeep ride back to the command center and looked up Captain Patten. She came right out with her curiosity: "Who exactly is this Roger Malcolm of Mitre? Where does he fit in?"

"He has some orders direct from Secretary of Defense McNamara. When I was still at Hickam and in charge of all flights down this way, he and his equipment showed up un-announced. I told him there was no way I could get him to Palmyra the next or any other day, whereupon I get a message direct from an aide to the SecDef at the Pentagon to do just that. I called Roger's boss, some crazy guy at Mitre named Frosty Lockwood. I asked him, 'Who *are* you?' He twitted me something fierce and shouted, 'Just do it and no questions asked.' Lockwood went on to tell me the Mitre Corporation is a think tank located in Bedford, Massachusetts, on contract with the U.S. Air Force to provide technical expertise in electronic command and control systems. I also asked about Dr. Malcolm, and he said, 'He's the smartest guy at Mitre, has a Ph.D. in nuclear power so we all call him 'Doc.' Now he heads up our team on Palmyra Island because it's critical to national security.' Now Miss Trowbridge," the captain continued with a broad smile on his face, "if you want to know anything else about Dr. Malcolm, I suggest you ask him directly. As Mr. Lockwood—Frosty said, and I can confirm: Roger Malcolm is one of their smartest staff members."

With those words in her mind, Emmie saw Roger coming toward her and was petrified. She thought, *I was truly nasty to him when we first met. What must he have thought? What can I say to him now?*

"Hi, Emmie, I hope you didn't think I was lost and gone forever. How are the kids?"

She looked over at the soccer game the kids were playing, collected her composure, and said, "Oh! Hi there, Roger. The kids are fine, and no, I figured that you would need to keep track of the Air Force and return to Christmas. How are things on Palmyra?"

"Luckily, we had only one serious problem, but my electronics guy solved it within a couple a minutes, so I felt I could come down here and double-check some of our results. But I also wanted to see how the kids were behaving at supper, movie, and bedtime. The last thing I would care to do is corral a bunch of live-wire children and keep them penned up for, what, twelve or more hours? Are you exhausted yet?"

"Oh, not quite. I do have most of their parents and six other teachers to do the 'corralling,' as you put it. I have a nice home with a comfortable room and the most wonderful couple looking after me. My big problem is strictly academic. I have no up-to-date textbooks, no modern lab equipment, and the encyclopedias are from the nineteenth century. I have to write on an old blackboard each days' lessons either the night before or the morning of what I have planned to teach—and I have kids in eight different grades!"

"Well, I don't know what I can do about that. There are no schools—no native people even—on Palmyra."

Suddenly a thought came to Emmie's mind. Something she heard Captain Patten say. With sort of a wry smile she asked, "Roger, don't you have a direct line to the secretary of defense at the Pentagon? They must have texts for all grades for all kinds of courses in all kinds of languages. Couldn't you call him and ask for some help for my kids? What about that 'unlimited budget' General Starbird has that you mentioned?"

Taken aback, Roger looked a little blank. He immediately thought, *Where did she learn that about me and the SecDef? That's top secret! Oh, I know, Captain Patten's been blabbing. But what can the SecDef or Starbird do for these little kids?* Then he thought, *She's pulling my leg. She doesn't mean it at all.*

There was an awkward pause. Emmie added, "I don't mean the top guy of course, but he must have plenty of assistants. What about this 'Frosty' that the captain is so in awe of?"

That triggered Roger's brain. *Of course, that is possible,* he thought. Then he finally replied to Emmie, "As a matter of fact, my boss, Frosty Lockwood, should be able to help. He is one of the most helpful guys in the world. He can go to the local school district, tell them you have these children who want to learn but have no books or materials, lean on their goodwill, and get a package of books that he can send to our man Dick Johnson at Hickam in Hawaii who can put them on a flight direct to Christmas. We ought to get your principal, Mr. Duxbury, in on it since I'll bet the high school needs books and materials in a bad way too."

"Oh, Roger! That sounds too good to be true. You're not kidding, are you?"

"I'm not kidding. Look, you have to corral your kids now, but do you think I could stay overnight on the ship with you and the kids? I came down here to oversee a very special test tomorrow, but it turns out that my 'need-to-know' has not been issued. So I'm going back to Palmyra in the morning. This evening you, Mr. Duxbury, and I could put together a complete list of what books and materials would be vital to get sent pronto down to your school. I'll put the list in a letter to Mr. Lockwood, send it via the shuttle to Dick Johnson at Hickam in Honolulu with instructions to send it on by airmail to Mitre in Massachusetts. I'm sure you should get whatever Frosty can beg, borrow, or steal in just a few days. Of course the books will all be in English.

I doubt that anyone in the U.S. has books in Gilbertese. Anyway, I'll alert Captain Patten to be sure your package does not get mixed up with the air force stuff."

Emmie looked at Roger with a little funny smile about staying over on the ship, but then said, "Oh, sure. There's lots of room, food, and spare bunks on the ship. We ought to be able to prepare that list in plenty of time."

That evening the two of them huddled with Mr. Duxbury in a small compartment off the ship's cafeteria while the movie played for the kids. They soon had quite a comprehensive wish list for the books and materials they wanted. The principal asked, "Are you sure your boss Frosty will be willing to get all this—and will he be able to? How can he ship it all by air and get it here with all these tests going off?"

"I'll leave that to him. He owes me a lot, as we say, 'big time.' He says, 'Rog, you're having all the fun while I'm stuck here behind my desk.' I tell him, 'If you would rather sniff the plutonium from twenty huge nukes, be my guest. I'll take over your desk.' That shuts him up."

Mr. Duxbury left the small compartment to quiet the kids and get them ready for bed. After an awkward pause, Emmie asked Roger, "I hear they call you 'Doc.' What's that for?"

"Oh, I have a Ph.D., and General Starbird calls me that for short, so it caught on around the office. At Mitre and out here on Palmyra they call me 'Rog.' Captain Patten tries to maintain a more formal greeting, so he calls me 'Dr. Malcolm.' How about you? What's your degree?"

"Well, I just have the American equivalent of a master's degree in mathematics from Girton College, part of Cambridge University. I was going to go on for my Ph.D. at Cambridge, but the postwar recession dried up the scholarships. I got involved in the postwar relief work in Europe and just never got back to Cambridge. After a job in statistics in the city, I decided I would rather teach and was taken on by my old school, Roedean. Then my wanderlust and thoughts of adventure in foreign lands got the better of me, and I volunteered for this job." She took a deep breath and hesitated.

Roger broke in, "Wow! A master's in math. That sounds a lot harder and more impressive than my piddling around with 'stinks and bangs' to get a degree in chemistry. You had to pass the Tripos, didn't you? How did you do?"

Emmie quietly said, "Oh, you know about our degree system in England." She took another breath. "I got a 'first'."

"Holy smoke! That's impressive. All I've done is a bit of routine science and sail around the world on a destroyer courtesy of the U.S. Navy."

"Oh, you were in the service too?"

"Yeah, I helped to shoot up some real estate in North Korea, dodged a few enemy bullets, and then had to hold the old ship together as the chief engineering officer. Mitre thought I knew something about nuclear energy and hired me two years ago since my Ph.D. came with a minor in nuclear engineering from the Oak Ridge National Laboratory. But academically you put me to shame with a 'first.' Even with the recession in England after the war, it's really too bad they didn't grab you to go on with your studies. Teaching little kids math seems a bit elementary."

Then she jumped right in to the heart of the matter. "Elementary or not, I like teaching the kids. By the way, Roger, do you have a family?" She held her breath.

"No, well, I have both my parents and two brothers living in Massachusetts, but no, I have never married." He went on quickly, thinking that here he was, thirty-four years old and still unattached. "I'm not homosexual, hardly that, and I've had many a date, but just never got up the courage to ask a young lady to marry me or just live together. I'm truly a workaholic. What with the three years in the navy and then getting my double Ph.D. and settling in at Mitre, I just didn't have time to woo a girl properly. What about you? What's your family situation?"

Now Emmie looked hard at Roger. Her thoughts tumbled about in her mind. *Should I tell him about my encounter with James? If I don't and he finds out, what would he think? Would he leave me flat? If I do tell him, would he get up and walk away from me anyway? Would that be the end of romance for me? Here I am, a thirty-two-year-old virgin. Would I ever have another such chance for love? What is this powerful attraction I feel toward him? Is it love…true love? Oh, my! I feel it…I feel him all around me! It is love…It must be! But wait…I hardly know him—not at all except what he told me just now. Could I…could I…well, live with him…forever? He seems to be heaven-sent to help me survive this chaotic place. Yes…yes. I just have to chance it.*

She gulped and went on. "Well, Roger, I too have both parents, but no siblings and never have been married or lived with a guy. Actually it wasn't wanderlust that got me into this situation but lust of a different kind. I got into an embarrassing situation with an attractive but married guy. My picture wound up on the front pages of the tabloids in London when he and his wife decided to divorce. I felt that I had to leave Roedean, the school where I was teaching, and just get out of the news for a while. I'm still so ashamed. I started to do what I knew was wrong, and got punished before anything really happened." She paused again to catch her breath. "Oh, Roger, I shouldn't be telling you all this. We hardly know each other, but you seem to be so very understanding. Here you have immediately agreed to get books and supplies for the kids. You helped me out the first time we met. I have felt since that moment that I would like to get to know you better. Is that too strange?"

Roger had to take a deep breath also. He was powerfully attracted to her, and he didn't really understand why she had made such a confession. But one thing he suddenly knew – he desperately wanted to kiss her and whisk her off in his arms. Luckily, he quickly recovered his senses and said, "Emmie, Emmie, Emmie, I just want to get to know you better. I don't really want to know more about what went on in your past, and I definitely don't think it matters. You clearly have a deep sense of right and wrong and empathy for others, particularly those less fortunate than you. You decided to help these little kids get a better education, and even after landing in the middle of this hellhole, you appear to be sticking it out. If I can help you even a little bit, I sure want to do so. I think you are lovely, pert, and really smart. I have never known anyone like you. So, what else should I know about you? What's it like to get a 'first' in math at Cambridge?"

Emmie broke down at this response, but after a bit dried her tears. "Oh, Roger, Roger, Rog…thank you, thank you, thank you. You must think I'm a weeping willow, but I truly began to think I was being cast out into the wilderness because of my sins. Can you really just ignore them?"

"Oh, sure, Emmie, for sure. I too have my sins, not for lust perhaps—well not yet anyway," he said with a smile, "but I certainly killed a lot of women and possibly children, not just enemy soldiers, with my gunfire in Korea. To me, as I think about it, war is the worst sin humans can indulge in. The population on both sides is whipped up by their leaders, the young and most fit men are sent to hurl themselves into the maelstrom, and they and many others die. That's one reason I'm here—to make sure that these incredibly destructive nuclear weapons are never used. Can you imagine just one of them wiping out an entire city? We must not let that ever happen again."

"Oh, Roger, I haven't begun to think about these tests. I've been so intent on my own misery. On the other hand, I must admit, I have tried to help people out. The unfortunate refugees in Europe were quite a challenge, but I think I did some good getting families back together. And I really don't mind teaching the little kids. Too many never get the chance to understand math and science as they should. Getting a 'first' is mostly just hard work and study, study, study. But there again, I think I did break some new ground. To go on to get a Ph.D. would have bankrupted my family. I truly feel good about having become 'just a teacher,' as many people say. But getting back to your sins, you were in the military. You had to obey. Don't you have any personal sins, just teensy-weensy ones?" Now it was her turn to smile sweetly.

"Well, I did lead one girl on for several years, and I'm sure she thought of marriage. But then I broke it off a bit too abruptly. I suspect she's never forgiven me. But I'm sure she wasn't the one for me."

Just then there was a commotion out in the cafeteria. "Oh, dear, I think Mr. Duxbury needs a hand. Roger, can you excuse me a minute?"

"Oh, sure," he answered, but the intimacy was broken. After a few minutes, he got up, went over to Emmie and said, "Good night. I'm turning in." The bunk seemed familiar to him from his time in the navy, but he found his mind stirring with thoughts about the conversation with Emmie, and sleep wouldn't come. *I'm dead-sure I love her, but what can I do about it? I'm not even supposed to be here on Christmas Island. Can I keep on catching the shuttle from Palmyra just to see her?* He twisted and turned in frustration, falling asleep just before the kids woke up noisily asking for breakfast.

For her part, Emmie too tossed and turned in her bunk in the women's area of the ship most of the night. She wondered, *Will he make good on getting us those books and equipment, or was he just stringing us along to make us feel good? Everything about him is just too good. Handsome, strong, great body, a team leader, war veteran, smartest man at Mitre, knows the secretary of defense personally, never been married, never had sex—oh, come on! Of course, his having been in the navy all those years I can't believe he's a virgin, not that I care. How could I have gone on and on about James and all that mess? He said it didn't matter, but surely it must. Is he in love with me? Suddenly I'm sure I'm in love with him. Maybe I should just come right out and say, "Roger, I love you." No, no. What a terrible idea. Oh, I don't know what to do!*

The next morning, Roger ate breakfast with Emmie and Mr. Duxbury. Their conversation was all about the kids and what Emmie might do if the books and equipment came in soon. They had to wait for Mahatma to sound the all-clear as soon as the Polaris missile live test detonated, which evidently had gone off according to plan. Roger rushed to catch the shuttle to Palmyra. He checked in with his team, and because they had no information on the test except its likely detonation time, they had not obtained any data. Roger told them, "Forget it. The powers that be really didn't want us to get any."

He composed a letter to Frosty, made a copy for Dick Johnson, and tucked the lengthy list of books and materials that Emmie and Mr. Duxbury had written into both envelopes. Roger walked over to the airfield runway, and soon the next shuttle appeared. After it landed he caught the attention of the pilot, handed him both envelopes, and asked him to give them both to Mr. Johnson of Mitre at Hickam. In Johnson's envelope, Roger had included a note for him to airmail Frosty's envelope on to him immediately.

While Roger was over at the airstrip, Hal murmured something. Joe asked, "What was that?"

"I wonder why Rog keeps running down to Christmas? After that first run when he brought back the test schedule, he hasn't really found out anything much down there. Do you think what I'm thinking?"

"What's that?" answered Joe.

"Well, I may be dead wrong, but what if Rog has found a woman down there on Christmas? Why else would he keep running back and forth like that? Whatever he has done or learned, he always comes back so happy-go-lucky."

Lee, overhearing Hal, said, "What? No way. Rog has always been all business at Mitre. Come on. Where would a woman come from at Christmas? There may be some natives there, but he wouldn't take up with a native woman, surely!"

Hal replied, "I'll bet you—I'll bet you a nickel that I'm right."

Joe said, "You don't have a clue if that's all you want to bet."

"Okay, a dime. There's nothing to spend any money here on Palmyra anyway, that's for sure."

Lee answered, "Okay, Hal, I'll take that bet. Here, Joe, hold the stakes."

"Come on, you gamblers," said Joe. "Knuckle down to business. We've still got to solve that problem with the seismic sensors." But he kept the two dimes.

Three days later a guy from the team from the Cambridge Research Lab (CRL) adjacent to their trailer came running up to Roger first thing in the morning. "Mr. Malcolm, we just got a radio message from Mitre in

Massachusetts asking us to get you on the horn immediately." Roger ran with the guy to their trailer, went in, and was handed the radio transmitter.

"Malcolm here," he said.

"Malcolm, you idiot," came his boss's voice loud and clear. Roger almost didn't need the radio to hear it. "You're supposed to be detecting bombs, not playing hanky-panky with some cute teacher. What in hell is going on?"

"I'm just being a good fellow trying to help educate the native kids on Christmas Island."

"Where do you see that in your orders from DDR&E? What are you doing on Christmas anyway? For chrissakes, Malcolm, stick to business! Do you think all I have to do around here is chase down, and probably pay for, a bunch of kids' books? Gawd-a-mighty, gimme a break! Over and out!"

"Wait, Frosty, wait." Roger could still hear his boss breathing heavily into the microphone. "I went down to Christmas to try to get the schedule for the next test. They wouldn't give the time of day until I get that 'need-to-know' request I sent off to you several days ago. So I'm wandering around and ran into that 'cute teacher' you mentioned. She's from England and just lambasted me about having to corral the kids to keep them from being blinded and fried by every test. Get me the 'need-to-know' and I'll stick to business." The microphone went dead and he didn't know whether Frosty had heard his last words. "Oh, well, back to the work at hand." Then he left to check on the seismometers again.

Word of the radio phone call got right over to Hal Leach from the CRL guys. As soon as Roger left the trailer, one of them sneaked past without Roger noticing him and climbed into the Mitre trailer. "Hey, you guys, did you hear the scoop on your boss?" Hal, Joe, and Lee surrounded him. "He's been diddling a cute English teacher down on Christmas, and now the whole task force knows about it!"

Hal pounded his desk and let out a great guffaw. "I told you so. You wouldn't believe me, but it's true. Rog has a sweetie down on Christmas. Pay up, you guys. I win the bet." They all trooped over to the CRL trailer, and the guys there confirmed it. Joe handed the two dimes over to Hal, who pocketed them with a wide smile on his face.

Lee said, "I can't believe it. Rog romancing a sweetie, and the only white woman around!"

A week later Roger got called to the airstrip, and the pilot had an envelope for him—his need-to-know. Unfortunately, it came with a disclaimer: his setup was to be classified at a higher level than anyone else's. None of them had a need-to-know about *his* instructions from DDR&E. He couldn't share his results with theirs. Even so, he promptly went around to each of the other teams on Palmyra to see what they were doing. He found out that none of them except the English were duplicating his setup. They were mainly designed to explore the diagnostics of the bomb, not measure its location, yield, and height of burst. But when they asked him what his team was doing, he had to fudge it. "Well," he would say, "we're measuring various parameters of the bomb that don't match with yours." When he couldn't say anything more, the other guys clammed up. *So much for need-to-know,* he told himself.

But he thought he might learn more down on Christmas Island and see Emmie again. He got down there on the sixteenth of May, checked in with Captain Patten, tried his need-to-know on a couple of the teams, didn't learn all that much, and then in mid-afternoon turned his jeep toward the school. "Where's Miss Trowbridge?"

"Oh," one of the kids replied, "she in school with Mr. Duxbury. She said not disturb. You her friend Doc, yes? Maybe go in, okay?"

Roger turned off his jeep's motor, took out the keys, and strode purposefully into the school. He heard Emmie's voice from outside the principal's office and went in anyway.

"Oh, Roger," Emmie exclaimed, jumping up. She flung her arms around him and kissed him madly on the cheek. "Look at all the books!" she cried out. "Your boss Frosty is fantastic. Mr. Duxbury and I have spent all morning since this crate arrived opening up this treasure trove and sorting it all out."

Roger held on to her just a little longer than the spur-of-the-moment kiss warranted but then replied, "I told you he would come through. You're right. He's fantastic. I told you he owed me big time. So now we're more or less even."

"But you're fantastic too. You came up with the idea of how to get these books, and you did it! Oh, Roger, you are wonderful!"

"Yes, Mr. Malcolm, you are wonderful," chimed in Mr. Duxbury. "How can we ever thank you?"

"Oh, really, Mr. Duxbury, just seeing you and Emmie so pleased with this treasure trove, as she put it, is thanks enough for me. By the way, who is that boy outside that knows me as Doc? He seems to be a lively and alert youngster."

"Oh, that must be 'Terry, *Te Raoi*' or 'Peace' in Gilbertese, although he is hardly ever at peace," said the principal. "His father is in the National Assembly of Kiribati, Mr. Tong, so he spends a lot of his time on the island of Tarawa, where the capital is located. When his father is away, Terry boards with the same local family where Emmie is living. His mother died a few years ago. Terry tends to be his own young man."

Roger stayed a while, helping to sort the books and other materials. Then he left, saying, "I have to check in with some of the other teams. I'll come by tomorrow before taking the shuttle back to Palmyra."

"Oh, Roger, stay with us tonight on board the ship again. It's not so uncomfortable, is it?"

"Okay," he replied, a bit taken aback. "As a matter of fact, the bunks aboard the ship remind me of my time in the navy, and they are more comfortable than those creaky cots in the BOQ." He left in his jeep, saying hi to Terry, who was busy playing soccer in the yard. Roger found all of the task force teams too busy preparing for the next morning's bomb test to pay much attention to him, so he returned to the school, picked up Emmie and Mr. Duxbury, and drove them to the ship. They ate in the ship's mess, and Roger and Emmie again sat apart in a spare compartment.

For some reason, at first their former level of intimacy was missing. Roger asked Emmie, "Tell me about your wartime experiences." She did so at some length, and then asked him about his time in the navy, which he did, also at some length but omitting any bit about his bullet wound. *No need to upset her about that old scar,* he thought. Suddenly Roger happened to look Emmie right in the eyes. He thought he saw a light of encouragement, even a bit of exasperation. *What am I doing prattling on so? I love this woman. I am madly in love with this woman.* He slid around to be beside her, reached out and pulled her toward him, lifted her chin up toward his, and kissed her full on the lips.

Finally when they were both out of breath, Emmie stammered, "Oh, Roger, I wasn't sure. I thought you might care for me, but I wasn't sure."

"Emmie, Emmie, Emmie, I care for you more than you can know."

"And I for you," she answered breathlessly.

He was about to propose to her when she pulled back. There was Terry Tong, staring at them. "Mr. Duxbury wants us all to go to bed. The movie's over, but we're not sleepy. Miss Trowbridge, what about one of your fun games?" Terry pulled on her, and she got up to help get the kids to bed.

Roger got up too, said good-night in passing, and went to his own bunk. The moment had passed. Again he tossed and turned. Now he desperately wanted to be close to Emmie. He got all aroused, had to satisfy himself, and finally dropped off to sleep, filled with erotic dreams. In the morning he managed to get her off for a passionate kiss, but all too soon he had to dash for the shuttle.

For her part, Emmie was also in a dither. Now she was sure of the love of both herself and Roger. But what did that mean? How often could they get together? What about his job on Palmyra and all too soon back in the States? What about her contract here on Christmas? Could their love survive long stretches of absence from each other? Again she had tell herself, *Oh, I just don't know what to do!*

Back on Palmyra, things began to go wrong. They missed recording one of the blasts. It turned out that a lightning bolt, which also sends out electromagnetic, or radio, waves much like a nuclear bomb, had struck near Palmyra just before the bomb went off, triggering the electronics with a false alarm. Joe Henry said, "We can put in additional filters to screen out the lightning, but then we might miss the bombs."

Hal Leach suggested, "What about putting in a second circuit with the additional filters and see if they screen out the lightning but not the bombs?" That didn't work, so Roger spent a lot of time considering what to do. Meanwhile he missed the shuttle to Christmas at the end of May. He didn't even get to send a note to Emmie.

Emmie went to Captain Patten. "Have you seen or heard from Mr. Malcolm?"

"The doc? No. As far as I know, he's still on Palmyra."

At the beginning of June Roger did get to send a note, expressing his love and explaining about being a workaholic. Captain Patten saw Emmie and explained to her that the whole task force was having trouble. There were no tests scheduled for ten days, until June eighth.

Chapter Nine

A Runaway Child

Roger decided to catch the late afternoon shuttle on the seventh. When he scrambled off the plane at Christmas, it was getting dark. One of the airfield workers saw Roger and called out, "Doc, Doc! Your girl has been looking all over for you. She's really upset about something."

Roger ran over and asked for the keys to a jeep. For once they were all in use. "Doggone it, wouldn't you know." Finally one came in. He grabbed the keys out of the driver's hand and roared off toward the school. *What could it be?* he wondered. *Is she upset that I haven't been down here for a couple of weeks?*

Emmie wasn't at the school. One of the other kids said, "Miss Trowbridge and Mr. Duxbury are out along the road south looking for Terry Tong. He's gone missing."

"Drat it," said Roger, "I must have missed them driving so fast to get here to the school." He swung the jeep around and headed back the way he came, slower this time, looking on both sides of the road. Then he saw them, down by the lagoon. "Emmie, Emmie, over here."

She ran over the rough terrain back to the road. "Roger, Roger, thank heavens you've come. Terry Tong ran off saying that he wanted to see the bomb go off. He said, 'All we do is watch movies. Why can't we watch bombs?' Then he ran off and we haven't seen him since. That was hours ago."

"Have you alerted the task force? They won't want a child wandering around the island."

"No," said Emmie. "We thought we would find him right away. We've been searching all along the road since then."

"I'll drive back and get them to organize a search party. Maybe Mr. Duxbury should come with me to organize a search in and around the school and ship as well as in the town just in case you missed him earlier. He may well be hiding back there. Mr. Duxbury, get the bigger kids to help out. They may have some ideas about where he may be. Meanwhile I'll come back, and Emmie, you and I can look further. I'll bring some big flashlights too. It's getting awfully dark." He drove as fast as he dared back to the task force command center, pushed his way in, and told the duty officer what had happened.

"We get that lost person every now and then," said the officer. "Give me this boy's description and I'll get out a search party right away. Where do you think he may be?"

"I hope he's right around here. The school principal, Mr. Duxbury, is here with me to help at this end. Give me a walkie-talkie and let me know if he turns up. I'll be down the road in my jeep making sure he's not out in the open down that way."

Soon Roger and Emmie were looking along both sides of the road with their flashlights calling as loud as they could, "Terry, Terry, *Te Raoi.*" Roger drove slowly, beeping the jeep's horn and shouting the boy's name in English as well as Gilbertese as best he could. "Let's stop and listen every few minutes to hear if he is responding," Roger suggested.

When they got well down along the lagoon road it was already past midnight. They crossed over to the beach road south and met a couple of jeeps coming north. Roger stopped them and asked, "Have you seen a young boy walking along the road or anywhere south of here?"

"No, nothing like that. All of the teams like ours are coming north, having set their instruments on automatic. The shot is scheduled for six o'clock in the morning, so only the guys left down there at the end of the island are the ones making sure the power doesn't go off and everything is all set to record the blast. They will leave at the twenty-minute mark when the bomber arrives and drive like hell to get as far north as they can before the bomb drops."

Roger thanked them as they drove off and turned to Emmie. "About all we can do is keep on looking, but I can't believe Terry got this far. We're miles from the school and ship." He used his walkie-talkie to check with the task force search party.

The voice on the other end reported, "Nope, no sign of him yet, but we still have a lot of places to look. One of the kids told us just now that his bicycle is missing. He thinks the other kid may have taken it. He may be way down at the south end of the island by now."

"Jeezus!" exclaimed Roger and told Emmie the news. "We're still a long way from there. I'll try to get hold of that last team that's down there on this walkie-talkie to ask if they have seen him."

After quite a delay in getting through to that team via the task force command center, the answer was, "No, we've seen no child down here, but most likely we've been too busy with our last-minute checks on the equipment to notice."

Emmie thought a minute and then said, "I don't think he would go all the way to the end of the island. Even this far seems unlikely to me. He's too smart for that. If he's not hiding around the school somewhere, he must be back along the road."

"Okay," answered Roger, "but let's go on just a bit further to be sure." Just then a loud hum sounded throughout the island and Mahatma came on the air to announce, "Test Alma is airborne. The countdown has started."

"Great Scott!" exclaimed Roger. "Is it that late? We better get going." He turned the jeep around and started back north, picking up speed.

"Go slower, Roger. We just have to find him," Emmie said, obviously in some distress. "I hate to think of him out here not knowing his danger." Suddenly the jeep's motor coughed and stopped. "I didn't mean for you to stop."

"God almighty, I think we're out of gas! I didn't check when I grabbed the first jeep I could find!" Roger got out his walkie-talkie and called the command center. "Sorry to bother you, but we just ran out of gas in our jeep. We're about five miles south of the lagoon on the western beach road, and we still haven't found the boy."

"We can't have anyone drive down to get you. Mahatma has us buttoned up here. No one is allowed out on the island once the countdown has started. Stay on the road, and we'll have the last team down on the southern tip of the island pick you up when they leave to come north to their bunker at the twenty-minute mark."

"Thanks much. We'll be walking north on the road, still looking for the boy." To Emmie he said, "We better not miss that last jeep. I'm afraid we're much too close to the bomb blast for comfort. Let's hustle as fast as we can."

They half walked, half ran—Roger called it the 'Boy Scout's pace'—pausing every now and then to catch their breath. Mahatma called out, forty-five minutes, then thirty minutes as the eastern sky began to lighten, and finally, when it was clearly dawn, twenty minutes.

Roger started looking for the B-52 bomb-carrying plane. Mahatma intoned, "ten minutes to bomb release," but Emmie kept her eyes searching the areas on both sides of the road. "Look!" she shouted, pointing off to their right. "Isn't that a bicycle?"

"Yes, I believe you're right." He suddenly realized that they were passing the culvert he had noted and looked at a few weeks previously. He broke away from Emmie and ran over to the bike. She followed closely behind him. The bike was just lying on the ground, no boy around it. But Emmie looked further.

"Terry, Terry!" she shouted in great excitement. "Roger, it's Terry over there on that mound!" The boy sat up, looked around, and in some haste got up and started to run off the culvert. "No, Terry, don't run away!" shouted Emmie.

"I want to see the bomb go off! Leave me alone!" he shouted back.

"That's why we're here," shouted Roger. "Let's watch it together. I'll tell you all about it. I'll tell you things none of your friends can know. We can all watch it from here." That seemed to work. Terry stopped, turned back, and came toward them. Roger stepped toward him, and in a quick move, put his arm around him.

Just then, the jeep carrying the last team from the south roared past on the road, not seeing them. "Oh, my God," said Emmie. "There goes our ride."

"I guess we will have to watch it from here. Terry, we are about to see the most awful sight that you will never forget."

Just then Mahatma intoned, "Five minutes to bomb release."

"Quick," responded Roger. "We better get under cover until the blast wave passes by. I don't know how strong this culvert might be, but follow me into this as a shelter quickly."

"Wait, wait!" said Terry. "I thought we watch together. How we watch from down in pipe?"

"That's just the point, Terry, When the bomb goes off the incredibly bright light will blind anyone whether you are looking at it or not. Shortly after that, the heat from the fireball could fry you, and then the blast wave may be strong enough to blow you away. Only after the heat and blast waves have passed over us can we come out of the culvert safely. Then we will watch the enormous fireball rise into the sky together without getting killed. Come on, we don't have much time."

They had to crawl on their hands and knees to get into its entrance and found themselves on dried mud encountering spider webs, discarded plastic bottles, and all kinds of junk.

"Oh, Roger, do we have to crawl through all this mess?" complained Emmie.

"Yuck," said Terry. "This is pile of dirt."

Roger said, "Quiet, you two. Yes, we have to get away from the entrance to this culvert, and we'll have to lie down in it when the bomb goes off." He shepherded the other two down to the entrance of the culvert and pushed them ahead of him. "This is far enough. We can still hear Mahatma but should be shielded from the blast wave. We have less than a minute or so to get as comfortable as we can. In fact, we have to huddle together as close as possible, face down. Here, Terry, you get between Miss Trowbridge and me. Emmie, put your arm around him and lie down. Pull him down and as close to you as you can." Roger did the same on Terry's other side. His face slid into the dirt, but he just reached out over Terry to pull Emmie toward him.

"Is this really necessary, Roger? This seems a bit much."

Just then Mahatma announced in even a more stentorian voice, "Bomb released."

Roger said, "Our lives may depend on it. Do it now! We have just twenty more seconds." He wasn't a praying man, but he prayed that the bombardier knew his stuff and wouldn't miss his aim point. Then he had one more thought. "Emmie, Emmie, can you hear me?"

"Yes, Roger, yes."

"Will you marry me? I love you dearly."

"What?"

"Will you marry me if we survive this?"

"Yes, of course. I love you dearly too. Yes, yes, yes. I could not live without you."

"What you two talking about?" murmured Terry.

"Detonation," said Mahatma.

Chapter Ten

Shot Alma

The thermonuclear bomb went off ten thousand feet over the Pacific Ocean at exactly 0602.24—that is, 6 hours 2 minutes and 24 seconds local time on the morning of June 8, 1962.

Roger felt the white-hot flash on his neck just as it raced at the speed of light past the opening to the culvert. The brilliance of the flash startled and amazed him even though he was expecting it, since he had his eyes closed tightly and buried in his arms. It was frightening in its intensity, and he instinctively hunched his shoulders up to protect his neck with his shirt collar—much too late to do any good, of course. He felt Terry try to jump up in surprise, but he held him down tightly. At that moment he also heard Emmie exclaim, "Oh, God!"

Within seconds the heat wave from the rapidly expanding fireball swept past the culvert with the thermal energy from a million tons TNT equivalent of exploding nuclear power. The temperature within the culvert shot up, baking them as if in an oven. Terry cried out, "I burning! I burning!"

Emmie cried out again, "Oh God, oh God, Roger. This is hell! I can't breathe!"

Roger felt the same but tried to calm the other two. "Tuck your mouth into your clothes to take a breath. This heat will pass by soon." But it seemed like an eternity.

After about twenty seconds of torment, Roger spoke out loudly, "Okay, now, we still have to wait for almost three minutes, perhaps only two and a half, for the blast and sound wave to reach us. Relax a bit, take some breaths, try to cool off, and I'll tell you when to huddle together again."

"I want out now!" Terry cried, jumping up. "Why can't I? I want see it now!"

Emmie jumped up too, slid past Terry, and embraced Roger. "Yes, yes, yes. Just in case you didn't hear me before that incredible flash and heat, yes, I will marry you, anywhere, anytime. I do love you."

Roger had to reach out and grab Terry at the same time that he was trying to kiss Emmie. His kiss went awry as he pulled Terry back. "That heat wave was bad, but the blast wave can knock you over and even kill you. It's the loudest bang you will ever hear or feel again. You may go deaf, or at least not hear anything for a while. The sudden pressure will squeeze your innards until they hurt and again take your breath away. We've all got to wait just a bit longer."

He turned to Emmie and finished his kiss, which she returned with vigor, and he added, "Yes, yes, yes, I do love you, too. Now, just to be sure we survive this blast, we have to huddle together again, but we don't have to worry about a flash of light or heat. It's a tremendous bang and squeeze—an overpressure crunch that may deafen us and knock the air out of us. Let's get into position to be sure we're ready."

What Roger didn't know was that the upper air currents had changed just as the B-52 approached the bomb release point. The bombardier had put into his bomb sight corrections for the winds aloft between the aircraft and the ground, but he had no way of knowing about the shift in the air currents between ten thousand and thirty thousand feet where the B-52 was flying. Also, the plane was "crabbing" as the pilot tried to fly a straight course. The plane and the bomb were blown quite a bit north as the bomb dropped; it actually exploded five miles further north than the aim point.

The blast wave reached the culvert about half a minute sooner than Roger expected. The bang deafened all three of them. The blast overpressure cracked Roger and Emmie's ribs, and its accompanying two hundred mile per hour wind sucked the air out of the culvert. As they tried to recover, the return wind a few seconds later stirred up the dust in the culvert, blinding them and giving their ribs another punch.

Two of them rolled over and sat up. Terry was the least hurt and got to his knees and then got up to a squatting position. Roger spat the dust out of his mouth, tried to cry the grit out of his eyes, and swore, "Goddamn it all to hell! My ribs must be broken." He tried to take a breath. "Ooh! That hurts! Emmie, are you all right?"

She didn't respond. She gasped, spit, cried, and gasped again. Finally she whispered, "My ribs are broken too, and I can't seem to be able to breathe. My lungs don't seem to work." She tried to sit up, cried out in pain, and lay back down, moaning, still in pain.

Roger's mind cleared just a bit. He knew they had to get help quickly. He reached around and found the walkie-talkie. "Here, Terry, take this outside the culvert, press this 'talk' button, and try to reach the command center."

"I not use this before. What I do?"

"Here, I'll turn it on. See this button with 'talk' written on it? Just press that and speak into this end. Speak loudly but don't shout."

"What I say?"

"Very slowly say, 'The Doc, Miss Trowbridge, and I are at the culvert on the west beach road. We are hurt and need help quick.' Then release the talk button and listen at the other end to hear if anyone answers. If someone answers tell me what they say."

Terry scrambled on his hands and knees out of the culvert, and Roger heard him speak into the walkie-talkie. He saw him release the talk button and listen intently. After a bit Terry said, "There no answer."

Roger crawled painfully out of the culvert and told him to try again and again until there was an answer. Then Roger crawled back to see what he could do for Emmie. *Not much,* he thought. *Better not try to move her.*

Suddenly Terry shouted, "They heard me! They heard me!" After a bit, Terry said, "The guy says they too busy now. All teams are busy."

"Tell them this is an emergency and to send the medevac chopper."

"Now the guy hung up," said Terry.

"Call him again and tell him again, louder this time, 'This is an emergency.'"

Finally Terry got through. "Ask him to put Captain Patten on the line," Roger said as he scrambled out of the culvert again and took the walkie-talkie.

After a good bit of back and forth, Roger heard Patten say in some annoyance, "What's this all about?"

"This is Doc Malcolm, captain. We got trapped out here looking for the youngster when the bomb went off. Although we got under cover, we got hit pretty hard by the blast wave. Miss Trowbridge and I may have a few broken ribs, or worse. We really need that medevac chopper right away."

"Goddamn you dumb binnies. Okay, okay, I'll wrestle up the search and rescue team—the 'SAR' boys. Where did you say you are?"

"We're at that big culvert about five miles down the west beach road, on the left as you go south. The young lad Terry and I will be waving our shirts when the search and rescue chopper comes along."

It took an agonizing twenty minutes or so for the chopper to arrive. While they waited, he turned toward Terry and said, "Now you can look at the fireball rising into the air. It's quite a sight, isn't it?"

"Yeah, it pretty, all yellow and red. It suck up whole ocean underneath"

"That's what they call the mushroom cloud. The brilliant clouds are highly radioactive—extremely dangerous." As the fireball rose higher and dimmed, white clouds appeared on top and around the fireball, the latter in a doughnut shape. The fireball glowed dark red and then purple. It started to drift to the northeast, rising almost to the stratosphere and carrying the evaporating and foreshortening mushroom cloud with it.

They heard the medevac chopper. Roger and. Terry waved, and they were spotted. They stepped aside as the medics jumped out and ran to the culvert. Roger was impressed by the way the medics were old hands at handling badly wounded soldiers and sailors. They got Emmie bundled up and out of the culvert without her wincing more than a couple of times, although Roger knew she was hurting very much. They cradled her into the chopper. Roger and Terry crawled in too and the medics followed, and in another twenty minutes they had landed back at the task force hospital.

This facility had been built and opened just a few weeks previously. Roger noted that it really was just four Quonset huts connected together. But after following the medics carrying Emmie into the facility he found it to be cool, clean, and well organized. They took her off to one emergency room, and an orderly took Roger and Terry over to another. They waited quite a while as Emmie was attended to, and then the doctor came around to look at them. He cleaned and put some bandages on Terry's scrapes, gave him a pain pill, and had him sit down while he looked at Roger. "Ooh, those ribs are clearly broken, Mr. Malcolm. As you may know, we can't do much in the way of putting splints on them. The best I can do is tape you up to immobilize them and let you suffer for several weeks as they heal themselves. But let's get some X-rays to be sure you don't have any other problems. That nuclear blast wave must have given you a real thump."

Roger said to the doctor, "I'm impressed with your facilities." Then he lay on his back under the X-ray machine, and an orderly snapped the photos.

"Yes," replied the doctor, "a task force of this size really needs a complete medical center. But we had so little time to get organized and shipped out here, it's a wonder we have as much as we have. Now, let's have a look at the lad here." He helped Roger get off the table and had Terry get under the X-ray machine. The orderly took the plates to be developed and read.

Shortly, as they put on their shirts, the doctor returned and told Roger, "Young Terry here is in amazing condition—a bruised back, stomach and ribs, and just a few scrapes. He can go on home. You, as you thought, have three broken ribs, but we can tape them up and you can go on your way also. You will be in some pain for a couple of weeks, but take a couple aspirin and tough it out. Your young lady, Miss Trowbridge, however, has a collapsed lung, three broken ribs, a badly bruised backbone, maybe a concussion, and perhaps internal injuries we're not able to spot here in the field hospital. We have treated her lung, taped up her ribs, and bandaged her head but recommend that she be flown immediately back to the hospital at Hickam in Hawaii. We'll dope her up for the flight, but they will have to decide what her true condition is and what to do about it. I don't think it's life threatening, but she definitely needs a better equipped hospital than this one."

Roger was appalled. *What have I done to the love of my life?* Turning to the hospital doctor he said, "Do you really have to ship her off? Who will look after her?"

"Oh, Hickam is used to soldiers and sailors arriving in various conditions. They have a staff of nurses who are dedicated to helping the wounded get well. I wouldn't worry about that."

"Well," said Roger now quite anxious, "when can I see her? Is she still in the emergency room?"

"No, we cleaned up her scrapes, bandaged them up as best we could, put in a drain to her lungs, put a soft restraint around her head wound, gave her a pint of blood, immobilized her in a stretcher, and sent her off to catch the next flight to Hawaii."

"What? Has she left already? I want to go with her. Where is she now?"

"The plane is probably loading right how. I doubt they will let you accompany her."

Roger bolted for the door, shouted, "See you later, Terry," and stumbled in great pain about half a mile to the airstrip. He arrived as one of the cargo planes was just pulling up its stairs. "Wait, wait. I have to go with you!" he shouted.

"What?" shouted the air crew chief, holding the stairs halfway up.

"Do you have a patient on a stretcher?"

"Yes, we do, but we have to take off."

"I must go with her."

"You're not on the manifest." And with that he closed up the stairs, the plane's engines roared into life, and the aircraft took off.

Roger slumped to his knees and thought, *Now what am I going to do?* Finally bracing himself, he walked back to the hospital and found Terry still there talking with the doctor. "Well, she's off," he said to them.

"Doc, are you very mad at me?" Terry asked Roger, looking down at his feet.

"Terry," Roger answered with a bit of a smile, "you are a wonderful young man. You are curious and want to see things for yourself, just like me. You are impulsive, headstrong, and do not know how dangerous the world can be. I'm not mad at you at all. I just hope you won't disobey your teacher again. You almost got all three of us killed, and Miss Trowbridge has been badly hurt. On the other hand, you handled that walkie-talkie like a real man. We all owe you a great deal for not panicking. Now let's get over to the school to let Mr. Duxbury know where you are so you can apologize to him. I suspect he will accept your actions as just what many a young man would want to do, but he may decide to hand out some punishment. Then I'll take you over to the family you are living with and calm their fears over your disappearance and tell them not to expect Miss Trowbridge for a while."

Roger got hold of a jeep and took Terry to the school and to his home. As soon as Roger completed those steps, he drove back to the command center and asked to use the radiophone to call Dick Johnson at Hickam. "Dick, things have been a bit crazy down here at Christmas. I'm okay, but that teacher you sent the books to, Emmie Trowbridge, got hurt and is on a plane to Hickam. When it arrives she will be taken to the hospital there. Please try to meet the plane and accompany her. She will need a friendly voice to calm her down. When she's settled in the hospital, get a message to me at Palmyra, and I will see if I can take some leave and get back there to be with her. We are sort of engaged to be married."

"What?" exclaimed Johnson. "Frosty Lockwood will go berserk! What about the team and the work you're doing? What have you been doing down there on Christmas Island? You're not even supposed to be there!"

"I know, I know. But I'm on my way back to Palmyra on the next shuttle plane. Just find her and help her out for a couple of days while I sort things out."

Roger noticed Captain Patten sitting there in the command center. He waved Roger over and told him, "You should know that Shot Alma missed its aim point by about five miles closer to the island. The bombardier has been sent to Siberia, and I sure hope it doesn't happen again. We lost most of our equipment down at the end of the island and a few decent diagnostics on the weapon. We do know that it went off at about eight hundred kilotons, but that's about all."

"I knew it blew much closer to us than it should have!" Roger exclaimed. "Jeezus! Excuse my French as my dad used to say, but it's no wonder we got hurt. The overpressure and wind speed must have been almost double what we otherwise would have felt. Goddamn! Poor Emmie, she really took a blow."

"Yeah," said Patten. "The medic at the hospital called me and asked that she be sent to Hickam pronto. Of course I agreed. Then I called Hickam and asked if they could arrange for her to be sent over to the Honolulu hospital if they couldn't treat her since she's not an American citizen. Doc, the task force was set up to handle 'most every emergency, and I thought Mahatma would prevent anyone from being caught out in the open. I sure didn't think anyone would be caught out so close to the blast. Well, it happened and you three survived, thanks to your quick thinking."

"Well, even so, we were awfully lucky. But what's Mr. Duxbury going to do without poor Emmie?"

"I'll go speak with him as soon as I can get away from here and to the family that boy is living with. Actually, Mr. Duxbury will just have to go on as before with the staff he has."

"Sure. Well now, I better be getting back to Palmyra. Who knows what disasters have happened there? And thanks, captain, for all you've done for us. If it hadn't been for Mahatma we certainly would not have survived. By the way, ten seconds before the bomb went off, I asked Emmie to marry me, and she said 'yes' just before the flash. That makes me, all in all, the happiest man on earth."

Chapter Eleven

Recuperation

Emmie woke up in the intensive care unit of the Queens Medical Center in Honolulu, Hawaii. It seemed to her that every part of her body ached. There was a breathing tube in her nose and throat, plus various intravenous lines attached to her arms. She couldn't speak and was thoroughly miserable. Two nurses hovered over her, and one said, "There, there, Miss Trowbridge, we're here for you. We'll be removing the tube as soon as the doctor arrives. Just relax and try to get some more sleep."

A few minutes later the doctor arrived, checked Emmie's records, had the nurses lift her into a sitting position, and listened to her heart and lungs. He motioned to the nurses and said, "Here, let's get this tube out of her nose and throat. She should be able to breathe on her own, so let's find out." Shortly, he spoke directly to Emmie. "Now, that's better isn't it? Take a few shallow breaths. Fine. Now some more, deeper this time. Even better. Okay. Can you talk to me?"

"Where am I?" she croaked softly. "What happened?"

"You're in a hospital on Honolulu, Hawaii. The U.S. Air Force brought you here. You were in a bad accident on Christmas Island, but you're going to be all right. A young man has been asking to see you. Should I let him know he can see you? Evidently he's not related to you so he couldn't be here before now."

Emmie nodded yes, expecting to see Roger.

"Well, let's get you into a regular hospital room, washed up and ready for visitors."

"Oh, please. Let me see him now. We're engaged to be married."

"He's not here at this moment, but we'll call him right away, and I'm sure he will be quick to get here."

Shortly Emmie had been moved out of intensive care and into a regular ward. One of the nurses left her and reappeared with Dick Johnson. Her shock at seeing a complete stranger was almost too much. "No, no, he's not the one! Where's Roger Malcolm, my fiancé?" She fell back onto her pillow and buried her head in it. After a couple of moments she recovered her composure, turned over, and sat up.

Dick quickly spoke up. "I'm Dick Johnson, the Mitre representative here in Honolulu. Roger asked me to help you. He's still on Palmyra Island. The planes haven't been flying there for a couple of days. I'm sure he will be here very soon. Meanwhile, would you like me to contact your parents? I believe they are in England, but we've had no way to reach them yet."

"Is Roger all right? He was injured by the bomb there on Christmas Island too. And the boy Terry. Are they all right?"

"Yes, yes. They are okay. Roger was patched up on Christmas Island at the medical station there that stabilized you and got you on the plane to Hawaii. Roger returned to Palmyra because that is where his team is. But he and his team are being relieved by another group from Mitre, so he will be flying back here to you soon. He told me that you are a teacher at the local school on Christmas and about your engagement to him, but of course I don't know what his and your plans might be."

"Can I talk to Roger? He must be as anxious about me as I am about him."

"I was able to reach him via a radiophone to another team on Palmyra that is close to his. I told him where you were taken and that I would check up on you. I will call him right away as soon as I get back to Hickam. Unfortunately I can't use the telephone here at the hospital to reach that other team. It's too bad that he doesn't have a radio on Palmyra."

Emmie replied, "What about my going back to Christmas Island? I'm still under contract there and the children need me—oh, damn those nuclear tests! Ooh." She uttered in pain and winced as she said the word "damn" and she vigorously hit the bed with her hand. "That hurts."

Just then a doctor walked in to the room. "Ah, Miss Trowbridge, it's good to see you here in a regular bed and out of intensive care. And this must be your fiancé."

"Oh, no," piped up Dick Johnson. "I'm a friend from the Mitre Corporation. Her fiancé is still down on Palmyra Island. But he may be arriving any day now," he added quickly.

"Oh, my," said the doctor. "That may complicate matters. Now, Miss Trowbridge, I have been attending to you and just now reviewed your records. You received quite a blow to the back of your head, leaving you with a severe concussion. You also had a collapsed lung, which was inflated and stabilized on Christmas Island, and have three broken ribs, which still hurt as you demonstrated as I walked in. I believe you should remain here in this hospital for us to ensure that you have no complications, particularly from the concussion, and then take a period of time to recuperate fully. We can recommend several rest homes here on Oahu."

Emmie struggled to sit up and look directly at the doctor. Dick took a step toward her bed and helped her adjust her pillows. "Ooh, yes those ribs are a real pain. But doctor, how long will all this take? And how much will it cost? I know that American hospitals are not free as they are in England. I am under contract to teach school on Christmas Island and should get back there right away."

"Are you working for an American contractor like Mr. Johnson here? Perhaps they have health insurance for you."

"No, I'm just a teacher in the elementary school down there. I don't know anything about health insurance. I was told that Kiritimati is sort of a British protectorate, but I doubt the British Health Service would cover me. But I just don't know. Ooh, at this moment I just don't care!"

Dick Johnson broke in. "I can get the U.S. command center at Christmas Island on the telephone. Perhaps Captain Patten can find out about your situation. He's aware of your accident, I believe. Meanwhile,I was wondering whether you ought to let your parents know about it. Do you know their phone number in London?"

The doctor quickly said, "I believe they already have been notified. The front office here at the hospital felt that, as a patient on intensive care, since no one in Hawaii appeared to be related to you, they ought to be told. We were told that you were from London, England, and we readily found the telephone number of your parents, actually in South Oxney, isn't it? I believe they may already be on their way to see you."

"Oh, double damn! Ooh! If only that didn't hurt so much. All they will want to do is scoop me up and get me back to bloody old England. Why am I being treated like a little girl? My injuries are not life threatening, are they? Mr. Johnson, help me get my clothes and help me get out of here!"

"I'm sorry," said the doctor firmly. "You're in no condition to walk away. Trust me. Without some pain relief your headaches will return and, as you've noticed, your ribs are still screaming 'pain' with every motion you make. We also are carefully monitoring your lungs since they sustained a crushing blow as well. The one positive thing is that you are not radioactive!"

"Oh, thanks, doctor," Emmie said with some sarcasm in her voice. "That's all I would have needed to become a complete basket case, to glow in the dark!"

"Well now, you need some rest. I'll call the nurse to help you get settled for supper and then retire for the night. Mr. Johnson, let's leave her be for a while. I'll come by at ten o'clock tomorrow to check on your progress, and we can discuss your next steps then. Mr. Johnson, I assume, will be here then too."

That night Emmie was quite restless, but she got some sleep toward dawn. When she awoke she felt better and had a good breakfast, and then she waited impatiently for the doctor and Dick Johnson to show up, as they soon did. The doctor listened to her heart and lungs, looked under the bandage on her head, and pronounced, "Miss Trowbridge, you are remarkable. I think you could be out of here by the end of this week. But you'll still need some more recuperation time." At that he walked out saying, "I'll check on you later this afternoon."

Emmie was furious. "I want to get out now! What right does he have to imprison me in this place?"

Dick Johnson said, "Well, the good news is that I was able to contact Roger, and he might just get here in a day or two. I'm sure he will have something to say about your stay here. Unless there is something else I can do for you, I'd better get back to Hickam and see if I can't accelerate something."

That afternoon, time passed slowly for Emmie. Finally both the doctor and Dick Johnson walked in. "How's the patient this afternoon?" the doctor asked cheerily.

"Lousy," said Emmie, sitting up and groaning the whole time.

The doctor checked her over again and said, "Your lungs are rebounding amazingly well, and your head wound is closing up nicely. Your radioactivity count has fallen as well," he added, trying to end on a joke.

The door opened suddenly again, and in walked Mr. and Mrs. Trowbridge! "Oh, my darling Emmie!" her mother squealed. "How did this happen to you?" She squeezed past Dick Johnson and tried to hug her daughter.

"Ooh, Mummy, that hurts. Just hold my hand for a minute, will you please? And Daddy, you too. How did you get here so quickly?"

"Oh, someone from the hospital called two days ago to tell us the awful news about your accident. We immediately booked flights, and here we are! But whatever happened to you? You're all bandaged up."

The doctor now called for quiet. "I must remind you, Mrs. Trowbridge, that Emmie has been severely wounded but is recovering nicely. She will need some further medical attention to see that her lungs, ribs, and head wound are not festering or otherwise giving her unnecessary pain. Then she may need additional rest to fully recuperate. I will leave now to give you all time to adjust to all of this amazing news. Please don't stay longer than another half hour."

Dick Johnson stayed awkwardly in the room. Mrs. Trowbridge turned toward him and asked, "Are you one of the attendants here at the hospital?"

Emmie quickly said, "No, Mummy, no. He's from the Mitre Corporation where Roger works. Mr. Johnson, please meet my parents, Mr. and Mrs. Trowbridge."

"How do you do," he said. "I've been trying to get Roger here from Palmyra Island just as soon as possible. He should be here in one or two days."

"Thank God," sighed Emmie.

Mr. Trowbridge shook Dick's hand as Mrs. Trowbridge looked completely mystified. "Who's Roger?" she asked.

"He's my fiancé."

"Your what?"

"My fiancé. We got engaged just before the bomb went off."

"What are you talking about?"

"Oh, Mummy, it's quite a story."

Dick Johnson took this opportunity to bow out of the room. "Miss Trowbridge, I'll let you explain the situation. I better get back to Hickam and make sure Roger gets here just as soon as he can make it."

* * * *

Roger's plane got to Hickam two days later. By a crazy coincidence, a plane from Hickam had landed on Palmyra, bringing Roger the filters for his diesel generator, now unneeded. Roger threw the keys to the Mitre trailer to Don Modano, who had arrived a few days previously. Then he ran to his tent, grabbed his personal gear, and ran back to the airfield. Throwing a quick good-bye to his replacement team, he jumped onto the plane. Only after it took off did he find that it was on the way to Christmas Island, not back to Hickam! It took Roger another two days to get where he desperately wanted to be. Dick Johnson was not there to meet him, being over at the Mitre office trying to find out if there was a round-trip flight to Palmyra he could get Roger on the next day or the one after that. He wasn't making much headway. Meanwhile, Roger got a taxi and had it take him right to the hospital. He rushed up to the hospital's desk and asked, "Please give me the number of Miss Trowbridge's room."

"I'm sorry, whose room?"

"Miss Trowbridge. I know she's here."

"We have no one by that name registered."

"But she must be here. Has she left?"

"Let me check the recent departures. Oh, yes. Miss Trowbridge was released to her parents' care this morning."

"Where is she now?"

"I'm sorry, but I do not have that information."

Roger found a pay phone and dialed the Mitre office at Hickam. "Johnson here," came the welcome voice.

"Dick, for crying out loud, what's going on?"

"Rog, where in hell are you?"

"I'm at the hospital, but Emmie's not here."

"No, she left with her parents earlier today. I've spent the whole time trying to reach you and get you on a plane back here. How'd you get here anyway?"

"By a slow boat to Christmas. But I'm here now. Let me grab another cab and get myself to the office."

As soon as Roger entered the office, Dick Johnson welcomed him like a long-lost brother. Then he quickly got right down to business. "Frosty was on the horn first thing this morning. He wants you to check in immediately."

"Wait just a darned minute. Where's Emmie and her parents? I think I've got a lot of explaining to do to them."

"That will have to wait. They should be getting in to LA about now, and from there they have first-class tickets to Idlewild and on to London. There's no way you can reach them at this moment."

"Jeezus, Dick, the love of my life gets creamed by a one-megaton blast and now she's gone? What in God's creation am I gonna do?"

"I suspect you're gonna have to put your love life on hold for a while and get back to Bedford to mend a few fences. Everett and Caz are about to give you the sack."

Roger let out quite a sigh and said out loud as he picked up the telephone and dialed Frosty's number at Mitre in Massachusetts, "Might as well get this over with."

"Where have you been?" shouted Roger's boss. "What kind of hanky-panky have you committed? What in hell's going on with you? Jeezus! Did you know that Willie Moore talked to Captain Patten on Christmas, got the scoop on your escapade, wound up getting an earful from Starbird as well as Harold Benton himself, called Everett and Caz and now they are not just livid, they've got the screeming-meemies—at *me*! And to top it all off, you disappear and drop completely off the radar! Get your fat ass on a plane and get back here just as fast as you can. No ifs, ands or buts. Holy crimoly! What I have to put with!"

"See you tomorrow, Frosty," was all Roger said as he hung up the phone. Turning to Dick Johnson, he added, "Can you get me on a flight to LA and on to Boston, pronto?"

Dick made a couple of phone calls and said, "Your plane to LA leaves in thirty minutes from the commercial field. Quick, I'll drive you over there. By the way, her parents live in South Oxney, near London. I never did get their phone number, but I'm sure you can as soon as you get the chance."

Chapter Twelve

The Nuclear Detection System (NUDETS) Gets Accelerated

Roger made the plane, and its connecting red-eye flight to Boston, and walked into his boss's office at 8:00 A.M. the next day. "What's up?" he asked quietly.

"It's about time. You really have the whole top brass here ready to give you the ole heave-ho. But I'll give you the scoop on the way down to DDR&E," Frosty said, apparently over his anger at Roger. "We're catching the nine o'clock shuttle out of Logan. I've got a limo outside. Let's go! Let's just hope Everett or Caz don't see us on the way out. They're still steaming over your malfeasance in office, as they put it politely."

"Wait a while. I've got to call London first."

"No time for that now, you clown. Get a move on." As they left, the telephone rang and rang. There was no one there to answer the call from England, Amy Stinson having just left the office to get some supplies.

As they drove, Frosty turned to Roger, checked to see that the window between them and the limo driver was in place, leaned over to Roger, and in the quietist voice he could manage said, "This is all top secret, need-to-know, eyes-only stuff. It's direct from the president and SecDef. They want to place three of your gizmos around D.C. within ninety days. I told Willie Moore that only you could do that. When I told him you were on your way, he laughed and said, 'Malcolm better have his asbestos BVDs on since I'm gonna scorch his hide first. If he doesn't wilt or go up in flames, I'll tell him about the other project—the one that saved his behind.' Even Everett and Caz don't know about this yet. If they knew you had arrived they would have heaved you out of this place pronto on your great fat fanny from the second floor, for sure."

Within the hour they were in Willie's office on the third floor of the Pentagon. Willie welcomed Frosty as an old, familiar buddy and turned to Roger. With a smile on his face he said, "Rog, you randy scamp, how did you do it—making off with the only white woman for a thousand miles, and probably a cute one at that? Write a book on your technique and you'll sell a million copies."

"She came on to me from the start, and it was truly mutual. But wait till you meet her and you can make up your own mind. Have you heard that she took a 'first' in math at Cambridge?"

"Pretty and smart, eh? Okay, maybe she can rub a little intelligence, if not common sense, into your brain." With that twist of the knife into Roger's midsection, Willie turned to business. "President Kennedy heard from his sources—I won't say which ones—but I'm sure you know that Khrushchev is plotting some move to further embarrass him if not take a position of strategic advantage. He's apparently emboldened based on his demonstration of thermonuclear weapon capability from his successful test series last August. Our tests, as you were witnessing, are proving to be no less successful, and we have a huge superiority in the numbers of weapons and total megatonnage. But the sources indicate that he might try some gamesmanship. We know that he hates our missiles in Turkey and Italy. We know they're obsolete and not too reliable, but their presence gives him far too little warning time if we ever did shoot them off. Are we liable to pull them out unilaterally? No, the Turks and the Italians would surely object. So what if he smuggled some of his short-range missiles into say, Cuba, Barbados, the Yucatan in Mexico, or anywhere else close enough for his short-range missiles to hit us. That would give him a first-class, number-one lever-arm to twist us anyway he wants. Would it be another threat to Berlin? All of Germany? A major reduction in our nukes? Or just removal of the ones close by him? And what about our Polaris subs just off his coast hidden under the sea? Pull them back? His range of options is huge and devastating. The one thing we simply have to know, when push comes to shove, is whether a nuke has gone off on our soil. As you know, Rog, from the Partridge committee, we want full coverage of the whole country. But our best guess is that Khrushchev will choose Cuba, so we need a NUDETS aimed around the East Coast, specifically at Washington, D.C., but with a range down to Miami and out to a radius of twelve hundred miles from Havana. And we need it fast. Our best guess is he'll move very soon—in two, three months."

"Jeezus, Willie!" interrupted Roger. "Now I have the goose bumps, as I suspect Kennedy, McNamara, and you have too. My ribs are still so sore from that one-megaton shot I got too close to, that I never want to be near one again. If Khrushchev or Castro shoot one onto the East Coast, even if we detect it, so what? You've got a million Miamians or even Washingtonians dead and the whole area radioactive."

"We have to be absolutely sure that a nuke has gone off and a pretty good idea of its location and yield. Then the president, or whoever is left to decide, has to figure whether to incinerate just Cuba or the whole Soviet Union. So the questions are, first, can we install and connect three NUDETS sites pronto? And second, can you do it?"

Roger pondered these questions for about a millisecond. "Willie, I just happen to have had a little advance indication from Frosty here about what you've been thinking, so my carefully considered answer is a firm yes. Of course, I will need an immediate, top secret line to the president of Mitre and to the commander of the electronic systems command to give Frosty and me the authority to buy, beg, borrow, and steal whatever we need. The NUDET system program office has already determined that the first NUDETS sites are to be at U.S. Air Force sites at Benton, Pennsylvania, Manassas, Virginia, and Thomas, West Virginia, so we'll use them. We'll have the guys at GE Syracuse build the same gear we have out at Palmyra in triplicate, put them in trailers, drive them onto the sites, connect them up, and check it all out. No sweat!"

Frosty interjected his backing, "We've got the team to do it. We proved it getting them out to Palmyra. Those guys will be coming back soon to augment what we have in Bedford. Just say the word, Willie, just give us the word."

"I rarely have much confidence when a contractor comes in and gives me a pitch. But yes, you guys have proved you can do it. I'll back you all the way. But only the SecDef can give the final okay." Willie paused, picked up the phone, and pressed one of the numbers. "Willie Moore here," he said. "We're ready to brief the secretary." A minute or so later a buzzer sounded on Willie's desk. "That'll be the SecDef. Come on quick!" The three of them trouped around on the third floor of the Pentagon along a corridor lined with pictures on the walls depicting military actions of all kinds to an office midway along where a secretary waved them briskly into an antechamber. Almost immediately, the door to the SecDef's office opened and a civilian said curtly, "In here."

Willie replied, "G'morning, Dr. Benton." Roger gulped. Harold Benton was the head of the Office of the Director, Defense Research and Engineering, or ODDR&E, for whom Willie worked. The four of them entered a conference room where Robert McNamara, the secretary of defense, sat at the head of the table. Dr. Benton introduced them to him and to Alan Howard sitting next to McNamara. Howard was another whiz kid from McNamara's Office of Analysis.

The SecDef quickly opened the meeting by saying, "Willie here says you Mitre guys can get a nuclear burst detection system aimed at the East Coast up and running in three months. Is that right?"

As Willie nodded, Frosty spoke up briskly, "Yes, sir. Our team on Palmyra Island, four hundred miles from Christmas Island, has shown we can do it that far and surely a good deal more—detection and measurement of a burst's location, yield, and height of burst. The detection can be reported to the NMCC, ANMCC, SAC, and NORAD within a few milliseconds after the confirmation of the burst by the optical and seismic sensors."

McNamara turned to Dr. Benton. "Harold, what about that? It's your project, isn't it?"

Benton replied, "Yes, it's mine and Moore's here, all right. I got a report from Captain Patten of Starbird's staff out there that he flew up to Palmyra yesterday and confirmed what Mr. Lockwood here just said."

Howard chimed in, "But wasn't there some interference with the static from lightning?"

"Yes." Roger put his oar in. "I was there when that happened on one shot, but the optical and seismic sensors should allow the real electromagnetic pulse from a nuclear burst to be confirmed."

"Well, Mr. Malcolm, I sure hope so," said McNamara.

"It's true that we don't have much in the way of statistics to get a handle on discriminating lightning from nuclear bursts," replied Roger, "but if we get the trial system up and running within three months, we can record every thunder storm that comes along and build up our confidence in the system."

"That depends on having more than three months to record just lightning bolts," said Howard.

"Yes," added McNamara. "As Willie here was authorized to tell you, we expect Khrushchev to act to provoke us fairly soon. That information, as you know, is not to be discussed by you outside this room. You are authorized to construct a trial three-site NUDET system right away, just to obtain data on possible interferences from thunder storms and other natural phenomena. You may not—repeat, *not*—say or infer anything else. Get that?"

"Yes, sir!" said Roger and Frosty in unison.

"You'll get your authorization from Dr. Benton, director of the DR&E here, by twix before you get back to Bedford, with accompanying authorization for the air force systems command and the NUDET system project office at Hanscom Field to give you whatever you need to meet our demands. Now clear out. I've got a dozen other fires to put out before noon."

As Roger and Frosty took a cab back to National Airport, Roger said, "Crime-in-ent-ly, what have we done! I give our chances of making our deadline about point-zero-zero percent."

"Ahh, me lad, begorra, have faith in the luck o' the Irish. You said it all: we just beg, borrow, and steal, as always."

"Look who's Irish now. Not I says 'the lad.' First I have to suffer the slings and arrows of Everett and Caz. They're not going to slough off my sins the way you and Willie did."

"Leave them to me. As soon as we get back to Bedford, call GE and catch the first plane to Syracuse tomorrow to get Henry moving. The more you're out of town, the better. I'll get Lee Turner to rustle up the three trailers, Dwight Bowen to design the interior equipment layout, with Modano to confirm it as soon as he gets back. Art Bryant can do the electrical interfaces and configure the computer codes needed. I'll lay it on Colonel Jones to arrange all the interfaces at the three sites with the air defense command."

"With that head start, my 'Kaintucky' friend, I think we just raised our chances for success from point-zero-zero to just point-zero percent. But don't forget the air force command post in the National Military Command Center, the NMCC, in the Pentagon. I guess Willie will handle that interconnection and the ones with the alternate NMCC, the Strategic Air Command—SAC—and the North American Air Defense Command, NORAD, as you promised McNamara."

"Shh! Holy bejesus, Rog! Stop talking so loud in that alphabetic slang. Any spy worth his salt could figure out what we're up to. Don't breathe a word about what we're doing. This is all national security stuff at the presidential and SecDef level, eyes only, no 'for'n' or anyone else but us has a need to know."

"Come off it, Frosty, you know surely that every spy worth his salt knows that as well."

Their conversation ended as they felt the plane gliding down to land at Logan Airport in Boston. Once back in their offices, before quitting for the day and after reviewing the historic events of the day in that secure location, Roger went into his office and asked the Mitre operator to get information in London, England. "Can you get me the number for Mr. Trowbridge in South Oxney?"

The answer came back after some delay and repetition of the name, "Is that Jerome Trowbridge in South Oxney?"

"Yes, I believe that's right."

"Just a minute and I'll ring that for you." The phone rang and rang. "I'm sorry, but no one seems to be at that number. Shall I try again?"

"No, I'll try again later. What was that number again?" This time Roger memorized it. As soon as he got home to his apartment, he tried the South Oxney number again. Again no one picked up. The next morning he left his apartment before 6:00 A.M. to catch the flight to Syracuse to get Joe Henry at GE working on the three-site NUDET system. At seven that morning his phone rang, but he had left an hour before.

That evening, upon his arrival back from Syracuse, he tried again from his apartment. It was Emmie! "Oh, Emmie, my darling, my darling. How are you? What's been happening? Oh, I can't believe it's really you."

"Roger, Roger, is that you? Is it really you?"

"Yes, oh Emmie, Emmie, Emmie, my love, my love."

"Yes, it's Emmie. At long last we've found each other. Where have you been? I thought we'd lost each other. But it's really you. Where are you? Are you still on Palmyra?"

"It's really me, and I'll never leave you again, never again. I'm in my apartment in Massachusetts. These past few days have been excruciating."

"Massachusetts! How'd you get there? Why aren't you here? Oh, yes, yes! The past few days have been excruciating for me in both mind and body, let me tell you!"

"That's right. How could I be so unthoughtful. How are you?"

"I'm much better, yes, much better. I've been discharged from the hospital and am home in my mother's loving care, recuperating rapidly. But all I want is to see you. Right now, my only ache is for you. But why are you in Massachusetts? Oh, I'm so confused!"

"Look, it's complicated. But I'll get a flight to London just as fast as I can. I'll let you know. Now tell me everything that happened to you after you left Christmas Island."

The next morning, Roger debriefed Frosty on his visit to get Joe Henry working on the design of NUDETS. Then Roger added slyly, "Oh, by the way, I am hereby requesting authorization to coordinate with the British counterparts to our team on Palmyra. I intend to fly to London for the weekend. They had some improvements to their NUDETS electronics that we should consider for our three-way D.C. system."

"You were supposed to do that on Palmyra," said Frosty, "not gallivant around wooing every woman you came across. Besides, the Brits are still out there with Modano and our team. Who are you planning on seeing in England? And to whom do we send your clearances? Do I smell a randy rat?"

"Okay, okay, there is one smart cookie waiting for me over there. She has no clearances or need-to-know, but I can't function without her. I'm bringing her back as my wife, but don't let her mother hear about that. She's the one that really has no need to know! And by the way, I already know what those Brits have in their electronics that we didn't."

That weekend, after the long flight to London from Boston, Roger called ahead from Heathrow Airport and found Emmie waiting by the phone at her parents' home. Within the hour, he knocked on their door. It opened with a bang, and Emmie launched herself into his arms. After a deep, long, soulful kiss she exclaimed, "Oh Roger, you're here, really here! I've been so worried. I didn't see how you could make it."

"Ooh, do your ribs still hurt as much as mine do? What a wonderful, painful welcome."

"It just doesn't hurt when it's you that squeezes me. But come in, come in and say hello to Mummy and Daddy."

Roger came, said hello, kissed Mrs. Trowbridge on the cheek, and shook hands with Mr. Trowbridge, who also embraced him warmly. Roger said, "I bring an equally warm welcome from America. From the tirades I got from all three levels of my bosses, not to mention the entire staff of the Pentagon, you'd think that I had just kidnapped the heir to the English throne. But they let me out of the zoo, and here I am to plan a wedding."

Then everyone started talking at once. Finally Roger held up both his hands and, waving them up and down, managed to get some attention. "Just to add to the consternation around here, let me say I'm Roger Malcolm. I have asked Emmie to marry me and she has said yes, and I am the infamous fiancé. All it took to convince her was a one-megaton thermonuclear bomb."

"Oh, good God," said her mother. "Is it true, Emmie? Is it true, my darling?"

"Yes, yes, yes. I love him so."

"Thank God," said her father. He turned to face Roger, reached out, and clasped him to his bosom again.

Roger made it a mutual hug and pulled back, grabbed the father's hand and said, "Father-in-law-to-be, what may I call you?"

Emmie quickly broke in, "Heavens! I haven't introduced you all to each other. Roger, this is Mrs. Natalie Trowbridge and over there is Mr. Jerome Trowbridge."

Emmie's father jumped in. "I've waited a long time for this opportunity to be the father of the bride, but Roger, the answer is that you may call me anything you like, but 'Jerry' will do fine. At work I'm called 'Jerome,' dating from World War One when 'Jerry' connoted the enemy. It didn't seem to matter so much in World War Two, but it's still 'Jerome' at work and 'Jerry' around home and among my friends—and relatives old, new, and most recent."

Roger looked him in the eye, keeping his hand clasped, and said, "Jerry, may I have your daughter's hand in marriage?"

Jerry almost shouted, "Yes, yes, of course."

Roger turned quickly toward Mrs. Trowbridge and said, "I do love your daughter more than I can say, or anyone can say, and I will do everything I can to make and keep her happy. So, may I call you, mother-in-law-to-be, 'Natalie'?"

Mrs. Trowbridge caught her breath, looked around at the group looking back at her, and finally said, "I truly don't know what to say except yes, of course. 'Natalie' it is."

Turning to Emmie, Roger said, "My love, give me a wholehearted kiss and welcome. May I say again, in front of all these witnesses, that I love you completely? Will you marry me?"

"Yes, yes, Roger. I love you completely too. I will marry you. Just be careful of my ribs when you kiss me."

To Emmie he replied out loud, "My ribs were broken too, so here's a doubly careful kiss." He leaned over the couch on which she was sitting to deliver the kiss they had both been saving up for the past several days.

When they both came up for air, he added, "So, now all we have to do is plan the wedding!"

"Oh, Roger," Natalie said quickly, "you have no idea what that entails. Please don't rush me. And isn't this all a bit, well, sudden? How long have you known our daughter, and she you? One month—two? We will be most pleased to have you stay with us and get to know Emmie and us. But a wedding? Perhaps we all should take a breath and enjoy getting together for a time first."

"Mrs. Trowbridge—Natalie—I should have said to make our arrangements for the wedding. I certainly understand that you, as the person who has the most to do, can't do that overnight. But having asked Emmie to marry me, and having had her accept my proposal, we will surely have a proper wedding. I'm sorry to have upset you. Take as long as you want. Also, I know we have to get to know each other much better. Just don't expect either Emmie or me to change our minds."

"We surely don't expect either of you to do that, Roger," said Jerry, interjecting himself into the conversation. "We know our dear Emmie has always made up her mind quickly. From what she has told us, you are some catch!"

Roger replied, "I don't know who caught whom, but with that settled, why don't we start getting to know one another?"

"While we do that, let's have some lunch," added Emmie, "and Roger can tell you all about himself and I can put in a few pointers about my life too. Mummy has a few tales to tell about wartime London, and Daddy might be persuaded to talk about some of his exploits that won't violate the Official Secrets Act."

After each of them had told their lifetime story, or the parts they thought appropriate to share, they all fell into small talk about how green the grass was and how pretty the garden looked. But then Jerry looked at Roger with a bit of hesitation in his bearing. "Roger, you should know what will come to light in the long run, that when Natalie and I got back to London after picking up Emmie in Honolulu, I took the time to check up on you."

"Oh, Jerry, I would be most surprised if you hadn't. But whom did you call and what did you find out?"

"I called Professor Jack Forest at MIT, whom I have never met in person but whom I had talked with many times during World War Two. I asked him if a Roger Malcolm had ever worked for him at MIT or studied there. He said, 'No, I can't recall that name, but I can have someone check our records.' So I added quickly, 'He seems to be working for a firm known as Mitre. Have you heard of it?' He said, 'Oh, yes, that's an offshoot from my group here. Let me call its president, Bob Everett, one of my former students, and find out what he can tell me.' Just an hour later, Jack called me back and said, 'Jerry, Everett knows Malcolm very well. He says he's one of their best technical guys. He's out in the Pacific on those U.S. tests, though he should be back very soon. One thing you should know, Jack: this Malcolm got mixed up with a woman out there and is being called back for possible disciplinary action.'" Jerry started to laugh. "I could hardly contain myself as I told Forest, 'That woman is my daughter.' Forest just about exploded. 'Jerry, I'm sure there is a perfectly sane and rational story behind all this. Now come clean.' So I told him what little I knew and that calmed him down. But Roger, see what you've started. It's an international scandal already, and at the highest levels. What do you intend to do about it?"

"Just what I've come here to do: Get married. What else?" Laughter prevailed then Roger said, "I need to stretch my legs after that long flight and delicious dinner. Emmie, why don't you show me around the neighborhood, if you can manage just a short walk?"

"Sure," she said, getting up from the couch with surprising alacrity. "Let's go."

After some more small talk, Roger stopped her, now out of earshot of her house and parents. "Have you heard anything from Mr. Duxbury or Captain Patten? What about your contract with the foreign service?"

"Thanks to your Dick Johnson, who gave me both their phone numbers and told me how to dial them. I talked to both of them. Mr. Duxbury told me to forget about coming back to Christmas for the rest of this term. He said the kids weren't about to learn much anyway with all of the bombs going off every other day. He added that he would be in touch with Mrs. Wentworth at the foreign service about my contract. He said perhaps I could come back next winter or spring and finish my obligation if I feel up to it. He expressed deep concern and sorrow about my accident and said he felt he should have been more strict with the kids, particularly Terry. He asked about you, and I told him we were engaged and would be married soon here in London. He wished us both the very happiest in our lives together."

"Well, that seems to make the way clear for us to share a life together, at least until you feel you ought to get back to Christmas Island. If ever."

"I don't know. I don't want to think about it right now. I just want to be married to you and spend the rest of our lives together forever and ever."

"In that regard, I've got a proposition I want to ask you about."

"What? I've already agreed to marry you. What more could you want, you devil you?" She was thinking how much fun it would be to jump into bed together.

"How about flying to my home tomorrow or whenever you feel up to it? I could introduce you to my parents and family, my boss Frosty, and Mitre, all at the same time."

"Tomorrow? But, Roger…"

"Wait, wait until I finish. To make it all legal, we will have to get married before we take off. Now wait, wait some more. I have a crass financial, as well as a moral, reason. Mitre won't pay for your flight unless we are really married. Being engaged, particularly the way we took that step as far as the Mitre brass goes, just isn't enough. I thought we could sneak off in the next day or two, go to the Justice of the Peace or whoever can legally marry us, and get the license and the air tickets, but not tell your parents. We can work with your mother on the wedding plans, and we'll come back in a few weeks to finalize them, arrange for the church and reception hall, send out the invitations, and then have the real wedding in all good time."

"Roger, no! That would be mean."

"I don't see why," replied Roger.

"What if she found out? She would think her wedding was just a sham. Besides, I can pay for my own ticket."

"Then I fall back on my moral reason. I don't want to go back to the U.S. alone, and I think you are as randy as I am. Furthermore, I would love to show you off to my family, to Mitre, and to the Pentagon as my wife, not my mistress."

"Most of the guys there probably think that already—that we spent the whole time on Christmas Island in bed together, aboard ship, on the beach, and inside that culvert."

"Wow, here I am, having been too frightened to ask a girl to go to bed with me for all my adult life, and now I want to do it legally and she objects! Would your parents object to my creeping into your bed tonight?"

"Probably not. I never told them how close I came with James, that guy in the hotel, but they know at my age I may have taken other lovers, although I haven't. Damn it, probably I should have. The trouble is, like you, I've been too busy to get asked. We're two peas in a pod."

"Yes, and I love the pod I'm in. I really want to be legally married right now! And I want to stick Mitre with the bill! What say, let's do it. Let's get married and then fly off. It will be exciting and we can leave your mother fretting over bridesmaids' dresses, flowers for the church, and the menu for the reception."

"Roger, you are wicked—and so am I."

Three days later, Mr. and Mrs. Trowbridge took the couple to Heathrow Airport for their flight to Boston, not knowing they were saying *au revoir* to Mr. and Mrs. Roger Malcolm.

Emmie was delighted with Roger's apartment, except she realized that if they continued to live there she would have to redecorate everything. Most of it was just too masculine! It was in Carlisle, Massachusetts, just five miles from Mitre in Bedford along local Route 225. It was also a short drive to I-95 (Route 128), the beltway around Boston that gave quick access (depending on the rush-hour traffic) north to Interstate 93 directly into Boston or south to Boston via the Mass 'Pike. The two-bedroom apartment was on the second and top floor of the new building with a screened porch looking west to Mount Wachusett, the highest point in eastern Massachusetts, over green fields and forests. The kitchen faced east, opening into a small dining room with the living room across the north side and the two bedrooms with large closets in each and the bath between them along the south side. A tiny office took up an area at the end of the living room. Every room was neat and spotless. The bed astounded her. It was a four-poster with a lace canopy over it, a large quilt thrown over the bed covers, and a backrest with two pillows for reading in bed. The bed was the only feminine thing in the apartment. She felt immediately right at home.

"Roger, this is priceless. I had no idea you were so romantic, particularly after the last several nights." Roger had studiously avoided sharing her bed in her parent's home, despite her open invitation. "How did you keep it so clean while you were off in the Pacific?"

"I arranged for a cleaning service to come in once a week. I don't like coming in to a dusty apartment any more than I suspect you do."

"Oh, this quilt feels so smooth and soft. I love the pattern."

"My great-grandmother on my mother's side sewed that quilt. I had to pry my mother's hands from it and promise I would never, ever jump on the bed with my shoes on."

Emmie laughed at that and flopped down on the quilt. Roger dropped the suitcases and flopped down beside her. They grabbed each other and kissed deeply. Coming up for air, he said, "not on my great-grandmother's quilt." He pulled her off, tossed the quilt aside, tossed the backrest and covers on the floor, picked her up, and tossed her back onto the bed. He fumbled with his shoes and socks, finally getting them off, unbuttoned his shirt, unbuckled his belt, slid down his trousers, tore off his underclothes, and jumped onto the bed beside her. She in the meantime had followed his lead with her clothes. Neither one of them had any actual experience with the complete sex act, but nature's instincts took over, and they both experienced the complete and utter satisfaction they had anticipated for their initial coupling.

Exhausted by their long flight from London and their exertions on the bed, they both quickly fell asleep. About two hours later, Roger awoke to feel Emmie stirring beside him, both still naked. Without a word he pulled her under him and they repeated their lovemaking—not as urgent or rushed as the first time, but even more satisfying. Roger next woke up with the dawn light streaming in. Emmie was already awake and crying softly. "Emmie! What's the matter? What did I do to make you cry?"

"Everything. Everything you've done is too perfect. You're the perfect husband with the perfect apartment and the perfect job, and you're the perfect lover. How can I match up? What do I have to do to be the perfect wife and lover too?"

"Just be yourself. You are smart, beautiful, caring, and also the perfect lover. For being innocents, we did all right last night. Let's do it again." And so they did! Finally, about 6:00 A.M., they both stirred again. Roger jumped out of bed, still naked.

"Oh, Roger! Where did you get those scars on your side and back? They look awful."

"Oh, that one in the middle of my back is from the sunburn I got after I left you to fly back to Palmyra the day after we first met. I wasn't smart enough to use a parasol the way you did to keep that vicious sun off my back. I went out in the noonday sun to fix the diesel generator for our project without my shirt on. I was only out there for a half hour. It still hurts a bit."

"But how about that scar almost the whole length of your side? That seems to have been stitched up all the way down."

"I was going to tell you it's from playing ice hockey when a guy skated down my side, but that happened to my coach, not to me. That scar is from an enemy bullet that gratefully missed hitting me dead on. Yes, I would have been dead but for sheer luck and, you might say, the grace of God. It's a long story, and now we have to get up. I'm due at Mitre by eight o'clock."

They both got out of bed, still stiff from the flight and sore from their injuries. "I'll make breakfast," Roger said, "since I know where everything is.

I called ahead to have my cleaning service stock the fridge. You can come to Mitre too. But first call your parents to let them know we're here and give them this phone number as well as Mitre's, written there on the board above the phone. You can catch up on the wedding plans and let them know what we'll be doing. At Mitre I'll get you a visitor's pass and you can meet our whiz of a secretary, Amy Stinson, and then my boss and the rest of the guys. Just close your ears when we first meet Frosty and he lets loose on me. The same goes if we get a summons to see Mitre's president, Bob Everett, and Charlie Zraket—the executive vice president also known as 'Caz.'"

Roger's car started right up after its long siesta, and they were soon at the Mitre headquarters building in Bedford. Roger had called ahead, and Emmie's visitor's pass was ready at the guard's desk. Amy greeted Emmie like a long-lost sister. Roger said, "She's the smartest one in the department, if not the whole company." Amy smiled knowingly, then she ushered them into the inner boss's office.

Frosty actually was the fine gentleman Roger knew he would be. "Nahce ta meetcha, ma'am. Whatcha doin' with this clown heah?" he said in his put-on Kentucky accent.

"Frosty, Frosty, Earl Forrest Lockwood, I do believe," Emmie replied in her best British accent. But in real earnest she added, "Frosty, you have no idea how grand a gesture you made for those kids on Christmas Island. What you had shipped down there, all in a matter of days, already has made the difference between just rote learning that most of them have suffered through, and real hands-on laboratory experience. And the books you sent are truly up-to-date. Some of those kids are going to win Nobel Prizes, or become prime minister, thanks to you."

"Aw shucks, ma'am. Warn't nothin' atall." Shifting to his normal voice he said, "Well, I couldn't do any less after what this guy"—he gestured toward Roger—"said about you and your situation. I was really pleased to help out. And congratulations on your engagement—"

"And wedding," put in Roger.

"What! That was quick! Oh, I see. Hitting up Mitre for the air tickets. Smart fella, this guy Malcolm. He didn't rush ya, did he? Now, Mrs. Malcolm—"

"Emmie, please."

"Now Emmie, close your ears because I am going to ream this guy up one side and down the other. He's got work to do, and so far he's let me do it all for him."

"Emmie," said Roger quickly, "here's a booklet that purports to tell what Mitre is all about. Amy will take you out to the lobby, and you can read all about us. Just don't believe a word it says. I won't be long." Returning to his boss, he said, "Where do we stand?"

"I'd be lying," replied Frosty, "if I said at 'bottom dead zero.' I've got everyone moving on what we talked about except Modano, who is still recording bumper thumpers on Palmyra. But your presence and actions are critical. So put on your national security, top secret, DX priority hat, and let's see what's next."

Roger said, "The first thing is to get GE aboard. I'll fly up to Syracuse again tomorrow, assuming you got ahold of Henry to check on his progress since I was there getting them started. We need to make sure that the higher-ups out there don't pre-empt them. I can go over with them the specific instructions on what Henry has started."

"Yeah, I told 'em and gave 'em a deadline of next week to have the soldering begin and two more weeks to deliver the gear mounted within electronic equipment racks here to Bedford."

Roger and Frosty went over the rest of the punch list in the same way—Turner for the trailers, Bowen for the layout within, Bryant for the communications and computer setup, and Curly Moore over at the systems program office under Colonel Jones for the air force coordination. Roger added, "Call a meeting of all hands tomorrow at eight A.M. I'll have some more instructions for the team then, before I dash to Logan to get the plane to Sizzicuse." Then he said, "Well, I'm off."

"Wait, wait. You have to get blistered by Everett and Caz first."

"That's what I'm going to do, but in company with a lovely young thing whose father is well connected with Jack Forest. Jack burst out laughing when Mr. Trowbridge told him his daughter was at the bottom of the entire scandal with Malcolm on Christmas Island. After the blistering, we're going over to meet my parents and take them to lunch. Sometime later this week or this month, I'm taking her in to meet Jack himself. I intend to get her to be accepted at MIT in the Ph.D. program in math and systems engineering."

"Jeezus, Rog, watch out! You'll get yourself overextended as usual. Remember, McNamara and DDR&E come first."

Roger stopped off in his office a made a couple of quick phone calls. Then dashing out to the lobby, Roger called to Emmie and said, "Let's go!"

"First we go upstairs to meet the president and executive vice president of Mitre." They were ushered in promptly, and the men turned out to be gentlemen too, saying all the right things to Emmie and scolding Roger very lightly. They didn't mention Professor Jack Forest's phone call the week before or the call from SecDef McNamara about the urgent need for a NUDETS along the East Coast. Roger figured they would watch him very closely from then on, stepping on him hard if he got out of line again. As they left the executive suite—"rug row"—Emmie whispered, "Where to now?"

"We're calling on my parents and taking them to lunch. Then in the evening we're having dinner with my two brothers and their families."

"No, no. My hair is a mess and I just have on this old travel dress."

"We'll stop off at our apartment and you can do your hair and change. We've got time. Meanwhile I can tell you what a dysfunctional family I have, particularly my two brothers," Roger said, laughing at his little aside about his siblings.

"Agh! This is too much, too soon."

"Get used to it. We like to talk about a 'Malcolm weekend' when we try to cram every kind of experience into forty-eight hours."

"It sounds like I'd better get used to it. By the way, as I sat there trying to read that Mitre brochure, a parade of guys came one or two at a time into the lobby through one door, past me and the guard's desk, and then back out through the door on the other side. Most of them said good morning and walked past, but two of them said, 'G'mornin', Miss Trowbridge.' How did they know my name? I just smiled sweetly and said good morning right back. I didn't mind being looked at, even if a few of the looks bordered on the lascivious. But I didn't get much chance to read that brochure."

Roger laughed. "That's Frosty for you—giving the team a chance to ogle a very pretty girl!"

Chapter Thirteen

The Real Wedding and a [Short] Honeymoon

The next day at the GE research laboratory in Syracuse, New York, Roger found great enthusiasm on the part of Hal Leach and Joe Henry; Leach was just back from Palmyra himself. They were already ahead of the timeline Frosty had given them. So they went to lunch with Emmie, who had again been relegated to the lobby with literature about the great 'Generous' Electric Company, as Frosty and Roger called it. Hal said, "I became suspicious of Rog when he right away made up some excuse to fly from Palmyra to Christmas. Then it became a habit, but I figured I wouldn't mention it, except for a little wager I made."

Joe Henry added, "Then we both heard a commotion over at the next team's site, where they had a radio telephone. We inquired and their whole team took turns telling us the gossip they heard from this guy Frosty. So Hal here," he said, pointing to Leach, "won his bet with Lee Turner for ten cents!"

"So no wonder I'm the center of an international conspiracy, and a gambling ring as well," Emmie said with a very pretty smile.

The following day, after breakfast and her daily phone call to her parents, Emmie again had to wait while Roger debriefed to Frosty, Caz, and the air force representative, Curly Moore. By 10:00 A.M. Roger got back to Emmie and told her, "Now you've got to learn to drive American style."

"Oh, I know how to drive, but I fear my British driver's license has expired."

"That's good, since you really have to get into practice driving on the right-hand side of the road. Then you'll have to take a written exam and a real driver's test. After that they may let you out on the road but only with me for sixty days. Finally you may be able to drive yourself alone. At that point we'll get you your own car. The most dangerous thing you can do in life is get into an automobile, particularly in Massachusetts." As they drove back to Carlisle, Roger added, "We can take the rest of the morning for you to get into the driver's seat at a big, empty parking lot and begin your practice sessions with me."

For the rest of the week this became the schedule: two hours at Mitre, one hour or more learning to drive, dinner at a restaurant, and then Roger driving Emmie around to get to know the area and see all of the places that Roger cherished from his childhood. After a light supper at their apartment, they watched TV or read a book. Each evening they soon repaired to their bed to catch up on all the sex they had missed before they met and married.

During the next morning's phone call, Roger agreed with Emmie and her parents that they would return to London in two weeks to make the final wedding plans. One day the next week, Roger stunned Emmie by asking, "Remember when you wanted above all else to get a Ph.D. in math?"

"Well, that's a dream long gone."

"What about talking it over with Jack Forest, your father's acquaintance at MIT? Or would you prefer Harvard? Come on. We can talk about it as we drive into Cambridge to meet him for lunch. He probably will take us around the MIT campus to show it off."

"What about being a good wife to you? Isn't that a full-time job?"

"It sure is. But I will be flitting around for the next couple of months after our honeymoon, often without you for security reasons. You undoubtedly will get tired of waiting for me out in some lobby, being ogled by every male passerby. It occurred to me that you could easily commute to Cambridge and see if you can restart your academic interests. If you don't want to just yet, or ever, I'll understand, but when your father mentioned Jack Forest as an old acquaintance, I thought that his pre-eminence in the computer field plus your excellence in math and computer skills might just fit together."

"I don't know, Roger. I've been away from academic math for years now. So much has changed. It was a real grind back then at Girton. You don't want a wife with her nose always 'at the grindstone, her ear to the ground, her feet making tracks, and her hand on the throttle,' as I heard Frosty say. I know what it takes to keep up with the incredible competition, especially at a place like MIT—the worst and possibly the meanest from that standpoint."

"Well, Emmie, we can at least meet the guy and thank him for saving my behind with Bob Everett." *And,* he thought to himself, *with your parents.*

Professor Forest was kindness himself, showing none of the terror he fostered in his students. "Ah, the young man and fiancée themselves," he said as they sat down at the MIT cafeteria. Turning to Roger he went on with a knowing smile, "Still at Mitre, Mr. Malcolm? Your president Bob Everett said you had been carrying on with a most unsuitable woman down at Christmas Island and he was about to sack you." Without waiting from a response from Roger, he turned to Emmie and chuckled to himself, adding, "Now I see why he was so shameless. You, the woman in question, certainly look most suitable to me."

Emmie laughed and immediately said, "I suspect my father has been talking to you. But anyway, he wanted me to give you his best regards. He says that the IBM computers are fantastic and all of Bletchley Park thank you for expediting them to England."

"Why, thank you so much, and please give him my best regards whenever you speak to or see him next. And luckily for you, young man, Bob Everett really thinks you can do just about anything and do it well. I understand your project down in the Pacific has been doing all that could be asked of it."

Roger replied, "Well, President Everett has thrown a lot of projects my way, but I have an immediate boss who is very perceptive, and we have assembled a crackerjack team."

"Well now," followed up the professor, "to what do I owe the honor of having lunch with you?"

Before Emmie could answer, Roger said, "Emmie here achieved a 'first' in math from Girton College, part of Cambridge University, as you surely know. She's undoubtedly brighter than I am, or most guys, but she was unable for a number of reasons to continue on to get her doctorate at Cambridge. She has achieved much in the way of social good since graduation, and trying to carry that perspective to underprivileged children in foreign lands, she ran afoul of the U.S. Air Force testing its entire family of thermonuclear bombs. We met, felt a strong bond of camaraderie, and became engaged as you have heard. We probably will live over here in Massachusetts after we are married. I suggested to her that, if she still was interested in getting a further degree in math or an associated science, she might do worse than trying to enroll at MIT."

Emmie chimed in, "Professor, I once dreamed of getting a Ph.D. in math and perhaps contributing something to that field, but there is no mistaking that I have been away from math for quite a while. So I told Roger that it is probably now a wild goose chase to consider it. But here we are. You have taught, worked with, and advised many, many students. Now having met you, I suddenly wonder if you could give me some advice about continuing my studies in math, computing, or an associated field."

"This is quite remarkable, that the daughter of Jerome Trowbridge should show the same interest and capability in math that he does. However, you are right to be cautious about starting up your studies again. The competition has become fierce both in pure math and in applied fields such as computer science, and all fields of engineering. But we have been making a determined effort to recruit women into science at MIT, particularly in math, so frankly you would have an edge in that regard. By the way, with whom did you work at Girton and Cambridge?"

"First it was Mary Cartwright, but she got promoted to be president of the college, so I was handed over to Professor Hardy, but he died, so Professor Littlewood took me on. I got quite a way with chaos theory, but he retired and I wound up with Philip Hall."

"Littlewood, did you say? Professor Littlewood? He was on my team over here during the war. He became indispensable to me. You really must be top flight if you had him as your mentor. And, of course, Mary Cartwright is legendary all over the world."

"Yes, they were both quite exceptional but after Professor Littlewood retired and then died, as far as I know only Miss Cartwright and Professor Hall are left who know me—and of course Professor Chebandrov at Edinburgh. He taught me all the math he could during the war when we both were at Roedean in the Lake Country."

"Well, you have quite a pedigree. Here's what I suggest you do. First, when we go back inside my lab building, I'll get my secretary to assemble a full package for a prospective grad student. That includes not only the application forms and the requests for student financial aid, but also a full course catalog and descriptions of the various schools and curricula at MIT. After you go back to London for your wedding, take some time to get your school transcripts from Girton, talk to any of your professors who can write a letter of recommendation, and get other supporting materials and recommendations such as your work in statistics. When you return to the U.S., think over your interests and come back in with an outline of what you might be interested in studying, whether it's a follow-up to what you were doing at Girton or whatever else you might take up. I'll introduce you to the relevant professors, and you can take some time to formulate your approach based on what you've learned. You should also spend some time in the library looking over the last few years' worth of math publications so that you can understand where the various fields stand now. Perhaps you might want to take some undergraduate courses first, to catch up with the field you choose."

Forest went on, "I hope I haven't put you off. You've already missed the cutoff for this fall's classes, so we're talking about next winter at the earliest. Now, pardon me, but I've got a class at one o'clock."

****

Roger and Emmie flew to London—the airfare now paid for by Roger, not Mitre—and were soon deeply in conversation with Emmie's parents, Natalie and Jerry, about the wedding.

"It can't be before the first week of September," Natalie said. We'll have it in the Anglican Church just down the road, and the reception will be back here in our home and garden. I've alerted the minister, Reverend Shallcroft, reserved the church itself, and talked to a caterer. I have a list of prospective invitees, which Emmie will have to update immediately. Also, Roger, you will have to add your side of the family and other guests. How does Wednesday, September fifth sound to you?"

Emmie replied, "It should be cool enough then for any wedding gown I might select to wear, so that's fine with me. And the only attendant I might want is Stacey Conover as my maid of honor. I really don't have any other friends around after what I've been through."

"Well," said Natalie, "we probably have enough of our friends who do know you, some quite well, to fill up our side of the church."

"And I've got some friends from Bletchley Park to add," said Jerry. "How about you, Roger?"

"I've got my two parents, but I'll have to ask my two brothers and their wives if they can afford the trip over here. My uncle and aunt, whom I lived with when I went to Northwestern, might be interested. They spent several years in London before the Second World War. Frosty Lockwood and his wife might come since he often has business here in England and Europe. He knows David Stirling quite well, the creator of the Special Air Service, the commandos of the British Air Force. His older brother, Lord Stirling, has a castle in Scotland where Frosty has visited David on occasion. Actually, my whole Mitre–GE team would probably enjoy such an outing, but I don't know who would pay for them to come. Other than those, I don't have much of a list. And that probably goes for Mr. Duxbury and anyone else on Christmas Island. General Starbird and Captain Patten are surely still completely involved with further nuclear tests."

"What about the date, September fifth?"

"That's just after the Labor Day holiday in the U.S., which is okay with me and probably my family. Then Emmie and I can take a nice long honeymoon."

"Oh! I hope so. But what about your top-level project?"

"I sure hope to have that all worked out by then, but as you suspect, you never know."

With that settled, Natalie and Emmie returned to deciding on a wedding dress and the menu for the reception. Later that night, Roger crept into Emmie's bed and, possibly sinning in her mother's view, enjoyed each other deeply. Before dropping off to sleep, Roger asked, "Emmie, my love, where would you like to go for our honeymoon?"

"Any place where you are."

"Oh, come on. You must have thought about it."

"How about David Stirling's castle?

"It's not his, and he's Frosty's friend, not mine."

"So…"

"What about Bermuda? It's more British than American, even though it's so close to our shore that it probably is overrun by Americans most of the time. My folks went there in 1924, the duke and duchess of Windsor in 1935, and my brother in 1952. We could see if it has changed since then."

"That would be fun, even if the duke and duchess aren't there anymore."

"We can talk about it more in the morning. I was thinking of taking twenty days wherever we go."

"Let's take forever, my lover to beat all lovers. Bermuda will suit me just fine."

****

Back at Mitre two days later, Frosty was particularly frosty when Roger showed up. "Do you know who's been on my tail since you evaporated from view? Just about everybody, Willie Moore and Caz in particular. I just can't keep all of the balls in the air myself. Grab a few, will you? And don't disappear again."

"I'm good until September fifth when you have to 'get me to the church on time.'" Roger sang that refrain from *My Fair Lady*. "Then I want twenty days for a real honeymoon. Emmie wants us to use David Stirling's castle in Scotland. Can you arrange it?"

"I'll give you a half hour for a quickie behind the church, and no, I can't arrange anything from David. He doesn't own it anyway. Who told you about him anyway? Jesus H.... Rog, your loose lips will sink us for sure."

"Just give me the update on our little project and I'll take it from there. Jesus H. yourself. This is duck soup compared to my Palmyra caper."

Roger worked long hours during August but kept up with Emmie's driving lessons, bravely letting her take the wheel as he showed her around eastern Massachusetts and lower New Hampshire. He also was able to keep up their lovemaking, which she enjoyed just as much as he. Then when the alarm went off, he jumped out of bed, made them both breakfast, collected her for dinner at any one of the many restaurants around, and set out a small supper. After a week or so of this regimen, Emmie objected.

"You know, Roger, I'll never learn to cook this way. Why don't you take a sandwich for lunch and come home for dinner after work that I'll cook and serve to you? I cooked for myself for many years when I lived alone, so all I have to do is multiply my menus by two. With your schedule, I really have a lot of time on my hands. I need to exercise my body and my mind more or I'll just get fat and stupid. By the way, I've received my transcripts from Girton as well as Roedean, and even Hatch End High School. I've got the promise of letters of recommendation from Professor Chebandrov, of course, and—what I didn't expect—from Professor Hall and Mary Cartwright, both still alive but quite elderly. Then I have a wonderful letter from Stacey Conover, who says also she'll be at our wedding. Oh! Professor Chebandrov says he will come down from Edinburgh by train to our wedding also. Isn't that fabulous! As soon as I get my driver's license and you can set me free to drive by myself, I'll go into MIT and use the math library to catch up on things. These fractals by Professor Mandelbrot at IBM have caught my interest. They're just what I might have gotten into if I had stayed at Cambridge. I still might be able to catch up since they're sort of an outgrowth of my thesis at Cambridge."

"That's just tremendous, Emmie, wonderful, great. When we get back from our honeymoon I hope you can catch up with Jack Forest and see if he would encourage you some more. And you must tell me more about these fractals."

By the end of August, Roger was quite pleased with their progress on the three-site NUDETS. Everyone took off for the Labor Day weekend, and the two lovebirds escaped to London, arriving on Sunday the third. Roger had made all the arrangements for their honeymoon and was prepared to be fully relaxed for the wedding. Unfortunately he had felt compelled to let Frosty know where they were staying in Bermuda. But their secret from Mr. and Mrs. Trowbridge held. Stacey came to stay with them, sleeping on a cot in Emmie's bedroom and preventing any lovemaking. Roger also had made the arrangements for his parents, Nanny and Dad, to fly over and stay in a nearby hotel, and he was paying the bills. He and Emmie met them at Heathrow on the fourth and shepherded them to South Oxney. Each of his brothers had telephoned that they did not see their way to coming over for the wedding but would make it up to Emmie when she and Roger returned. His uncle and aunt were off in Palm Springs for their holiday and couldn't come. Frosty just said, "Someone's got to mind the store, so have a great time. Don't even think of me, much less Mitre and the SecDef. And watch out for that British damp grass behind the church."

The day of the wedding dawned clear, sunny, and warm even for September in London. Roger dawdled a bit reading *The Times* as Emmie struggled with Stacey to get into her wedding dress without mussing her hair, laughing nervously at each other. "What's so funny?" Roger shouted through the door to their bedroom. He had been shunted to his father-in-law's room to put on his cutaway. He then made himself the butt of many future jokes by requiring Natalie to *do* his white bow tie. Just then, his parents arrived from their hotel. They had all met the previous evening when they went to the church for the wedding rehearsal, followed by the rehearsal dinner given by his parents at a nearby restaurant. They went in two cars to the church just a short distance away, Roger with his father and Jerry, and Emmie with her mother, Roger's mother, and Stacey in the Rolls Royce limousine Jerry had hired.

"God, what a princely—or is it a 'princessly'—royal sum that four wheels with a steering column cost!" Jerry muttered to Roger as the limousine drove off. Actually, "pricey" is more to the point. Roger was too immersed in his own thoughts to reply while Jerry drove the three men to the church in his old clunker. They went into the church through a rear door and were shown to a small chamber off the nave and told that the verger would come in to escort them into the church at the appropriate moment. He soon appeared and took Mr. Trowbridge around to the front since the limousine with Emmie was just driving up. Roger could hear the commotion of the guests arriving. He turned to his father and asked if he had ever been the best man at a wedding. His father started to tell about the Colgate–Palmolive merger wedding when his college roommate, from the Colgate company's fortune, had married a young woman from the Palmolive fortune. Just then the verger reappeared and whisked them off to stand before the congregation, with the minister as the organist playing the "Wedding March" from Mendelssohn.

Roger looked out as Emmie's father escorted her slowly down the aisle. Roger could hardly contain himself from shameless tears as he viewed the loveliest woman he had ever seen coming toward him with a radiant smile, as she too was almost overtaken with emotion on seeing Roger in his finery. Luckily, they both had the sense and courage to ward off their sentimentalist feelings and were soon announcing their wedding vows. They had agreed beforehand not to kiss and ruin Emmie's makeup after the minister had pronounced them man and wife, but it lead to a slightly awkward moment when the congregation didn't know what to expect. So Roger took Emmie's hand and simply started leading her down the aisle, and all was well as she kissed her mother and father, then Roger's Nanny and Dad, and smiled beatifically at each of the attendees as she passed them along the way.

The wedding reception back at the Trowbridge's house went off without a hitch, but, trying to be as inconspicuous as possible, Professor Chebandrov at one point took Roger aside and told him something that would, you might say, save the world. "Roger, let's go out in the garden for a little quiet walk." After the professor led him quite a distance off, he said, "Mrs. Trowbridge was wonderful to invite me to your wedding. Congratulations and best wishes for a long and happy marriage. Now, Emmie wrote to me recently and told me much about her experiences on Christmas Island and a bit about you. What I want to talk to you about is quite different. I inferred from her letter that you may be connected to the highest levels of the defense department in the United States."

"Well, I've met the secretary of defense just once. I doubt that he even remembers me. All I can say is that I work for the Mitre Corporation which has contracts with the defense department."

"In any case, I've been told something that, to me, is extremely disturbing."

Just then Emmie called out. "Roger, we've got to cut the cake and open the presents. Some of the guests have to leave."

"Be right there, my love. Well, Professor, hold that thought. Come into the house, and after certain customs are observed, I promise I'll listen to everything that's on your mind."

About an hour later, Roger and Professor Chebandrov continued their discussion, and the professor said, "I had a colleague back in the 1920s at Lomonosov University in Russia who was quite smart in math but turned more to engineering. I lost track of him. But evidently right after the war he became involved as a central figure in the Soviet atomic energy program. He stuck to the engineering part of it and survived all of the politics that ensued. Four years ago he became attached to Chairman Khrushchev as his technical advisor for nuclear weapons. He was assigned in 1958 to work on the nuclear weapon test ban treaty that your President Eisenhower was so interested in. He actually came over to the U.S. and met with officials in your state department trying to come up with a treaty both countries could agree on. He then came to England to discuss the British part of the treaty, and even came up to see me in Edinburgh, just overnight.

"We went for a long walk that evening and he told me that he was extremely worried about Chairman Khrushchev. My friend said that Khrushchev was really not all that interested in such a treaty. He was just going through the motions. He got my friend to authorize and conduct an accelerated program to build new and bigger thermonuclear weapons, which he thought was very provocative to the U.S. and a huge waste of money. He said he had the temerity to ask the chairman, at great risk to his own life, 'Why spend so much money on so many new weapons when, if you sign the treaty with Eisenhower, you won't be able to test them to be sure they will work?' The chairman just smiled and said, 'Comrade, that is not your concern. Just make sure they *will* work.' He could not say more because his life was already at great risk, and so was his family's. Oh, Khrushchev said one other thing that is important: 'Comrade, do you think that those old U.S. nuclear missiles in Turkey and Italy, the Jupiters, will work?' My friend said, 'Yes, I have no reason to doubt it, even as old as they are.' The chairman went on, 'Well they are a great nuisance to me. I wish someone could tell me how to get rid of them without starting World War Three.' Without thinking, my friend replied, 'Swap some of ours for theirs.' The chairman replied, 'Thank you, comrade. That is great advice. You may go—and get started on those new weapons.'"

"Well," said Roger with some impatience, "so what? Khrushchev sure demonstrated his disdain for the nuclear test ban treaty with those nuclear tests over Novaya Zemlya, didn't he? The only positive thing is that it brought Emmie and me together. I truly owe him that."

"No, no. Listen to me just a bit more. I was in my hotel room in London last night, hoping to get a good night's sleep before your wedding. There was a knock on the door and a bellhop gave me an envelope unmarked except for the hotel name embossed on it. Inside was a torn piece of paper with a scribbled message on the stationery of Lomonosov Moscow State University that simply stated, 'Negotiations have started.' The message was written such that you couldn't trace the writer or how it got to my hotel in London. I ran right out after the bellhop and asked, 'Who gave you this envelope?' The bellhop said, 'The front desk, sir.' So I went down immediately and asked the clerk there, 'Who gave you this envelope just now and how did you know it was for me?' The clerk responded, 'Oh, yes, I do remember since it was a bit unusual, sir. A small boy came running in, avoiding the doorman who is supposed to keep small boys out of the hotel, came right up to this desk where you are standing, and said, "Please give this to Professor Chebando right away." I took the envelope, and he ran away as fast as he came in. We have no Professor Chebando registered, but I immediately figured it must be you, sir. Was I wrong?' I said, 'No, not at all. Thank you very, very much.'"

"You're saying that your former classmate in Moscow has sent you a warning that Khrushchev may be about to start some type of negotiation to get the U.S. to pull its Jupiter missiles out of Turkey and Italy. Is that it?"

"That is anybody's guess, but I would surely take it seriously. You must warn your secretary of defense that the U.S. must double its guard and invigorate its intelligence to uncover what 'Comrade' Khrushchev may be up to and be ready for it. Here is the envelope with the message inside. Keep it in a very secure place. I really have no further use for it, and it might just convince your people of what I have told you."

"What's this friend of yours name, anyway?"

"That I cannot and will not tell you. Any hint of what he has told me, and what I just told you, to anyone inside or outside of the Soviet Union would mean his instant death and probably mine. Perhaps your CIA would know or be able to find out, but I doubt it."

"Professor, I'll do my best, but it will have to wait until the end of my honeymoon."

****

The honeymoon was going great.

They were staying at the Inverness Hotel, not far from the main city of Hamilton, Bermuda. Roger and Emmie were both relaxed and could enjoy all of the interesting and lovely things about Bermuda. Emmie said, "Look, we can rent motorbikes. That could be fun."

"No, no. It could be fun until one of us, more likely me than you, goes head-over-teakettle. This bicycle built for two is much more fun and much safer. You can ride in front and let me do all the tough pedaling."

"More likely all the tough coasting. I'll take the rear and make sure you do your share." Roger laughed at that but rented the bike for two, and they agreed to swap places each day. So they rode all over the island and had picnics at Gibb's Hill Lighthouse, St. Peter's Church, Fort Hamilton, the tiny Somerset Bridge, Victoria Park, Botanical Gardens, and historic places in between. Finally Emmie said, "I've seen enough historic sites, let's go shopping." They were able to walk down to the fabulous shops in Hamilton and bought English silverware, Waterford crystal stemware, Wedgewood china, and a sterling silver tea and coffee set.

"Stop, stop. Emmie. You've already run up a bill that will take a mortgage on our firstborn to pay off!" So they retired to their room at the Inverness, hopped into bed, and after doing what comes naturally to newlyweds, took a short nap.

Later as they were resting in bed, Roger had a thought. "You know, Emmie, my dad told me about this place where he and Nanny honeymooned. I was worried that it would be a ghastly remnant of past glory, but they've fixed it up wonderfully. The funniest thing is that early on the morning of our wedding, Dad snuck around to a chemist's shop in South Oxney and, red-faced with embarrassment, bought a box of condoms. He slipped it into my suitcase. I wonder what he did for birth control back in 1924? Not much, I guess, since brother Sid arrived less than thirteen months after their wedding, but they must have figured something out since I didn't arrive for another twenty-three months, and Walter all of forty-two months in 1931. Condoms were unlawful in 1924, at least in the U.S."

"Well," replied Emmie, "I've observed that you've been taking care of me in that regard, except for that first night in our apartment. I don't think I'm pregnant, but after all, who cares?"

"You mean I can stop putting those blasted things on whenever I get randy?"

"Well, not quite yet. I want to be with just you for a while without that blasted, as you would put it, morning sickness business."

Roger did not question that reasoning, and they continued their existence, carefree but with precautions.

They topped off that day with a horse-drawn carriage ride to the Elbow Beach Hotel for dinner and dancing almost until dawn. Another evening Roger said, "Let's really be naughty." He showed her the way to climb over a ridge from their hotel and walk down to a sandy beach on the less inhabited, less popular north shore of the island. Roger looked carefully around in the early darkness, saw no one, and dropped the large beach towels he had brought from the hotel. Then he slipped off his bathing trunks. He chided Emmie, "Come on. I'll bet you never went skinny-dipping. Quick, join me!" She promptly did. They waded slowly into the very slight surf, and when they got just past the breaking waves, Emmie caught her breath.

"Ooh, that's cold."

Roger replied, "That's the '*ooh* line,' where the cold water just reaches your skin below your waist. Come on, let's jump into the deeper water." As they emerged from their plunge, Emmie noticed that she was in the midst of luminescence in the gentle waves.

"Roger, look at the tiny lights in the foam."

"Yeah, those are one-celled animals called amoebas that fluoresce when disturbed. They're harmless and quite a wonder to see." Then the two of them swam out to where they could still just touch the sandy bottom, and bounced up and down, giggling and then laughing like two teenagers. The Bermuda water in September now felt warmer than the air. They clutched each other, standing so just their heads were above the surface. They pawed and nuzzled, and, as Roger put it, "I wouldn't care if the whole world were watching. Emmie, you are truly the most fantastic wife a man could have. Just the touch of you warms me all over. Especially the part of me that really counts."

"Roger, you naughty of naughtiest boys. You really are the devil who made me do it! I will take it that you mean your head is the part that really counts."

"I'm not saying which 'head,' but before I do the devil's mischief on you, let's get back to our warm bed and see what the other naughtiness the evening will bring!"

The next morning, while still in bed with Roger stroking her back, Emmie felt his long scar again and asked, "You never did tell me the long story about that bullet wound. How about telling me now?"

"Well, I feel a bit ashamed about it. You see, our destroyer accompanied a small group, a squad, of marines each night to go ashore well behind the enemy lines in North Korea to gather information." Roger continued describing his encounter with the enemy, ending with the moment that the four marines appeared on the run, turning to shoot back at the enemy. "I stood there as if watching a war movie while all five of the marines jumped into their boat and shoved off into the waves. Suddenly, seeing the enemy appear, I recovered my senses and quickly scrambled to jump aboard my boat already in the water and almost out of my reach. It was just that slight hesitation, that distinction between the 'quick and the dead,' that almost got me. Just as I got into the bow of my boat and stood there shooting back at the enemy, they shot at us. They hit our engineer in the chest, so our cox'n, one of our shipmates, took over, and started the boat engine at full speed backward. That sudden motion by the boat threw me forward and down just as the bullet meant for me hit the right-hand side instead of my chest. Well, the wounded marines, my engineer and I all survived, but all will bear the marks of the encounter from that moment on. If I had reacted just a moment earlier so that the boat got under way quicker, well…"

"Oh, Roger! I don't want to think about it. What if…"

"No, no, Emmie, No what ifs. I should not have said that 'if.' I should have stuck to the ice hockey story. Just hug me again, and keep on hugging me, and we'll be all right. But now you see why I am so against war. I'm not a pacifist, but I will do everything I can to find a way to avoid more wars."

After a short silence, Roger added, "Now after breakfast, I want to know more about your story of helping those refugees in Europe." They returned to their room, and Emmie told him in more detail her tales of being evacuated from London as a ten-year-old, then getting her 'first,' and finally helping her former Girl Guide put refugees together with their families or into jobs in Europe. She ended by telling him about her statistics experience, particularly with computers.

"I really grew up on that experience," she added, "and learned a lot about computers and how to use them in non-military, non-financial applications. But that seemed awfully sterile, you might say, so then I turned to teaching. Roedean, as I have told you, is quite a prestigious school and I truly enjoyed the children, the other staff members, and the whole atmosphere. Then that terrible business with James just blew me away. I probably could have passed it off somehow, but at the moment it devastated me. So I fled to—where? How lucky can a ruined woman get? I fled right into your arms! Oh, Roger, Roger, what bliss I've found! Please hold onto me forever."

Roger listened intently and cradled her into his arms. "You must do the same with me, Emmie, my love. You have had a fantastic career, giving as much as you've received. You deserve as much love as I can give, and then some." They kissed passionately. It was nearly noon before they set out on their bike for a picnic, this one at the botanical garden.

After ten days, they were hardly started on their relaxation and interest in what Bermuda had to offer. At breakfast the next day, Roger was calmly sipping his second and last cup of coffee for the day when the owner of the hotel approached their table carrying a telephone with a long cable. "Excuse me, Mr. Malcolm, but you're wanted on the telephone. It seems to be quite urgent. It's a Mr. Lockwood. I don't know why he didn't just call your room."

"He knew I just would not answer. Oh, Lord! Emmie, this is bad news."

"Hello, Frosty. What's the good news? Emmie and I are having a ball here."

"Get your balls in motion in this direction, Malcolm. The big, big, big guy wants to see us tomorrow, if not sooner." Roger looked around to the adjoining tables and saw everyone looking at him. Frosty could be heard across the room.

"Oh, that guy, Well, he can wait ten more days, can't he?"

"You friggin' better not think so. Som'pin' has come up that just plain won't wait!"

"What about just five more?"

"No!"

"Two more?"

"No."

One more?"

"No! No! No! If there are no commercial flights you can make *today*, he'll send or divert a military plane to bring you direct to his office—'fly right in the window,' he said."

"Keerist-a-mighty, son-of-a-seacook, ding-dong dooly whistle, dang nabbit, Frosty. I am not a swearing man, but that's how I feel. Emmie is nodding that she agrees two hundred percent with me, and she can swear blue thunder."

"God-a-mighty damnitalltohellandgone, Frosty," Emmie added so that Frosty and just about everyone in the breakfast room could hear.

"Put Rog on, Emmie. Put that lazy good-for-nothing son of a sea cook on." To Roger he shouted, "Stop jawin' and get movin'. Time's a-wastin'. Rog, this is real and this is trouble. The *man* is counting on you. *Over and out.*"

"Emmie, you didn't hear what Professor Chebandrov told me, but I think we better 'scramabouche' outta here! The world is about to tremble!"

Chapter Fourteen

Emmie and Roger Brief the Secretary of Defense

They made the flight to Washington's Dulles Airport the next morning, and as they exited the airport they were ushered into a limousine by Major Alten of the Air Staff. Roger recognized him and introduced him to Emmie, and off they went to the Pentagon. The major accompanied them directly up to the third floor and down the hall where a secretary; Harold Benton, director of DDR&E; Frosty; and Col. Ed Holden of the Joint Staff were anxiously waiting for them. Frosty, Harold, and Roger were ushered into Secretary of Defense Robert McNamara's office. Emmie, Major Alten, and Colonel Holden had to wait in the secretary's antechamber. Bob Everett, Charlie Zraket, and Alan Howard were already chatting with Secretary McNamara.

"Gentlemen," the SecDef said with an extremely worried countenance. "Please take your seats here around this table." The SecDef immediately launched into what was on his mind. "Our intelligence, as well as MI5 in England, have picked up very strong signals that Khrushchev is planning some sort of move against us here in the U.S. It is probably already under way. We need your NUDET system on line and operating within a few days. Can you do it?"

Frosty immediately said, "Yes, sir. We have the equipment on all three sites and checked out separately. We just have to connect the phone lines and exercise the full system. The one thing we need is access to the Air Force, Army, and Navy command posts, the National Military Command Center, and any other command sites you want."

"Harold, can you see to that?"

"Yes, sir! By tomorrow before the end of the day. Yes, sir!"

Turning to the Mitre President, the SecDef added, "Bob, do you want to add anything to what we just heard? We have to be damn sure."

"I'd bet the farm on Frosty Lockwood and Roger Malcolm any time."

"What about that, Charlie?" SecDef motioned to Caz.

"I went over the whole system with Frosty yesterday and again as we flew down from Boston this morning. Outside of what he mentioned, we're set to go."

"Go to it then. That'll be all."

As they all got up and left the room, Roger hung back. "Excuse me, sir. I may have some intelligence that you don't have."

"What's that?" said the SecDef turning around to look at Roger. "What do you mean, something that I don't have?"

"You may call me completely off base and a kook besides, but for an incredible coincidence and an incredible story, I have something to tell you that may just help in this situation."

"Well, out with it. I don't have all day to listen to stories. Alan, come back in and listen to this, will you? Shut the door behind you."

Roger took a deep breath as the three of them stood there. "Chairman Khrushchev's chief adviser on nuclear weapons—let's call him 'Boris'—visited with his former colleague in Russia, Professor Chebandrov, who was then and still is at the University of Edinburgh. Chebandrov was previously my wife Emmie's mentor in math, and she and her family have been close friends since then. Emmie's my wife sitting outside. At the time of this encounter, arranged surreptitiously by Boris, he was in England following a visit to the U.S. negotiating the nuclear test ban treaty. Boris told Chebandrov a story deeply troubling to himself. I don't know Boris's real name, but your test ban treaty folks will know.

"The story in essence, and this was some years ago, was that Khrushchev was not serious about the treaty and ordered Boris to start immediately developing and building more and bigger thermonuclear weapons. Boris said that he demurred, but the chairman persisted. Then he told his adviser that what he really worried about were the U.S. Jupiter missiles in Turkey and Italy so close to the borders of the Soviet Union. He said they were a problem and a danger for any nuclear confrontation with the U.S. They decreased his response time to any threat almost to zero. He asked the adviser what to do about it, adding that he surely wanted to avoid World War Three at all costs. Boris said that he thought briefly and then said to the chairman, 'Negotiate a swap of some of ours for some of theirs.' Khrushchev simply said, 'Thank you, comrade. That is great advice. You may go—and get started on those new weapons.'"

"Swap ours for theirs? We'd never do that," Howard replied immediately.

"Wait, wait, let me finish. The professor got a message ten days ago that said, 'Negotiations have started.' Chebandrov, in London for our wedding, took me aside after our wedding reception and with no one around to hear, told me what the message was and how he got it." Roger recounted what the professor had told him about the letter on Lomonosov State University stationery. "The professor added, 'Roger, you must tell your secretary of defense what I just told you. Here, take the envelope with the letter. Perhaps it will help convince your people about what I have told you.' Unfortunately, Emmie and I took off for our honeymoon in Bermuda, and I had no idea that what I had just found out should have been relayed immediately to you. Perhaps the CIA can make out some fingerprints on the envelope and scrap of paper, but Professor Chebandrov and I, and others, may have smudged them too badly."

"Well, as I said, we've obtained some intelligence along those lines," said McNamara. "But this could be important verification. May I see the letter please?" Roger handed him the envelope, and the SecDef took out the scrap of paper. After scanning it, he showed it to Howard and then put it on top of his desk. "We'll keep it safely, but I believe we already know who 'Boris' is. We may need it again."

"On the other hand," replied Howard, "we still have to consider disinformation. What do we know about these two chums? Could we speak to your wife, Roger? Perhaps she could tell us more about Professor Chebandrov at least."

McNamara stepped to the door, opened it, and said, "Mrs. Malcolm, could you come in please?" Emmie was soon seated beside Roger and Howard, all looking at the SecDef. It was obvious to Roger that she was thoroughly perplexed, even sorely worried. "As you may know, we have asked your husband and his team at the Mitre Corporation to install a system similar to the one he took to Palmyra Island around Washington, D.C. The purpose is to detect any nuclear bomb that may have detonated within our country and report that fact immediately to the president. He then must make that awesome decision as to what response should be made, and against whom. I needn't tell you what the consequences might be for such an attack upon us."

Emmie spoke up, interrupting the SecDef. "Exactly what do you mean by 'response'?"

"Well," replied McNamara, "the president must decide almost immediately what nation, or group, was responsible for attacking us with one or more nuclear weapons, and whom to confront or attack in response."

"Oh," said Emmie, "do you mean drop one or more nuclear bombs on someone?"

"Well, yes, it all depends on how many were dropped on us. That is why we need your husband's system so urgently. It is designed to answer some of those questions."

"Oh," said Emmie again, obviously not satisfied with the answer but willing to listen further to the SecDef.

"Getting back to what concerns us at the moment, it turns out that your mentor, Professor Chebandrov, may have received some intelligence concerning the intentions of the Soviet Union. Your husband has told us a little about him, but we need to hear about him directly from you. When did you first meet him and how was he your mentor?"

Emmie straightened up in her chair and recounted her wartime experiences and how she was able to excel in math.

"Did he visit you frequently in London after you graduated from Girton?" asked the SecDef.

"No, only once or twice when he came to London for a meeting of the International Mathematics Association. He stayed overnight with us just once, but I believe he dropped by on another occasion."

"Was he acquainted with your father as well?"

"Well, yes. They talked about how to help me with my studies at Girton, and later how I might get a fellowship to pursue a doctorate at Cambridge. It turned out that they had acquaintances in common whom they asked to help me. Unfortunately, it turned out that my family and I couldn't afford my further studies."

"What does your father do?"

"I don't really know. He studied math at Cambridge and now does some kind of computer work at Bletchley Park north of London."

Both McNamara and Howard visibly reacted to the mention of Bletchley Park. "Did the professor ever visit your father at Bletchley Park?"

"No, not that I know of, and I'm sure my father would have told me. He never told me about anyone visiting him there, much less what anyone did there."

"Did the professor ever mention a college chum of his at Lomonosov State University in Moscow?"

"No, never. I only heard of that university from Professor Chebandrov when we first met in 1943. As I recall, he only mentioned it in passing and how he left there to go to Berlin and then to Edinburgh. I don't remember him ever mentioning any colleagues in either Moscow or Berlin, and he would never, ever refer to them as 'chums.' He is quite reserved and works pretty much alone on his math research. He has mentioned colleagues at Edinburgh, but I can't remember their names. He may have social friends there, but again, I don't know any of them."

"Did the professor talk at all that you know of with your father about his work or about math in general?"

"Oh, I know that my father would never talk about his work, as I said, even with me, the only one not at the park who might have understood him. He took an interest in my math studies, but never related them to his work."

"Is there anything you know of that might indicate that the professor might not have told the full story of how he came to be at your primary school during the war?" asked McNamara.

"Or could be persuaded to make up or embellish a story for any reason?" added Howard.

"Oh my, no," said Emmie quickly. "He has always been completely straightforward with me. He told me how he came to be at the Roedean School in Keswick quite early in our relationship, and he did so freely and without any hint of making it up. He chuckled at the incongruity of being considered an enemy alien yet being so anti-Nazi. Yet he seemed very pleased to have obtained the position of math teacher at Roedean. He never said or inferred that it was beneath him. Of course he was delighted when the war ended and he could return to the University at Edinburgh. During our time at Roedean and on every occasion since, when I have asked him for advice or help, he has done so very promptly. I could never have achieved a 'first' at Girton without him."

"Well," said McNamara, "that puts him in quite a nice light, I must say. Thank you, Emmie, if I may call you that. You have been extremely helpful." Getting up, he opened the door to the room and saw her out, closing it after her.

"Nice light, eh?" Howard said, with more than a hint of disbelief. "Let me draw a slightly different picture. Chebandrov may be one of those pure math types who is politically naïve. Or he may be a full-scale deep 'comrade' embedded in the UK university system. 'Boris' or whatever his name is may or may not exist, but someone very easily could have cooked up this scheme to put us off. What's the natural conclusion to draw from this story, as Roger here puts it? Khrushchev somehow puts some old, short-range missiles into—where? Cuba comes to mind. So he and Castro threaten us with a nuclear strike unless we pull our Jupiters out. Tit for tat. Quid pro quo. We'd be either crucified in the press or lose Miami. We might lose Miami anyway. And then, as Khruschev put it, World War Three starts. Let me remind you, we have a ten-to-one advantage in throw weight over the Soviets. Good-bye, Soviet Union! He's not going to do that."

"You're getting all worked up, Alan," sighed McNamara. "We all know that. What we have to figure is how do we stop him from getting any nukes close to our shores, and if they show up there, how do we get them out?"

"I'd just threaten him with seven thousand megatons of nuclear weapons aloft and undersea, plus the Jupiters. That's the kind of language he surely understands."

Roger got up, saying, "I don't think I can add to this discussion except to say Boris mentioned a negotiation. Mr. Secretary, that's what you and Mr. Howard might just keep in mind. Meanwhile, I'd better get back to Mitre and make sure we have our system tested and ready."

"Thank you, Doc. That's what Starbird tells me he calls you."

"Yes, sir," replied Roger snappily, realizing that McNamara had obviously checked up on him. "I may not know my thermonuclear elbow from my sternum, medically speaking, but The Man seems to appreciate my advice."

The next day at Mitre, Frosty told Roger, "Regarding our ability to test the three-site NUDET system, Lee Turner is quite amazing. He found a huge capacitor bank at the army's Aberdeen proving ground that they use to check whether a strong electromagnetic field might trigger the fuses in their planes carrying nuclear weapons around the huge radars in the Arctic or their tactical weapons for the army. Lee found out that they occasionally connected this 'gazapper,' as they call it, to a helicopter. The chopper hoists a copper wire up ten thousand feet and having charged the capacitor with a large direct current diesel-electric generator to its capacity, many thousands of volts, the guys on the ground throw the switch and it goes *gazap!* They get a radio signal like a lightning bolt—or a nuclear blast. Lee says he'll get it up to see if all of our sites detect it. If so, we can test our NUDET system almost for real. A week later, Roger drove down to the proving ground not far north of Baltimore, Maryland, and watched it work. He heard, and felt, many a wonderful *gazap!*"

"Lee, this is terrific!" exclaimed Roger.

Roger turned to Lee Turner and asked, "When can we test our whole system?"

"Next Tuesday or Wednesday. I'll let you know Monday."

On Wednesday, Roger told Emmie that he would be gone for the day and left his car for her to do some shopping around Carlisle or wherever she wanted. Roger and Frosty flew down to Washington, rented a car, and drove to the Pentagon. Roger had called ahead to notify Willie Moore and Colonel Holden of the Joint Staff, who were waiting on the steps and jumped into the car. Roger drove them to the air force site in Manassas, Virginia, not far south of the Pentagon. Roger said over his shoulder as he drove, "This should really show what we can do with NUDETS operationally."

Willie replied, "I sure hope so. The SecDef has invested a lot of his time into this. The president is also very concerned. I got confirmation this morning that the communications to the Pentagon and the other sites have been connected." As soon as they arrived at the site, they all jumped out of the car and crowded into the trailer with the electromagnetic receiver and other electronic gear.

Lee Turner became the guide, saying, "I'll have the *gazapper* guys fire it off for a minute or so. Watch the 'scope to see if we receive the radio pulses here. Then we can check over here with the other two sites to see if they got them also. Finally we can see the plot of the ground-zero locations on the printer over here." The four of them grouped around the electronic read-out devices as Lee talked on the telephone with the group at Aberdeen. Almost immediately the signals started to arrive. Lee then added, "I got here earlier and had the *gazapper* fire off a number of shots. They came in loud and clear at all three sites, and the computer calculated the ground-zero locations of them all. Here is a computer plot of the results. I've had an ellipse drawn around ninety percent of the locations. It's about a mile on the major axis and three-quarters of a mile on the minor axis."

"As I understand the accuracy requirements, Willie," said Roger, "that seems to meet them, doesn't it?"

"Of course, we wouldn't know whether the Pentagon or the Capitol building just got evaporated," said Colonel Holden, "but maybe that doesn't really matter. If CINCSAC, the Commander in Chief of the Strategic Air Command, finds out, in the next twenty minutes, good-bye Soviet Union!"

The group discussed the situation the colonel had brought up. However, soon Willie said, "Well, enough chit-chat over the hypothetical; back to work."

As Roger drove them back to the Pentagon, he turned to Willie and said, "I'll send you a report on this result first thing in the morning, with a recommendation to have Harold Benton of DDR&E approve our system for immediate operation."

"Sounds okay by me."

"And oh, one other thing. I would like to have access to the various service command posts in the Pentagon as well as the National Military Command Center. I am still concerned about the problem with lightning strikes in this area and want to be sure that we are not going to generate any pesky, or dangerous, false alarms."

"That also is okay by me."

Later on, after flying back to Boston and taking a limousine home, Roger noticed that Emmie was unusually quiet. He asked, "What's the matter? What did I do to make you clam up?"

Emmie said, "What do you mean 'clam up'?"

"You know—suddenly get all quiet."

So Emmie took the bit in her mouth and asked Roger, "Are you guys serious when you talk like that?"

"Like what?"

"Like the world is coming to an end and none of you seem to care at all," she answered frostily. "Maybe I misunderstand the 'game,' as I heard Colonel Holden calling it as he was chatting with Major Alten in McNamara's outer office while you big boys were discussing nuclear war with the 'SecDef,' as you call him. 'All we need to convince Mr. K to back down is seven thousand megatons of nukes aloft and undersea.' But then having heard directly from Mr. McNamara what your system is for and what the president has to decide about nuking some entire country, I suddenly can envision the consequences. You and I have seen all those multi-megaton nuclear bombs go off over Christmas Island and felt the devastating effects from just one. Now you and the others are talking about dropping nuclear bombs on countries and even full-scale nuclear war. It all seems to me to be very much for real. I married you as a serious, caring man. Now it seems that you are one of *them* again. You and all of your cohorts here are completely mad! I tell you, I'm getting very, very scared. That's the 'clam'—or as we say in London, the 'cat'—that has my tongue."

"Emmie, dear Emmie. I suddenly see your point, and it's well taken. Please don't think that I don't think about what I'm doing! Please *do* think that I for one am trying my best to see that nothing like the end of the world happens. I'm sure President Kennedy and SecDef McNamara are trying too. The problem goes all the way back to President Truman and President Eisenhower. And Professor Chebandrov told me—and this may not be repeated to anyone—that his chum from the Lomonosov University told him that Chairman Khruschev likewise very much does not want to start World War Three. Yes, we are all mad, but madly trying to get our two nations past this moment when we each have the capability to destroy the other."

Chapter Fifteen

The Cuban Missile Crisis

On October 22, 1962, Roger and Emmie watched the evening news along with most everyone else in the U.S. as President Kennedy announced that the Russians had deployed nuclear-tipped missiles in Cuba. He added that the U.S. Navy had been ordered to establish a quarantine line around Cuba to keep any more missiles from being delivered. The Cuban Missile Crisis was under way. "Jeezus H!" shouted Roger. Then calming down, he said, "Sorry Emmie, but I told them that would happen. Now we've got to find a way to negotiate with Khruschev to get him to take the missiles out of Cuba."

"This is serious, isn't it?" asked Emmie.

"You bet your boots it is. Perhaps Frosty has some ideas to work with the Pentagon to make sure no one goes off half-cocked and orders an air strike against Cuba—or against the Soviet Union."

The next morning at Mitre, Roger and Frosty talked about what they should do. Their air force system program office and all of Hanscom Air Base, not to mention the entire U.S. military, were on alert and feverishly moving forces around in response to rapid-fire orders from the Pentagon and subsidiary commands. Frosty said, "I think the best thing for us to do is hunker down and not get in anybody's way."

"No, no," replied Roger. "I'm going to fly down to Washington and get into the NMCC and the Air Force Command Post at the Pentagon. I'm terribly concerned that our NUDETS could suffer a false alarm just when it could be fatal—trigger the president to send off our bombers and missiles."

"You really think that's possible, or even likely?"

"Yeah, it happened to us once on Palmyra. It certainly could happen again, even in October when thunderstorms are rare."

"Well," added Frosty, "write if you get work."

Roger called Willie Moore, which took a long time with the panic reigning in the Pentagon; actually, it took two days to get through. Finally he reached Willie and told him what he wanted to do and asked for emergency access to the command centers in the Pentagon. Willie said, "I'll see what I can do, but this is unheard of during times like these." The next day Willie called back and said, "Okay, Roger, thanks to the SecDef you've got your access, come on down."

Roger then drove home and told Emmie what he was up to. "I've made reservations at a hotel in Washington for both of us while I check out our NUDET system at the Pentagon and make sure nothing like a false alarm happens at a crucial moment. Now we both have to pack right away and catch the shuttle from Logan Airport to DC."

She quickly said, "But what am I to do while you're checking on NUDETS? My first visit to Washington was just that day trip to see McNamara in the Pentagon. I'd really like to see the city itself. Of course, I have no idea about where I should start."

"Well, first, as soon as I've gone off tomorrow morning, I want you call your folks to find out Professor Chebandrov's phone number and give him a call. If you can reach him, start off telling him how wonderful it was for him to get to our wedding and reception. Tell him that our honeymoon in Bermuda was grand and that now we are settling into married life in Massachusetts. Finally, tell him—and this is important—tell him, quote, 'Roger has done what you asked him to do and he will contact you later today.' After that, you could take a cab to the Smithsonian and even walk over to the National Gallery of Art. You can get lunch there. Then by four o'clock, catch a cab to get back to the hotel no later than five. I'll leave a number at the hotel desk where you can reach me if any emergency comes up. But I'll be sure to come back to meet you here at about five P.M. and after my phone call to the professor, we can have dinner. After that," he added with a knowing smile, "I wonder what we could do to pass the time?"

"Oh, you rascal you! But I'm looking forward to this trip, aren't you?"

"Emmie, we're just this far from nuclear war," he said holding up his thumb and forefinger pressed together.

"Oh," is all she could think of to say.

They quickly packed some clothes for a several-week stay and took the Boston-Washington shuttle, and soon that night they were settled in a hotel in Georgetown.

The next morning, Saturday, October 27, Roger went off right after breakfast in the hotel dining room. Emmie went up to their room and called her parents to tell them how nice their apartment was and how she was learning to drive on the right-hand side of the road. Then she added, "Roger's over at the Pentagon about this Cuban missile crisis. He said, not to worry, that he's sure it will work out without a war. By the way, we're at a hotel in

Washington." She gave them the hotel's phone number. "Roger wants to talk to the professor. Do you have his phone number?"

Mr. Trowbridge found it and read it off to her saying, "That's his number at the university. Here's his home phone number."

Emmie tried to get the professor at the university, and he answered immediately. "Emmie, so nice to hear from you. How's married life over there in America?"

"Wonderful, except it's so hard to drive on the wrong side of the road." The professor laughed. "But another reason I called is to tell you that Roger has done what you asked him to do, and he will call you back about five P.M. our time."

"What's that? What has Roger done? Pardon the absentminded professor in me, but I can't quite recall what I asked him to do....Oh, wait a minute, oh yes, oh my, that's serious stuff. Yes, that is excellent. Be sure to have him call me as soon as he can. Five o'clock where you are in Washington? That's ten o'clock in Edinburgh. Have him call me here at my office since I have a paper to finish. I'll still be here then. Well, it is so wonderful to hear your voice. Please call again any time."

Emmie checked her wardrobe and called the front desk to order a taxi, but she was told to just come down and go out the front door and the doorman would hail a cab. Very soon she was wandering around the Smithsonian Museum of Natural History, fascinated by the exhibits. Later she did walk over to the National Gallery, had lunch at the cafeteria, and wandered around the exhibit halls, admiring the world-class collection of paintings and sculpture.

At 5:00 P.M., she and Roger arrived at the front door almost simultaneously. When they got to their room he told her, "I finally managed to get into each of the command centers I need to. Everywhere it's sheer madness, complete chaos. I really hope the air force doesn't drop any bombs somewhere and start World War Three. Now, do you have the professor's number?"

"Yes, here it is. But do I get a kiss first?"

"Oh, wow. Married for just a month and forgot my husbandly duties already!"

When he came up for air he dialed the overseas number. The phone rang and rang. Suddenly it was picked up and a gruff male voice said, "Police Inspector Gerald, who's this?"

"Roger Malcolm, a friend calling from the U.S. Is Professor Chebandrov there? It's most urgent that I speak to him."

"Yes, he's here, but no, you can't speak to him."

"What?" replied Roger. "Please, tell him I'm calling him about what he asked me to do the last time we were together. It truly is an extremely urgent matter. I really *must* speak to him."

"You're calling from America, you say? Well, I guess it's all right to tell you. He's been shot dead!"

"What? What did you say? He's dead! Oh, my god. No, no, it can't be. Is this Professor Chebandrov's office at the University of Edinburgh?"

"Yes, and he's surely dead. Would you know anyone who could have done it or ordered him to be shot?"

Roger answered too precipitously, "Yes, the Soviet KGB," and then immediately wished he had not blurted that out.

Emmie had recoiled from standing next to Roger when she heard him say 'dead.'

"What is it? Roger, what is it?"

"The professor's been shot dead in his office. The police are already there." Into the phone he said, "Inspector Gerald, when did this happen? My wife just talked to him on the phone earlier today."

"When exactly was that?" Roger turned to Emmie and asked her when she had called him.

"Just about twenty minutes after ten A.M. our time here."

Roger told the inspector, "Twenty minutes after three P.M. Edinburgh time."

"Well," the inspector replied, "he was shot just about forty minutes ago. The janitor heard the shot, rushed up here to the professor's office and found him lying right beside his desk chair. He said the whole room was a mess, but there was no evidence of the killer. He rushed out to look for anyone in the corridor or stairwell, but saw no one. He shut and locked the door to the professor's office, went immediately back to his own office, and called the police. We were here within ten minutes."

"God, I can't believe it," said Roger. Emmie had sat down on their bed and fell back, sobbing.

"Why did you say the KGB did it, just now?" asked the inspector.

"I have no reason except that he had been contacted surreptitiously by a close adviser to Chairman Khruschev of the Soviet Union about three years ago and again this year on September fourth, just before our wedding in London. He asked me to relay some information he had obtained from that adviser to our secretary of defense, which I did shortly before this Cuban missile crisis erupted."

"Who was that adviser, and what did he tell the professor?"

"I do not know the adviser's name and I cannot tell you what I told our secretary of defense except that it concerned nuclear-tipped missiles and possibly Cuba."

"Look here," said the inspector, "this is a case of murder. I have to know everything there is to know to help solve it. You must tell me. Or is the law different over there in the U.S.?"

"I truly do not know the name of the adviser, and under our laws in the U.S. I must protect national security information, which this surely is. If you want to know more, contact the British embassy here in Washington, DC. and have a properly vetted intelligence officer take my deposition there. I may be reached either at this hotel or through the office of the secretary of defense."

"All right, all right."

"By the way," Roger went on, "you said the room is a mess. Do you think it was a common burglary or was the killer or killers looking for something, such as an envelope or a piece of paper?"

"I'd say it was the latter, the piece of paper. Only the desk drawers and papers on the desk and tables in the office were thrown around. I suspect the professor returned to his office when the killer did not expect him and confronted the killer, who then shot him and rushed out to avoid detection."

"Thank you, inspector, you've been of great help. But to add to your efforts, I have begun to wonder if my wife and I may be a target of the KGB, or whoever did this terrible deed. Also, since my wife got the professor's phone number from her parents in London, they may be at risk. I'll take care of my chances here, but you might have the London police put some type of protective surveillance on Mr. and Mrs. Jerome Trowbridge of South Oxney."

"That may take some doing, but if I can, I will try to arrange that. And thank you, Mr. Malcolm. You have perhaps saved me and my men quite a bit of time looking up blind alleys. Please let me know if you think of anything else that might help our investigation of this tragic murder. Good-bye and good luck."

"Good-bye, inspector, and best wishes for a quick arrest of the killer." Turning to Emmie, Roger said, "We've got to get out of here."

Emmie sat up, wiped her eyes with a tissue, sighed, took a deep breath, and groaned, "Roger, oh! Roger, what's going on? After all we've been through I thought that now we are married we could have a quiet time for our lovemaking. Suddenly there's a doomsday missile crisis that takes us apart, and now a terrible murder of poor Professor Chebandrov. Oh, my dear professor— that's all I ever called him. We were really much closer than I was to my dad. I can't imagine him gone, and what a way to die!"

"Yes, yes, my love. This is an incredible tragedy. But it may get much, much worse if we don't get out of here right now!"

"You really think the KGB is behind this and would try to kill us too?"

"I've no idea, but I don't want to find out. Leave everything and let's go."

"Where?"

"To the Pentagon to talk to SecDef McNamara."

Roger took Emmie by the arm as she grabbed her pocketbook, and he pulled her gently out the hotel room door, locking it as they went through, and pulled her again toward the stairs. "We don't want to have anyone see us getting off the elevator, and it's only three flights." He walked her down and then added, "Now walk beside me very casually toward the hotel restaurant." They entered, and he had the waitress show them to a table at the back. As soon as she left them, he got up with Emmie, and they both walked deliberately out the rear door. "I know this part of Georgetown, so just keep up with me, faster now." He led her east past Dumbarton Oaks and turned just in time to see a car coming toward them, slowly as if looking for something— or someone, he thought. "Quick, down this street." He rushed Emmie along down several blocks to M Street, checking behind him for anyone or any car that might be following them. That car suddenly appeared behind them again. He hailed a taxi going west, which fortunately pulled in and stopped right in front of them almost immediately. "Please take us as quickly as you can to the Pentagon. Keep going west to the Key Bridge. Let us off at the river entrance."

"There's bound to be a traffic pile-up at Key Bridge. I It's rush hour in D.C., or didn't you know? I'll show you a much quicker way."

"Okay," said Roger, "but I sure don't want anyone to know where we're going if I can help it. I'll be watching behind us to see if we get followed."

"Oh, a spy, eh? Well, okay. Give my best to the CIA. I'll show you how to shake your pursuers!" The driver went slowly west behind the traffic along M Street, put his blinker on as if to turn right, then as the stop light turned yellow, suddenly cut into the middle lane, passed two stopped cars, and turned left onto Wisconsin going south, cutting off the oncoming traffic at the light. He accelerated south on Wisconsin and asked, "See anything suspicious?"

Roger, looking back the whole time, answered, "Well, there's still a line of cars that came across Wisconsin behind us as the light turned green. I don't know whether anyone in it could be after us."

The cab driver then cut sharply left onto South Street, found it amazingly empty of cars, and with a laugh, hit the accelerator further and swerved again sharply to the right to join Thirty-First Street, throwing Roger hard against Emmie. As they both pulled on the seat back in front of them to straighten up, Emmie said, "Roger, that hurt. Do we have to play at being spies like this? We're more likely to get killed by this cab driver than the KGB."

The cabbie joined a line of traffic, and still going south, followed Thirty-First Street along onto Virginia Avenue as the traffic thinned, and he stopped at the light at Rock Creek Parkway. When the opposing light turned yellow, he cut right, zipped south along the Potomac River and around to swing up onto the Arlington Memorial Bridge. "Anyone behind us?" he asked.

"Sure," replied Roger, "but I can't tell if they've been following us."

"I'm going this way since the traffic rarely piles up going toward the Arlington Cemetery." He left the bridge turning onto Washington Boulevard on which the traffic was all going the other way leaving the Pentagon, pulled off into the Pentagon parking lot, found an opening between the cars leaving for the day, and pulled up smartly at the river entrance. There was no car behind them, but one car Roger did not see came as far into the parking lot to note their destination and then made a U-turn and exited with the other traffic leaving. He wouldn't have known that car was headed back to the hotel Emmie and Roger had just left.

Roger thrust two twenty-dollar bills into the driver's hand and said, "Wow! That's a ride I'll never forget. Thanks. The KGB must still be looking for us way back up Wisconsin!" He jumped out, hauled Emmie after him, and ran up the steps into the building.

"Wait!" cried out Emmie. "My stomach is still back in the cab where you slammed me into the door. I just hope my ribs aren't broken again."

Ignoring her complaint, Roger went on, "We'll go right up to McNamara's office on the third floor." Still dragging Emmie, he sprinted up the stairs. When they arrived, the door opened as if expecting them, and Alan Howard came out. "Hold the door, Mr. Howard. We've got news for the secretary."

"Oh, you two again. What's the rush now? Anyway, he's not in, but be my guest. You can wait inside."

Roger walked quickly in, followed by Emmie and Howard. "We've got to see Secretary McNamara right away," Roger said breathlessly to the SecDef's administrative assistant. "This is extremely urgent." Emmie slumped into a chair by the desk, also out of breath.

"Wait a minute," said Howard. "What's so urgent this time?"

"Professor Chebandrov has been shot dead, just a few hours ago, in his office at the University of Edinburgh," replied Roger.

"So?" said Howard.

"So it seems to me that somebody high up in the Soviet Union doesn't want the professor to corroborate what the adviser told him about Khruschev wanting to negotiate."

"Aren't you speculating just a little too much? Maybe some burglar just tried to rob the professor and when he resisted, shot him."

"Still, I think the secretary ought to hear about this and decide for himself," added Roger, getting a little agitated. Turning to the administrative assistant, he said, "Could you call the secretary and find out if he could see us right away? I still believe it's extremely urgent."

"He's with the president at the White House, but he's scheduled to leave just about now. Let me call the White House appointment secretary and see if you can meet him somewhere." She pushed one button on her phone, asked to talk to Secretary McNamara, and was put through. "We've got Mr. and Mrs. Malcolm here, and he says they have some urgent news for you. Can you meet with them somewhere soon? Oh, fine. I'll send them right over." Turning to Roger she said, "He said for you to come right over to the White House. He's about to leave to go to dinner and an evening reception, but he said he'll wait for you in the antechamber to the Oval Office. I'll call for a car and driver to take you and will have the guards on the gate waiting to let you in."

"This is madness," retorted Howard. "They're probably trying to figure out how many air strikes are needed to take out all the missiles in Cuba—and Castro besides."

"That's exactly why we have to talk to both the SecDef and the president," Roger replied heatedly.

"Well, I'm coming along then," answered Howard just as heatedly.

'Time's a wasting," said Roger, and he opened the door for the three of them to stride out, just as the administrative assistant called after them that the car was waiting at the river entrance. Fifteen minutes later, they were ushered by a Secret Service officer into an antechamber to the Oval Office in the White

House, often called the Roosevelt Room. The officer stayed with them as the president's personal aide, Kenneth O'Donnell, looked in and then left.

The president's private secretary, Evelyn Lincoln, came in from her office across the hall and asked, "May I get you two anything? Coffee, tea, or a cold drink?"

"No, no," answered Roger, "we won't be staying more than a minute or two."

Just then, down the hall at the Cabinet Room where the ExComm had been meeting, the door opened, and McNamara held it open as the high-ranking members walked out. The SecDef came with them to the antechamber and brightened up as he saw Roger and Emmie and greeted them effusively by name. "Let me introduce you to these gentlemen, most of whom I'm sure you already know by sight," he said as they passed by. "This is Lyndon Johnson, the vice president; Dean Rusk, secretary of state; General Maxwell Taylor, chairman of the Joint Chiefs of Staff; John McCone, director of the CIA; McGeorge Bundy, national security adviser; George Ball, undersecretary of state; Charles Bohlen and Llewellyn Thompson, both former ambassadors to the Soviet Union; and Ted Sorensen, the president's speechwriter."

They all murmured, "Pleased to meet you" and walked off, obviously wondering who these two with Howard were.

McNamara told Roger and Emmie, "I'll be right with you," and then he turned back toward the Oval Office, went in, and closed the door behind him.

Inside, President Kennedy slumped in his chair behind his desk, his smile fading, allowing an expression of deep pain to cross his face. His brother Robert Kennedy, the attorney general, was sitting in a chair across from the president. "Bob," the president said to McNamara, "I have never been so glad to see those guys leave. That ExComm is too large. There's too much palaver. Where were you at the end of the meeting?"

"I went downstairs to the Situation Room, where the Joint Chiefs were huddled with some of the others. They all want to bomb Cuba immediately. They are planning five hundred sorties for Monday morning!"

"Yeah, I know. Everyone is saying that, every member of Congress and even Ike. This nightmare has my mind in a whirl and my back in a vise. God I'm tired, and my back is truly killing me!" Speaking to his brother, the president said, "Bobby, can you get hold of Dr. Travell to see if she can come right in? I'm going to need some help if I'm to get through the next forty-eight hours in one piece." Turning to McNamara, the president went on, "By the way, have we heard anything from Penkovsky? It would surely help if he could let us know what Khrushchev is thinking."

"I asked McCone about that," said the SecDef. "He said, 'No, and now I'm worried.' It's been over a week now since our source there in the Kremlin slipped us those prints showing the details of the Soviet missiles in Cuba, and we've heard nothing since. I'm truly afraid that the KGB tracked our knowledge back to him and he's a goner."

Just after that exchange, the president's spine doctor appeared and said to McNamara, "Mr. Secretary, would you bring the president's rocking chair over next to his desk? I think I can relieve some of his pain with his usual back massage." McNamara hustled to oblige the doctor. She got the president up from his desk, had him do several of her usual stretching exercises, and then settled him onto a fluffy cushion on the seat of the chair. She rather vigorously started to manipulate his back as he rocked.

McNamara suddenly remembered Emmie and Roger sitting outside in the antechamber. "Mr. President, while we have this moment, could I bring in two people that you really should hear from? It bears directly on what we were just talking about."

"I don't really feel like meeting anyone at all right now, Mac."

"I can see that, but these folks have been through something that may make your pain seem, well, not trivial, but less all-consuming."

"What could that be? You don't really know what I'm going through right now."

"What about being badly injured and barely surviving a thermonuclear blast much too close at Christmas Island?"

"Oh!" the president exclaimed in wonder. "Well, okay, bring 'em in. Ooh, doc, that does make me feel better already."

The SecDef stepped to the door, opened it, and said, "Mr. and Mrs. Malcolm, will you come in, please?" Howard started to join them, but the SecDef pointedly added, "Not yet, Alan, not yet." After Roger and Emmie entered, he closed the door behind them, leaving a most annoyed and frustrated Howard outside. The SecDef introduced President Kennedy and his brother to the couple. "Jack and Robert, this is Emmie Malcolm from London and her husband, Roger, from the Mitre Corporation in Bedford, Massachusetts." The couple greeted them, and as the president sat in his rocker he warmly returned their greeting, as did the attorney general.

The President added, waving to the person behind him, "This is Dr. Jane Travell, my back specialist. She's the one who truly keeps me going." She greeted them, and then discreetly left to return to her tiny office adjacent to the Oval Office.

The president waved them to sit down in the chairs grouped around his desk and continued rocking as he sat beside it. The SecDef went on, "They have both been with General Starbird at the nuclear tests off Christmas Island in the Pacific. Both were severely injured in a tragic mishap from a one-megaton thermonuclear weapon burst. But that is not why they are here." The SecDef summarized the situation with Professor Chebandrov and Khrushchev's adviser leading up to the letter with the words, "The negotiations have started." The president nodded. The SecDef continued, "I see that you have put two and two together and come up with who that adviser may be. McCone told me that person was in London at the time he could have sneaked off to see Professor Chebandrov in Edinburgh and even might have been able to smuggle that scrap of paper about the negotiations to the professor in London just last month. Roger here was good enough to share this situation with me and Alan Howard before the missile crisis erupted. Alan thinks the letter and all that went before it may just be elaborate disinformation to put us off. I've given the envelope and the scrap of paper to the CIA for examination, but I think we ought to know more before we dismiss it out of hand. Roger, what is this news you have brought us?"

"The professor was murdered a few hours ago—shot dead in his office at the University of Edinburgh," Roger said as calmly as he could.

"Goddamn it!" exclaimed the SecDef, slapping the desk so hard his hand stung.

"Whoa," said Robert Kennedy.

"Goddamn it to hell and gone is right!" added President Kennedy. "This whole crisis gets more and more vicious. What do you think this means, Bob?"

"That puts it front and center. Maybe those hard-liners in Moscow really are putting the pressure on the chairman. It sure fits with the contradictions between his secret letter last night and his public statement this morning, and it reinforces what Khrushchev's adviser said, 'Negotiations have started.' But of course it may, as Holden says, be an involved plot of some kind, just to put us off."

The president turned to Roger. "Let's call the adviser 'Boris' as you've suggested. By the way, he practically developed the Soviet nuclear weapon arsenal all by himself. He is well known here, particularly for his efforts on the test ban treaty. It must have really hurt him to have been forced by Khrushchev to develop those massive bombs and then break the tacit test ban agreement between the chairman and President Eisenhower, not to mention me. He truly took an enormous risk to slip that note to the professor, if that is what transpired."

"But Mr. Malcolm, what do you think?"

"I don't know what you and your team that we just passed in the antechamber have been considering in the way of options, but I can think of only two: one, start the bombing and pray it doesn't lead to World War Three; or two, negotiate the swap of our Jupiter missiles in Turkey for Khrushchev's missiles in Cuba. Howard calls that tit for tat or quid pro quo, and that will make every American mad at you, Mr. President. But also, remember, the adviser quoted Khrushchev as saying, 'I don't want to start World War Three.' Maybe tit for tat isn't all that bad."

"Oh, thanks. We either get nuclear holocaust or I lose the next election—or worse, I get impeached," the president replied.

Emmie jumped into the fray. "Mr. President, Roger and I barely escaped being killed by just one of your thermonuclear bombs. Have you ever witnessed one of those going off?"

"Er, no, as a matter of fact I've never seen a nuclear bomb explode."

"As a matter of fact, neither have I," added the SecDef.

"Nor I," added Robert.

"Well, first there is the blinding light, able to blind a person miles away who just happens to look in that direction, or perhaps doesn't even have to look at it. As the result of a potentially fatal misjudgment on our part, we were in a culvert, a large pipe half-buried in the ground, facedown with our heads in our arms, and the flash was awe-inspiring. Then the less intense light from the expanding fireball grows and grows and grows. The heat, which Roger tells me can ignite wood for miles around, quickly becomes unbearable. Just when you think you are going to burn up, the blast wave hits with an incredible *bang* louder than any fireworks or explosion I have ever heard. Roger equated it with a sixteen-inch gun going off right beside him. The overpressure, as they call it, is what did the damage to our ribs and lungs, breaking three ribs of both of us, and collapsing my right lung. Also, a piece of concrete culvert fell off above me, struck me at the back of my head, opened a severe wound, and gave me a concussion. At about the same time, the hurricane-force wind roars by, seemingly a hundred miles an hour or more, or two or three times that. The heat is quenched somewhat, but the wind stirs up the dust all around, even in our culvert—choking, blinding, gagging dust. After it dies down, the wind comes roaring back with almost the same ferocity, sucking the air from your lungs. After all that, the fireball grows some more, cooling from yellow to orange to red and rising up into the sky and forming the characteristic mushroom cloud. Finally, it turns purple as it reaches the stratosphere and drifts off with the upper winds carrying its radioactivity to contaminate the entire planet. That's from just one megaton.

"Of course, you know all about that. But Colonel Holden mentioned, perhaps inadvisably, that you have seven thousand megatons in the air and under the sea ready to blast the Soviet Union and other Communist countries to radioactive rubble. Undoubtedly, Cuba has some missiles with nuclear warheads ready to rain destruction down on the Unites States, and, if the Soviet Union can launch its missiles, many thousands of megatons will come along over here.

"So what am I getting at? Professor Chebandrov told Roger that his colleague from Moscow had heard from Chairman Khrushchev's lips that he doesn't want to start World War Three. That all he wants is to get your old Jupiter missiles out of Turkey. Boris told the chairman that all he had to do was negotiate. 'Swap some of ours for some of theirs,' he told Khrushchev. The professor may have given his life to get that word to you. Isn't it worth trying that negotiation to avoid the nuclear holocaust? Maybe as Roger said, tit for tat isn't all that bad? Mr. President, please, please try that course. I spent three years in Europe after World War Two trying to reunite families separated by the incredible chaos when it ended. The misery, the sadness, the emptiness felt by the millions of people displaced by that war were heartbreaking to me. Do you really want to chance a far worse devastation? Tell me, 'No, Emmie, no.'"

Roger gulped at this break with protocol. *What was the president thinking now?*

The president hunched forward, as did the attorney general. "What do you think, Bobby?" asked the president.

"That is the most compelling speech I have heard since this crisis started," said Robert Kennedy.

"I fully agree," said the SecDef, turning a wide smile of approval toward Emmie.

The president straightened up with a look of determination, "Look, let's cut out all the blarney. I don't want to go back into the Cabinet Room at nine o'clock with all those guys nit-picking the life out of what we're trying to send to Khrushchev. I know what I want to say. It's based on what I have here from Adlai Stevenson at the UN and Lyndon, Mac, and you too, Bobby. Here is my decision. We offer to agree to trade the Jupiters just as soon as he, Khrushchev, stops the Soviet build-up and dismantles the missiles in Cuba for our, that is UN, inspection. That seems to be the nub of what he wants, so let's give it to him. Let's negotiate to trade his missiles for ours. But—and this is the essence of our agreement—there will be no written quid pro quo, no mention of a trade in any memo or statement of any kind outside of this office or to Dobrynin directly. That's where you come in, Bobby."

"I get it," said Robert. "I can take your written message to the Soviet ambassador Dobrynin. He has immediate access to Chairman Khrushchev. I can probably get in to see him right away this evening and make such an offer to withdraw our Jupiters verbally. I would first state our acceptance of the chairman's conditions set out in his first message yesterday: namely, to give our assurance not to invade Cuba, and to end the naval quarantine as soon as the Soviet missiles are being dismantled and prepared to be shipped back to the Soviet Union. I would have a document signed by you to that effect. Then I would tell him verbally that the U.S. would take the Jupiter missiles out of Turkey and Italy, but that this action must be kept completely secret, there would be no public quid pro quo, I will add that secrecy on this latter point must be absolute. I will emphasize to Dobrynin that the situation was extremely serious and that within twelve to twenty-four hours the U.S. might have to initiate an attack. I will add further that if the Cubans are shooting at our planes, then we are going to shoot back."

"Okay, Bobby. I agree," said the president. "Let's go with that. Get Evelyn in here with Ted Sorenson and we'll dictate the memo, along with a corresponding memo to U Thant at the UN who is also involved directly with Khrushchev, while you make arrangements to see Dobrynin right away. We'll also send it directly by secure message to Moscow. And no quid pro quo, get it," he added while winking broadly. He turned to the others, got up and led them toward the door. "A secret stays a secret if only one person knows it. Here we have four people plus me and Dobrynin who know it. If the quid pro quo gets out, I'll personally throttle all four of you."

As they departed, Roger whispered to the president, "I trust that my wife didn't upset you by speaking out the way she did. That's not at all like her."

"No, no, not at all. My wife does that all the time," the president said with a smile. "No, your wife's little speech there convinced me what I should do. Bobby, Mac and a couple of others have been leaning that way for several days, but the military, Congress, most of my team, as you put it, and even Ike have said without a bit of hesitation that we have to bomb right away. The air force said it would take five hundred sorties to do the job on Cuba if we only use non-nuclear bombs. Do you think Khrushchev would stand for that? Thank God for Emmie! The whole world will owe her an incredible debt of gratitude if we get out of this without bombing. Now let me get that memo together for Bobby to take to Dobrynin right away. Time is truly short."

As they trooped out, Roger said to McNamara, "You may realize that Emmie and I could potentially be the target of whoever shot the professor. Do you think you could arrange for us to be kept in a safe house until this all blows over? Sorry for the pun."

"Oh, certainly, I understand fully. As we go out I'll make some calls, and the Secret Service will make the arrangements."

"We'll have to go back to our hotel first to collect our things," said Emmie.

"A secret service agent will go with you while you do that," said the SecDef.

Within an hour, Emmie and Roger were on their way in a Secret Service limousine with two agents. They drove around the back of the hotel and made a dash for the door to the restaurant with one of the agents. The three of them ran up the stairs to their room. Roger turned the key, and Emmie brushed past him and gasped. The room was a complete mess. All of their belongings and everything else in the room had been gone through and turned upside down.

The agent grabbed the phone with a handkerchief and called down to the desk. "This is agent Blandon of the U.S. Secret Service. Please have your manager come up to room three-fourteen immediately. There has been an attempted burglary here."

"Emmie, don't touch anything!" exclaimed Roger. "We'll have to do without for a day or two."

The agent said to them both, "You may look around to see what may have been taken, but don't leave any fingerprints, and disturb things as little as possible."

The manager arrived and drew a deep breath. "We've had burglaries before, but nothing to cause as complete carnage as this."

"Take your toiletries and nightclothes and one change of clothing for tomorrow, but leave everything else." Turning to the manager, the agent continued, "Seal the room. We'll have one of our teams come in immediately to do a complete inventory and survey. Mr. and Mrs. Malcolm, let's go!" About two hours later they were settled in a very pleasant room in a nice house in the Virginia suburbs at the end of a long driveway through some deep woods, likely heavily guarded against intruders.

As the couple were escorted to their room, Roger quietly suggested to Emmie that she call her parents in London. "They may be wondering where we are. And we should check to make sure that the London police are on the job protecting them. Give me their number and I'll have our 'host' make the call."

Emmie took the phone from the man who dialed the number, and her mother promptly answered. "Mummy, what a relief to hear your voice! Are you and Daddy all right?"

Natalie answered brightly. "Why shouldn't we be all right? Well, we did have an odd thing happen last night. Let your father explain."

"Emmie," said Jerry. "About eleven o'clock last night just after we had gone to bed, I heard some noise outside. You know that we usually sleep with our window open. So I quickly put on my trousers and shoes and went to the door. I was just about to open it when somebody knocked on it. So I opened it a crack and it was Constable McCratchy, you know, of the local constabulary. He said, 'Don't worry, Mr. Trowbridge, we got him.' I asked the constable to come in, but he said, 'No, no, we have to make sure there aren't any others lurking about. Just close the door, lock it, make sure all the doors and windows are shut and locked, and we'll let you know tomorrow morning what has been going on out here. Not to worry, just lock up and go back to sleep.' This morning the constable came by and told us very little, actually. He said, 'I was asked by my supervisor a day or so ago to post a policeman or two in this area to look for any suspicious characters who might sneak around. Well, one of my men spotted one, and challenged him. The sneak pulled a gun on him and said, "Move off, copper, or you'll be sorry." The other one of my men heard that, snuck up on him and batted the gun away with his billy club, pulling him down as he swung the club. My other man whistled for help and I just happened to be near and ran up to put the cuffs on the sneak. I called for the paddy wagon and we hustled him off. I thought you might have heard the commotion, so I went up to your door to find out.' I asked who the man was and what he was doing, and the constable replied, 'He seemed to be a foreign type, didn't say anything, and when I reported the incident to our higher-ups I quickly got a call from Scotland Yard to send him over there, which I did. They haven't said a word to me since, although I did call. When we searched him at our station, he had your address on him, a set of lock-picks, a short rope for tying someone up, a wicked knife, a small flashlight, a nasty cosh, and, of course, the gun. We'll stick around your neighborhood for a couple of more days, just to be sure there are no more of his type trying anything.' And then he told your mother, "Sorry to worry you, ma'am, but these days you can't be too careful. He was a bad 'un all right, but I trust he won't see the light of day for many a year now.'"

* * * *

At 9:00 A.M. the next day—Sunday, October 28—Khrushchev's reply was broadcast: "The Soviet government…has issued a new order on the dismantling of the weapons which you describe as 'offensive' and their crating and return to the Soviet Union." Although the Joint Chiefs were skeptical of Khrushchev's offer, the crisis was over.

Epilogue

After returning from their interrupted honeymoon in Bermuda, Emmie opened a bulky envelope addressed to her. It included the notification that the Massachusetts Institute of Technology would be pleased to have her enroll in their graduate department of mathematics. It also included the forms for her actual enrollment and those to apply for financial assistance, along with a note from Professor Forest welcoming her into the university's Graduate School of Mathematics. She let out a yell, "Roger, I'm in!"

"What, where are you 'in'?"

"MIT," she spoke back to him in a quieter tone. "Can you believe it? Me, an aging woman, accepted into the most prestigious school in the world!"

"You got into Harvard?" twitted Roger.

"No, dummy, MIT! I'm a mathematician, not a hockey player," she twitted back.

She immediately called Professor Forest to thank him for getting her into MIT. He said, "No, Emmie, it was solely on your accomplishments and on what you said you had in mind to study for your Ph.D. Your acceptance is strictly on your merits. But I want to add that you will not be working in my computer lab but with Professor Schwartz in the theoretical math department."

"Oh, that's okay. I looked him up and I agree that he's more suited to my interests. But I will make an appointment to meet him and check it all out."

Pleased as she was, Emmie wrestled with her conscience regarding her contract to teach math to the young students on Christmas Island. "Roger, you know how I feel about my contract with the British foreign office about teaching on Christmas Island. I'm going to write to Mr. Duxbury and see if I shouldn't return to honor that pledge."

"Why don't you call him on the phone? I can show you how to do that through the Mitre switchboard."

"Oh, I don't want the entire Mitre company listening in."

"No, I can work it so no one but you and Mr. Duxbury can hear each other."

Well, Mr. Duxbury was overjoyed to hear from Emmie. "We have persevered down here while you were gone, but it would be marvelous if you could return. I think you only need to be here for one year to meet any contractual obligations, though even that could be waived if you were sure you didn't want to come. But everyone here would be as delighted as I would be if you did return."

So, she met with Professor Schwarz and determined that he would be right for her as her mentor toward getting her Ph.D. Then she floored him by requesting permission to postpone her acceptance of the appointment to MIT in his department. "You see, Professor, I made an agreement to teach youngsters math and science on Christmas Island way down near the equator in the Pacific Ocean. My work there was interrupted by an unfortunate accident during the American nuclear tests. I truly feel that I should take a year and complete my contract."

"Well, your work here is not yet on any kind of schedule, so if you are determined to teach on that Pacific Island, I will certainly not stand in your way. I will welcome you here at MIT in about, what did you say? About a year?"

"Yes, that should do it. I will certainly keep you advised, but right now I think a year from now will be fine." Returning to their home she made plans to return to Christmas Island the first of January 1963 and complete her contract.

In a surprise move, Roger said, "I'm not letting you out of my sight for a whole year. We just started on our love affair. I'm going to take a leave from the Mitre Corporation to go with you!"

When they arrived back at Kiritimati, Roger observed that the U.S. Air Force had cleared out from the island following the last thermonuclear tests but left a huge amount of dust, debris, and equipment behind. The equipment included such items as jeeps, bulldozers, cranes, and the air strip with its control tower and a fully operational marine port. Also left in reasonably good shape were numerous living quarters, offices, and associated buildings.

Emmie found that Superintendent Duxbury was indeed overjoyed at having her back and showed her that he had inventoried all of the wonderful books and scientific equipment that Frosty had managed to ship the year before. He had stored them in a large closet with abundant shelves to hold them properly. He, of course he had used them while Emmie was away. "I'll be able to jump right in," she said, and so she did. The children and their parents were overjoyed as well.

The rascally boy Terry Tong was joined by his father and his siblings from Tarawa, the father having completed his government work there, and the family took possession of one of the nicer living quarters abandoned by the U.S. Air Force. Roger found that he could be useful making sure that the jeeps and other equipment left behind by the air force were in working order and training the Kirimatians in how to drive them and operate the other equipment that might be useful.

The year passed peacefully and, in the not-so-young couple's minds, rather quickly. But they were actually much relieved to be able to return to their apartment back in Massachusetts, where they soon established the wonderful married life they had both hoped for. Roger was back doing vital work for Mitre, and Emmie was working assiduously on her Ph.D. program at MIT.

Meanwhile, Natalie and Jerome Trowbridge began to think about their situation. A few months into 1963, Natalie said to her husband, "Jerry, merry-old England is just not that merry. We've still got rationing, your income has stagnated, the roads and railroads are in poor shape, and the whole country is struggling. What we thought we might be able to do when we got to this age—travel, have vacations in the Lake District or Scotland, and so forth—seems awfully unlikely. What do you think?"

Jerry was not entirely surprised by this statement from his wife. He paused a while, really just for effect, and then said, "Look, we're old, our house is old, the country is old. Let's go to America!"

"Oh, Jerry, do you really mean that? Oh, wow. I wonder what I should wear? I'll have to get an entirely new wardrobe!"

The next day, Jerry called MIT. "Jack, Jack Forest? This is Jerry Trowbridge. I heard what you did for my daughter and her shady husband; do you think you could do the same for a shady father?"

"Is this the Jerry Trowbridge that saved World War Two for the Allies?" he said jokingly. "And I understand from the Mitre people that your daughter and her 'shady' husband just saved the whole planet from World War Three. Of course I can help you out. Send me your particulars, not offending the British Official Secrets Act, of course. I can fill that part in. Let me send you the appropriate forms to fill out and as soon as I get them back we'll be in touch to see what can be worked out."

"Wow! That sounds terrific. Natalie and I just agreed that we ought to migrate like some birds to be on hand if and when the grandchildren arrive!"

And so, in the autumn of 1963, Roger and Emmie were joined by her folks. Jerry had to 'settle' for a professorship in applied engineering—meaning computer design and development at Harvard University. Emmie started what turned out to be a very time-consuming and arduous return to the academic life, but she soon found her niche in developing some spectacular developments in Mandelbrot sets, or fractals, developing a close relationship with Professor Benoît Mandelbrot at the IBM Thomas J. Watson Research Center. Roger returned to Mitre in Bedford, Massachusetts, where he was promoted to associate department head to Earl F. Lockwood in the Strategic Analysis Department. Roger worked on the problem of letting the president know in an instant what the enemy (that is, the Soviets) was doing. Frosty worked on the U.S. plans for any response the president might order. Willie Moore remained their close tie to ODDR&E at the Pentagon.

At night, Emmie and Roger worked assiduously on the problem of giving their parents a grandchild.

Postscript from the Author

Since my actual experiences with the nuclear tests in 1962, as described in fictional form above, I have come to believe firmly—as I have Emmie expressing to Alan Howard regarding nuclear weapons—"So what use are they? Why not get everyone to scrap the damn things?"

Such sentiments occurred to me as I watched the mushroom cloud from Shot Alma in June 1962 drift off northeast from Christmas Island toward South America and on around the world. It occurred to me then, how many cases of cancer would eventually be caused by the leftover plutonium and other radioactive fission/fusion products from that 800-kiloton bomb? What about the radioactive stuff from all the other nuclear bombs set off in the atmosphere by the U.S., Soviets, and others since 1945? Thank goodness for the treaty to end atmospheric testing of nuclear weapons that was negotiated and signed by President Kennedy on October 7, 1963.

However, considering the present situation, I believe that our incredibly large stockpile of nuclear weapons, as well as those of the Soviets (now the Russians) and all other nations (Britain, France, China, India, Pakistan, Israel, now North Korea, and perhaps others), are extremely dangerous to have around. In effect, they are useless except perhaps in the final Mutual Assured Destruction mode, which may well destroy or at least severely damage the entire planet.

Of course, unilateral disarmament would be just as dangerous, allowing almost any nuclear-holding enemy to extort our compliance with their demands. Also, not only are active and recently dismantled nuclear weapons dangerous, so is all of the fissile material in existing nuclear reactors and their highly radioactive pools of spent nuclear fuel rods. Added to that source of fissile materials are the many research reactors and other types of radioactive elements such as medical devices. The ability and possibly the existing intention of non-state groups or state-supported groups to hold us hostage with existing fissile or radioactive materials they might obtain is truly a further major problem. Also, today's very real threats from gangs of terrorists such as Al Qaeda, who may well at this moment be trying to obtain a quantity of such materials, are always in our nightmares.

What is to be done to deal with these terrible threats? It will obviously take a most difficult, global, and protracted effort to be achieved by a series of treaties based on the current nuclear proliferation treaty. The first treaty must be to negotiate the further gradual dismantling and removal of the fissile material from all existing and obsolete nuclear weapons. The development, manufacture, and stockpiling of new ones must be strictly forbidden. The plutonium and enriched uranium can be burned as mixed oxide fuel in present-day and future nuclear electric power plants following a certain amount of redesign and/or reconfiguration. This procedure will allow for the generation of electricity from the fuels that required so much electricity to produce in the first place.

The second treaty must be to increase the security from terrorist attack of all nuclear-electric power plants. As part of this treaty we must reprocess the stored fuel rods to separate the unburned plutonium and uranium to make additional mixed oxide fuel to generate electric power as noted above. This again will recapture part of the energy that went into manufacturing the original fuel rods. The reprocessing procedures can also be used to separate the short-lived from the long-lived radioactive fission product elements. The short-lived, more highly radioactive elements must be stored in extremely well protected facilities. The long-lived, less highly radioactive fission products could be safely stored in Yucca Mountain or a similar permanent facility. The separation of these two groups of fission products should allow for considerably easier design of the storage facilities. Above-ground storage silos might be appropriate for some of these materials, at least temporarily—again, with enhanced security.

Of course, the detonation of a nuclear device of any type as a weapon, whether it would be of Hiroshima size (about ten kilotons TNT equivalent) or up to a "city buster" of a megaton or more, would be catastrophic. But if any retaliation, and any re-retaliation, in kind were prevented, the world would survive. Although the city would be destroyed, the nation would be able to rebuild and continue as did Japan after 1945. The above treaties are designed to prevent this situation from occurring.

The third consideration is whether we must undertake to prevent unauthorized individuals and groups from stealing fissile fuels from research reactors, medical devices, or other facilities, which are widely distributed around the world and not necessarily highly secure. The possibility of a dirty bomb containing radioactive materials but without a nuclear explosion going off in a city would be a terrible catastrophe. The city and its environs could well be uninhabitable for many, many years. But again, the nation would certainly survive, as Japan is currently demonstrating following their terrible tsunami and partial reactor meltdown. Even so, very close monitoring of all sources of radioactive materials must be further enhanced.

These three efforts to include all nations in such treaties, and to provide for their effective enforcement, will strain the diplomatic skills of every country and the United Nations, as well as regional groups such as the North American Treaty Organization (NATO). The difficulties of the International Atomic Energy Agency to enforce the nuclear non-proliferation treaty, and its struggle to determine the nuclear capabilities of Iraq under Saddam Hussein, Iran under Ahmadinejad and North Korea under Kim Jong-un, provide several examples of the problem.

However, the first and primary effort must be to rid the world of the megaton-sized city-busters—in particular those weapons which at this moment are operational.

Richard Stiles Greeley, Ph.D.
A Concerned Nuclear Chemist and Engineer
St. Davids, PA 2013